Born in North London, the eldest o[...] child but managed to disappoint h[...] grammar school. It was suggested th[at...] frivolous, she would be better suited in a school where no [...] demands were made on her. A course at secretarial college led to the one career she never wanted – office work – but at least her ability to touch-type at speed proved useful when, years later, she began to write short stories.

Now retired and living in the village of Shenley, close to the M25 and St Albans, Leila has had success with her poetry and short stories but it's the craft of writing novels which she most enjoys and, keen to pass on her knowledge, runs workshops for gifted young writers at her old primary school.

To Dawn
Best wishes
from Rosie B

Girl in the Hat Shop

Leila Cassell

SilverWood

Published in 2016 by SilverWood Books

SilverWood Books Ltd
14 Small Street, Bristol, BS1 1DE, United Kingdom
www.silverwoodbooks.co.uk

Copyright © Leila Cassell 2016

The right of Leila Cassell to be identified as the author of this
work has been asserted in accordance with the Copyright,
Designs and Patents Act 1988 Sections 77 and 78.

All rights reserved. No part of this publication may be reproduced,
stored in a retrieval system, or transmitted in any form or by any means,
electronic, mechanical, photocopying, recording or otherwise,
without prior permission of the copyright holder.

This is a work of fiction. Names, characters, places and incidents
either are products of the author's imagination or are used fictitiously.
Any resemblance to actual events or locales or persons,
living or dead, is entirely coincidental.

ISBN 978-1-78132-565-0 (paperback)
ISBN 978-1-78132-566-7 (ebook)

British Library Cataloguing in Publication Data
A CIP catalogue record for this book is available from
the British Library

Page design and typesetting by SilverWood Books
Printed on responsibly sourced paper

All that is necessary for the triumph
of evil is that good men do nothing.

Edmund Burke, 1729–1797

Willesden Green, 1928
I am eight years old when I make my first big mistake. I tell my mother I can see someone who isn't really there.

Everyone's come to meet my new baby brother. I've had my cheeks pinched a hundred times. Uncles, aunts and cousins, I know them all but there's one guest that I don't recognise. So I ask my mother and I don't point because I know that's rude. I just ask her, very politely, who is the lady with the black scarf round her head. My mother stares at me. Then she clutches her heart, grabs my arm really hard and drags me away to the corner of the room. I tell her that she's hurting me. She takes no notice.

'There's no one there. You can't see anyone. Do you hear me?' She lets go of my arm, holds my face between her hands and twists my head towards the centre of the room. 'See,' she hisses in my ear. 'What did I tell you? There's no one there.'

I can't understand why she's so angry. I don't understand why she's pretending there's nobody there. I ask her again. 'Standing next to Jack's cradle, see?' She shakes me so hard that I start to cry.

Daddy comes over to see what's happening. 'Hetty,' he says, 'what on earth are you doing?' My mother doesn't say anything. She runs out of the room and shuts herself in the kitchen. But the lady is still there.

Chapter 1

January 1940

Mrs Feldman, President of the Willesden Synagogue Ladies' Guild, surveyed the scene and beamed with pride. The dance floor bounced and vibrated beneath her plump, satin-shod feet as the band played a spirited version of "Jeepers Creepers". Young guests jitterbugged and jived. The old bobbed and glided. Across the room, Mr Feldman climbed on to the stage and whispered something to the bandleader. The bandleader smiled and handed him the microphone. Mr Feldman tapped the microphone twice and cleared his throat.

'Rabbi Shultz, ladies and gentlemen, I'm sure everyone would like to join me in thanking my beautiful wife, Rosa, and all her wonderful helpers for making this evening such a success. Mazel tov, ladies. God save the king.'

The bandleader raised his baton, Mr Feldman nodded and the band began playing "Raisins and Almonds", his wife's favourite song. As he sang the Yiddish lyrics, his voice wobbling with emotion, Mrs Feldman's chin trembled and her eyes glittered with tears.

The lullaby had just reached its tear-jerking finale when someone tugged her arm and whispered, 'Don't look now, Rosa, but I think Fay Abrams is a bit upset.'

Mrs Feldman glanced over her shoulder at the young woman sitting at the back of the hall. A pale, thin creature whose looks might have been marginally improved by a touch of rouge and perhaps a little more attention to the thick, wiry hair which she wore dragged back from her face and anchored tightly in place with tortoiseshell combs. Dabbing her eyes with a tiny lace handkerchief, Mrs Feldman sighed, opened an enamelled compact, dusted her nose with a pale pink powder puff, snapped the compact shut, slipped it into the tasselled bag that hung from her wrist and sailed across the floor towards the table where Fay sat, holding the collar of her coat against her cheek, her eyes dark hollows of misery.

'Not dancing, Fay?' she said brightly.

Fay shrugged, her fingers playing with the ring on her left hand, twisting it back and forth. The young man sitting beside her leapt to his feet and gave a little bow.

'Mrs Feldman,' he said, 'perhaps you'd do me the honour? Fay doesn't feel like dancing this evening.'

'I'd be delighted, Bernard, but not right now. I wonder… would you mind doing something for me? Would you be a dear and have a word with Rabbi Shultz? Look at him. His face is turning beetroot.'

Mrs Feldman watched Bernard weave his way through the throng of guests towards the rabbi, who was now leaping and whirling around the dance floor. She dragged a chair next to Fay, positioned it at an angle where she could keep her eye on proceedings, patted Fay's hand and said, 'Listen, darling, it's none of my business and God forbid you should think I'm prying—'

'He's not coming back.' The girl's voice was flat and expressionless. 'He's going to die face down with a bullet in his back. I've seen it and every time I close my eyes I see it again. And the noise. The terrible noise.'

Mrs Feldman was horrified. Her hand fluttered above her heart. 'Pah! Pah! Pah!' she said, making little spitting noises to shoo away the evil eye. 'May God forgive you.'

'Forgive me for what, Mrs Feldman? You think I want to know what's going to happen? You think I asked for this?'

'Listen, *buballah*. These are difficult times and it's only natural that we imagine the worst but you mustn't think like that. Believe me, I know just what you're going through.'

'No, you don't. You have no idea what I'm going through. Tomorrow morning he'll board the train in his uniform. I'll wave and blow him a kiss and that's the last time I'll see him alive. And there's not a darn thing I can do to stop it.'

Desperately trying to catch Bernard's attention, Mrs Feldman put her hand on Fay's sleeve. 'Fay, darling, why don't you take off your coat? We haven't done the tombola. You might win something.'

Fay shook her head. 'You haven't understood a word I've said, have you?'

Mrs Feldman was wondering whether she dare leave the girl on her own for a few moments when she saw her pick up a narrow slip of paper that lay on the table in front of her. She wrote something on it and folded it into a tiny square.

'Give this to Bernard and tell him...' Fay's eyes filled with tears. 'No. Don't tell him anything. I'm sorry, Mrs Feldman. Please excuse me.'

'Pah! Pah! Pah! May God keep the poor man safe from his meshuga fiancée,' she muttered, as Fay disappeared towards the exit door.

She stared at the strip of paper lying in her gloved hand. It was from a cracker. She had been determined there would be crackers. They were a bit plainer than she would have liked, but all the same she had done well to get them. She unfolded the paper, smoothed out the creases and read the motto. "Don't make love at the garden gate. Love is blind but the neighbours ain't." When she turned it over and read Fay's pencilled message on the back, she gave an involuntary shudder. *I'm blessed to be loved by you but I'm cursed by something I can't explain. Forgive my behaviour.*

Mrs Feldman made an arbitrary decision. She screwed the paper into a tight ball and dropped it into the ashtray.

Bernard's parents and his sister sat shiva at their house in Walm Lane, the three of them huddled together on low chairs. Mr Ebstein, grey-faced, unshaven, his shirt torn; Mrs Ebstein, her eyes red and swollen, hair uncombed, shabby cardigan ripped above her heart, and Rita, Bernard's sister and Fay's dearest friend, looking numb and dead-eyed as if she didn't understand what was happening. Fay was his fiancée, but, being neither wife nor family, she was denied the right to sit with the mourners.

She watched as the steady stream of visitors came and went with gifts of food. She heard them murmur the prescribed words of condolence – "I wish you a long life" – and wondered how the prospect of a long life, after they had just lost their only son, could possibly bring comfort to his parents. Rabbi Shultz said prayers for the dead and it was then that Rita began to sob. Fay gave her a clean handkerchief and stroked her hair, but her own eyes remained dry.

She'd been grieving from the moment she'd seen those terrible images, weeks before Bernard died. How puzzled and confused he'd been by her behaviour. She wished it could have been different. She wished she could have shown him how much she treasured every precious moment they spent in each other's company. She wished she'd been sweeter, more loving and affectionate. But how could she, plunged as she was into a private world of despair? She couldn't tell him what she'd seen. Her visions had become something she'd learned to endure in silence, always praying that each one would be the last, that one day she'd be normal like everyone else and that given time she'd grow out of it.

When she looked around to see if her parents were ready to leave, Fay saw them talking to Mr Feldman. Mrs Feldman, head on one side, hands spread in a theatrical gesture of pity, was pushing through the crowd towards her. There was no escape. Rosa Feldman looked up into Fay's face with an earnest expression of sympathy.

'Fay, darling, what can I say? You're young. And you have your whole life in front of you.' Fay didn't respond. She stared at her, forcing Mrs Feldman to say more than she meant to. 'Listen to me. Saying that you're cursed, well, it's not right. You mustn't think that way.'

She reached out to touch Fay's hand, but Fay didn't want to be touched. Not by Mrs Feldman, not by anyone. Fists tightly clenched, she held her arms stiffly by her side.

'You read my note. It was for Bernard, not you.'

'Well, to tell you the truth I was worried about you.'

Before she could stop herself, Fay bent her head and with her mouth close to Mrs Feldman's ear, she whispered, 'But it happened, didn't it, Mrs Feldman? Just like I said it would.'

Mrs Feldman glanced nervously behind her. 'It was God's will,' she murmured, and Fay wondered if Mrs Feldman secretly believed that God had nothing to do with it, and that by saying he would die, Fay had somehow made it happen.

Chapter 2

It wasn't that her mother was a bad cook, but she'd got it into her head that what Fay needed in her hour of darkness was good, plain food. The kind you might offer an invalid. The kind that would tempt none but the starving.

'Eat. You look like a matchstick with the wood scraped off,' she said.

'Leave her alone, Hetty,' said her father. 'When she feels like eating, she'll eat.'

'Lou, can't you see? She's wasting away.'

Her father smuggled in secret treats – a portion of chips, a salt beef sandwich from Blooms. 'Don't tell your mother,' he whispered, and to please him she managed to swallow a few chips or take a bite of the sandwich, while he stood on guard in case Hetty walked in and caught them.

Alone in her room, Fay lay on her bed. Miss Greenwood, the manageress of the hat shop where she had worked since she left school, had told her to take all the time she needed but her mother's clumsy attempts to cheer her up had already begun to be more than she could bear. She could hear her footsteps on the stairs and pretended to be asleep.

'Fay. Listen to me. Are you listening?'

Fay sighed and opened her eyes.

'I'm going to send your brother up to keep you company. You're not hiding yourself away forever. It's not good for you.'

Moments later, Jack tapped on her bedroom door carrying

a jigsaw puzzle of a country cottage. 'Will you help with the sky?' he said. 'There's an awful lot of it.'

Fay told him to go away. He made a model of a windmill with his Meccano set and brought it in to show her.

'It's a proper working model. Look, Fay. You turn this handle and it goes round and round.'

'Very nice, Jack. Now do you mind leaving me alone? And don't forget to shut the door behind you.'

Dry-eyed, she stared at the ceiling. Ten minutes later her mother was back in her room. Fay turned her face to the wall as her mother sat on the chair beside her bed.

'Now, you just listen to me, my girl. All this moping around isn't good for you. Life's full of disappointments so you might as well get used to it. One disappointment after another. Believe me. I should know. You might not think so but things could be a lot worse. A whole lot worse.'

Fay went downstairs, telephoned the shop and assured Miss Greenwood that she was more than ready to return to work. Dressing the next morning, she was shocked by how much weight she'd lost. The waistband of her skirt was so loose she could have stepped into it without undoing the buttons. The skirt hung on her and Miss Greenwood was such a stickler for neatness. She'd made that clear from the start. Clear diction, good manners, nice shoes and a modest style of dress.

'This is Mayfair, my dear. Our clients expect high standards,' she'd said, and when she told Fay that the job was hers, she'd gone with her parents to Swan & Edgar and turned up on her first day, all kitted out in a smart business suit.

Today, staring at her reflection, she almost changed her mind about her fitness to return to work. The bulb that hung from the bathroom ceiling, shielded by a green glass shade, cast an unflattering light at the best of times but never before had her skin looked quite so sallow, her eyes quite so dull. Trying to add a little colour to her face she pinched her cheeks hard and bit her lips, but it made no difference. Her thick hair looked lifeless and wiry, so she anchored it back from her face so tightly that her head hurt.

On the bus, she avoided making eye contact with the other passengers. She stared out of the window. Beneath the railway bridge in Kilburn High Road, tucked between a jewellers and an ironmongers shop, stood the premises of Samuel Ebstein & Son, quality tailors. As she passed it, she imagined she could still see Bernard, his mouth full of pins, a tape measure round his neck, a piece of tailors' chalk in his hand, his head bent over a length of finest worsted.

It was there that he had made the coat. Rich bottle green, fitted at the waist, with a large velvet collar.

'I hope you like it,' he'd said.

She'd tried it on and stroked the collar against her cheek. He'd pinned a tiny posy of violets to its lapel. She'd kissed him and thought herself the luckiest girl in the world. Now he was gone and she wondered how long the business would survive with just the old man working all by himself in the little shop under the bridge.

At the hat shop, Miss Greenwood took one look at her and asked if she was quite sure she was ready for work.

'You know, Miss Abrams,' she said, 'we could spare you for another few days. Business is still very slow.'

'I'd rather be here, Miss Greenwood. I need to keep busy.'

Miss Greenwood looked doubtful. 'You really should invest in some make-up. It would perk you up no end.'

Whether Miss Greenwood's concern was entirely genuine or whether she was more worried what her customers might think, Fay was not certain, but, eager to make up for her absence and determined to persuade Miss Greenwood that she was more than ready for work, she told her how much she'd missed being in the shop and asked about the customers who'd come in while she'd been at home.

'To tell you the truth it's been rather quiet. That young salesman wanted to know where you were.'

'Which young salesman?'

'Mr Cassell. Handsome young fellow but inclined to be rather bold, I think. That actress you so admire bought the velvet cloche.

Merle Oberon? The one who played Cathy Earnshaw. It's a shame you missed her. I know how much you enjoyed that film.'

She had enjoyed it. It was the last film she and Bernard had seen together. They'd sat in the dark holding hands and when Cathy had died in Heathcliff's arms, Bernard had wiped Fay's tears and tilted her chin and kissed her. She would like to have known what Miss Oberon had been wearing, what she'd said, whether she was tall or short, but before she could ask, a chauffeur-driven Bentley glided silently to a stop outside the shop and Lady Langbourne, in a mink coat and a hat decorated with a long bird of paradise feather, swept into the shop in a cloud of perfume.

She peered at Fay. 'My dear child, are you ill?' she said.

Miss Greenwood frowned. 'Miss Abrams, perhaps you'd like to make a pot of tea for her ladyship.'

Leaving the door open behind her, Fay disappeared into the kitchen at the back of the shop. She heard them talking.

'The poor child looks positively consumptive,' said Lady Langbourne.

'Miss Abrams has recently suffered a loss, my lady. Her fiancée was killed in action.'

When Fay returned carrying the bone china tea set on a lace-covered tray, Lady Langbourne patted her hand and said, 'Miss Greenwood has just told me about your sad loss. I'm so sorry. All we can do is pray that this dreadful war ends quickly before many more young men lose their lives. You know, dear, it's our duty, every one of us, to do what we can to keep morale high.'

Easy for you to say, my lady, thought Fay, wondering if one of the wealthiest women in London had any idea what real suffering felt like.

As if she could read her mind, Lady Langbourne spoke gently. 'We all have our crosses to bear, Miss Abrams. It's how one deals with trouble and sorrow that's the measure of one's strength of character.'

She chose one hat and ordered a second in another colour. The chauffeur took the hatbox from her hand and opened the car door. Lady Langbourne settled back and raised a gloved hand as the

Bentley glided away. She was the only customer that day.

'You may as well go home early, dear,' said Miss Greenwood. 'Get home before the blackout and put your feet up, and for goodness' sake try to eat something.'

'I'd rather stay until closing time, if it's all the same to you.'

'And I'd rather you went home and got some rest.'

'I'm not tired, Miss Greenwood.'

'Please don't argue with me. You're to go home and let your mother take care of you. I'll see you in the morning.'

Fay walked slowly towards Marble Arch. At the last moment, just as the bus arrived, she turned away and went back down Oxford Street, past Selfridges, where Rita worked, and into Lyons Corner House. She sat alone at a table near the window. She had one cup of coffee, managed to eat a little more than half of the Welsh rarebit, ordered another coffee and sat watching the people bustling by. The light was already fading when she finally boarded the bus.

The street was in complete darkness. Fay fumbled for the key and as the door opened, she came face to face with her mother. She was standing at the bottom of the stairs, clutching her chest.

'What is it? What's happened?'

Hands flapping as if she could not speak, her mother pointed upstairs. 'He's been attacked. Your brother's been attacked.'

Fay pushed past her and raced up stairs. She turned the handle of his door. It wouldn't budge. He'd barricaded himself in. Fay rattled the handle.

'It's me. Come on, Jack. Let me in.'

'Go away. Leave me alone.'

'Please, Jack. Don't be silly. Let me in.'

'I'm not being silly. I don't want to talk to you. I don't want to talk to anyone. Just leave me alone.'

She rattled the door handle again. 'Open the door.' He didn't reply, and she was sure she heard muffled sobs. 'All right, if you don't want to talk to me at least help me with this jigsaw puzzle. Please, Jack. There's such a lot of sky.'

There was a scraping noise as he moved the chair he'd wedged under the handle and a second later the door opened. Hiding his face with his hands, he flung himself down on the bed. Fay sat beside him and put her arm round his shoulder. He was trembling.

'What happened?' She held his hands and pulled them gently away from his face. There was a cut above his eye and his lip was swollen. 'Who did it, Jack? Tell me who did it and I'll beat the living daylights out of him.'

He closed his eyes and she saw the glint of tears under his lashes.

'They called me a dirty Jew. They said I killed Jesus and then they bashed me and they said that Jews drink babies' blood.'

'Who were they? Were they boys from your school?'

'They said if I told they'd...'

'They'd do what, Jack?'

'I can't say it, Fay. I don't want to tell you.'

Fay stroked his hair back from his forehead and whispered, 'Come on, Jack. What did they say?'

'They said they'd chop the rest of my willy off.'

'Did they indeed? Rotten bastards,' she said. 'Tell me who they are.'

'You don't know what they're like, Fay. They're much bigger than me. Practically men.'

'How old?'

'I don't know. Fifteen or sixteen.'

Fay was growing angrier by the minute. Jack was twelve, tall for his age but still just a kid. If he'd been in a fight with another boy, a boy his own age, she knew he would have dismissed it as just one of those things. Part of growing up. This was different, and it hurt to see how miserable he was.

'They're just bullies, and they didn't just pick on you because you're a Jew. They picked on you because you're smaller than them, and that shows you what rotten cowards they are, doesn't it?'

He nodded. She took his hand and pulled him to his feet.

'Come on, let's go downstairs before Mum has a heart attack.' At the door, she slipped her arm around his waist and as she did, she remembered what Lady Langbourne said. 'We'll show 'em, Jack. We'll show 'em what it means to have strength of character.'

Chapter 3

The Langbournes' London residence was a short stroll from the shop. A three-storey Regency house in an elegant square at the top of Portman Place, Fay had been there several times before. Not actually inside the house. She usually only got as far as the front door but, over the housekeeper's shoulder, she had glimpsed the grand staircase and the fine paintings that hung on the walls. On other occasions when Miss Greenwood asked her to deliver Lady Langbourne's order, the housekeeper took the hatbox, closed the front door and Fay had returned to the shop. So, she was surprised and slightly nervous when the housekeeper invited her in and informed her that Lady Langbourne was waiting for her in the study.

It had rained all morning. Fay's shoes were wet. She wondered if she should remove them but the housekeeper ushered her inside and led her straight into a room overlooking a walled garden. Lady Langbourne was seated at a desk in front of the window, addressing a small stack of envelopes. Holding the black cord of the hatbox with one gloved hand, Fay bobbed her head.

'Good morning, my lady. One narrow-brimmed, damson felt hat, trimmed with osprey. Would you like to try it on?'

'No, Miss Abrams. No, I don't think so. I'll do that later. Give the box to Elsie, and she'll take it up to my dressing room.'

The housekeeper smiled and left the room. Fay stood there, uncertain whether she was expected to show herself out or wait for the housekeeper to come back. She cleared her throat and was wondering if she should make some comment about the weather when

Lady Langbourne put down her pen and waved her hand towards a little gilded chair. Certain that Miss Greenwood expected her to hurry back, Fay perched on the edge of the chair with her hands folded in her lap.

Lady Langbourne frowned. 'Miss Abrams, you still look rather pale. I hope you're looking after yourself. It's so easy to allow grief to take one over.'

'I'm doing my best, my lady. Miss Greenwood is ever so kind and just being in the shop takes my mind off things.'

'I'm quite certain it does, Miss Abrams. Keeping busy is one of the best ways to cope with sadness. But even so, it's not the only way. You may feel that it's too early to be thinking about yourself. You may even think it's vain and foolish but I always find that there's nothing like a new hairstyle or even a new hat for brightening up one's spirit.'

Fay did think it was vain. And foolish. And none of Lady Langbourne's business. But what could she say?

'I'm sure you're right, my lady,' she murmured, and wondered how much longer she would have to sit there.

'Miss Abrams, I want you to have this little scarf. It's rather pretty and I am truly sorry for your loss, dear. I really am.'

Wrapped in white tissue paper, the scarf was dark green chiffon, fringed at each end with black and green beads.

Fay shook her head. 'No, Lady Langbourne. It's terribly kind of you but I can't possibly take it.'

'You'll hurt my feelings if you refuse, and what's more I will be disappointed if you put it away in a drawer and never wear it. I don't believe in saving things for best. Wear your best every day.'

'That's a very nice sentiment, Lady Langbourne. The scarf is lovely and if you're absolutely sure… Thank you. I shall wear it all the time.'

'I'm quite sure, Miss Abrams. I want you to have it. Now, I know Miss Greenwood will be expecting you back at the shop but if you could spare me a few more moments…?'

Now what? thought Fay, and wondering what on earth Lady

Langbourne could possibly have to say to her, a salesgirl and a junior one at that, she murmured, 'Well, she'll probably be wondering what's happened to me.'

'I shan't keep you long, Miss Abrams. Now, I know that you may not share my beliefs, dear, not everyone does, but until one has actually experienced evidence of eternal life, it is something which one might dismiss as nonsense. And the fact is it's not nonsense at all.'

Fay ran her hands nervously over the tissue paper and concentrated on smoothing out the creases as Lady Langbourne explained that one of her dearest friends was a gifted medium and clairvoyant.

'I don't know what I would have done without her. With Miss Bartlett's help I found the strength to bear the loss of my only child, my beloved daughter, and I believe you would benefit too. Keeping busy and treating yourself to a new hat is all very well but nothing compares to the comfort that comes from real evidence of eternal life.'

'I don't know about that, my lady. Orthodox Jews believe that the dead shouldn't be disturbed. They should be allowed to rest in peace.'

'And are you orthodox, Miss Abrams?'

'Orthodox? No, Lady Langbourne. That isn't how I'd describe myself at all.'

'Well, as I said, we may not share the same beliefs but I thought I should mention it and if you are in any way interested, Miss Bartlett is giving a demonstration of her gift at Caxton Hall, next Friday at half past seven, should you wish to give it a try.'

The door opened and the housekeeper stepped into the room.

'Elsie, Miss Abrams is just leaving. Will you show her the way?'

Fay thanked Lady Langbourne again for the gift and followed the housekeeper to the front door. Ten minutes later she was back in the shop.

Miss Greenwood examined the scarf. 'It's lovely,' she said. 'How thoughtful of her. I can't say I share her ladyship's views, though I do believe Sir Arthur Conan Doyle was an avid supporter of the spiritualists' movement.'

'Really?' said Fay. 'I'm not certain that's much of a recommendation. I seem to remember hearing that Sir Arthur believed there were fairies at the bottom of the garden.'

Miss Greenwood laughed. 'Does that mean that you won't go and see Miss Bartlett?'

Fay wasn't sure. For the past day or so she had noticed a certain tension in her shoulders, that tingling in her scalp that usually signalled the onset of another vision. If Miss Bartlett could do anything about that, if she could tell her how to make them stop, then Fay would be first in line for a front-row seat. But eternal life? She loved Bernard. She missed him terribly, but did she need the kind of comfort that Lady Langbourne was talking about? Life was complicated enough and sometimes just being Fay Abrams was about as much as she could cope with, but she hadn't dismissed all of her ladyship's advice.

On her half-day, Fay walked down to Cricklewood Broadway and withdrew twenty-five shillings from her savings account. In Woolworths, she bought a pot of Bourjois Rouge for Brunettes, a tub of Dubarry face powder and blew two shillings on a Gala lipstick in Scarlet Rose. "Gala lipstick, the liveliest lipstick in town," so the advertisement said. "Used in moderation, an asset to wartime morale."

At home she shut herself in the bedroom and after studying the photographs from the pile of *Picturegoer* magazines she kept at the bottom of her wardrobe, she picked up the scissors and cut her hair, lifting it at the sides with a couple of combs and allowing it to fall in waves around her jawline. She checked her reflection, hesitated for a moment, picked up the scissors again and cut a fringe, curlier than Claudette Colbert's shiny bangs, but immediately her long, narrow face took on a rounder and softer appearance. Having applied the make-up with an inexpert but discreet hand, Fay dressed in a pair of navy slacks and a pearl grey jumper and went downstairs.

'Oy vey,' said Hetty, hands flapping as if she might pass out at any moment. 'What have you done to yourself? My daughter's a *kurveh*. Just you wait till your father comes back. He'll have a heart attack. And while I think of it, I suppose it was your stupid idea that he should take Jack to the gym.'

'Dad didn't think it was stupid. Nor did Jack. It will be good for him. Being with other boys. Doing a bit of boxing. More use than those jigsaw puzzles.'

'And what kind of thing is that for a Jewish boy to be doing? Punching people.'

Fay smiled. 'Mum, Joe Weisman runs the gym. He's Dad's oldest friend and you couldn't get more Jewish than Joe, could you? Jack will be fine. You'll see.'

When her father came home, he took one look at her and let out a long, low whistle.

'Fay, is that really my girl? This elegant young woman?'

'Mum says I look like a prostitute.'

'Hetty, what a dreadful thing to say.'

'Well, just look at her. How long is it since poor Bernard died? And she's painting her face already. You think that's right? What will people say?'

Fay shrugged. 'I don't care what people say, Mum. No one knows what I feel inside and I don't need to wear my sorrow like a badge for everyone to see. Anyway, someone told me that one's strength of character is measured by how one deals with sorrow. I'm dealing with mine by cutting my hair and putting on some make-up.'

Hetty stared at her, then slamming the door behind her, she shut herself in the kitchen. Cupboard doors banged, pots clanged, accompanied by the sound of her slippers slap-slapping angrily on the lino floor.

Her father grinned at her and winked. 'Well, *buballah*, I don't know about one's strength of character but I must say one's looking very pretty.'

Chapter 4

'You know, Lionel,' said Mrs Feldman, as they walked arm in arm to synagogue, as they did every Sabbath, he in his Crombie overcoat and trilby hat and she dressed from head to toe in her best clothes, 'it's a great pity that we don't have more young women in the Guild.'

'Not everyone is as dedicated to good causes as you, my love.'

'Well, they should be, especially in these difficult times.' In Heathfield Park they were joined by other families making their way towards the synagogue. 'Look, there's Mr and Mrs Abrams and their boy. I see their peculiar daughter isn't with them. I shall speak to Mrs Abrams after the service, Lionel. I'm quite sure the girl could do with something to take her mind off things.'

Lionel made no comment. As she strolled into the synagogue, Rosa Feldman acknowledged greetings with a nod and a wave of her gloved hand. Taking her regular seat, she glanced around and did exactly what the other ladies were doing – a thorough examination of how each was dressed. There was poor Mrs Ebstein with Bernard's sister, Rita, both dressed in appropriately sombre attire. And Mrs Levy wearing that awful green frock again. Had the woman no idea how unflattering it was?

Never certain which part of the service she was supposed to be reading, she turned the pages of her prayer book and tried to concentrate. When Lionel opened the ark and carried the Torah on his shoulder, she watched with pride, but once his part was over, her thoughts drifted back to the telephone conversation she'd had that morning with her sister. Rosa and Lionel had not been blessed with children, a fact that caused her no regrets at all. Especially when she'd spent fifteen minutes of her time that could have been better spent listening to her sister wail and sob that her lovely boys had been snatched from her bosom and sent off to fight and God alone knew whether she'd ever see them again.

'You're not a mother. You can't imagine the torment I'm suffering,' she'd cried.

What could she say? Pull yourself together? No. That would have sounded heartless. The king himself had called for a week of prayer 'for our soldiers in dire peril in France'. There was no point telling her sister not to worry. After all, that's what mothers did; worry themselves sick about their children, even when they'd grown into hulking young men. Rosa wished she could have found just a few words of comfort but it seemed that everything she said made matters worse. When she tried to tell her sister that the boys would be home before she knew it, she'd howled like an animal in pain.

'In a box, Rosa? In a box?'

Now, sitting in the synagogue with Mrs Abrams only a few seats away, the thought crossed her mind that if Fay Abrams really could see into the future, perhaps she could take a quick look into her crystal ball and predict a happy outcome for her two nephews. It was an utterly ridiculous idea. She couldn't imagine what made her even consider it. It was all superstitious nonsense. Her sister needed to keep busy, and all the Abrams girl needed was something to keep her mind more usefully occupied.

The service over, she was standing outside with Lionel when Lou and Hetty Abrams emerged with their son. Leaving Lionel chatting to the rabbi, Rosa walked across and spoke to them.

'Good Shabbos, Lou. Good Shabbos, Hetty. Jack, my boy, I'm sure you grow another inch each day. Where's your sister today?' It was then that she noticed the nasty bruise above the boy's eye. 'Dear me,' she said. 'You've been in the wars, haven't you? What happened to your poor face?'

Jack looked at his father. Lou shrugged. 'A little accident, that's all. He tripped and fell.'

'And Fay? Is she well?'

It was Hetty who replied. 'In case you're wondering why she's not in shul today, Mrs Feldman, it's because unfortunately she doesn't get every Saturday off.' Had she imagined it or was Hetty's manner rather frosty?

'She's back at work, already? Good for her. Nothing like staying busy to take your mind off things. And you, Jack, are you looking forward to your bar mitzvah? How are you getting on?'

'I've learnt the first part off by heart, Mrs Feldman, but I'm still struggling with the rest of it.'

'And when is the momentous occasion?'

'Ten months, three weeks and four days away.'

Rosa smiled. 'Plenty of time, darling. You'll be saying it in your sleep by then. I wonder, Jack, would you mind if I have a quick word with your parents?'

Waiting until the boy had wandered over to speak to the Ebsteins, Rosa lowered her voice and said, 'I've been thinking it might be nice if Fay was to become more involved with the synagogue's social activities. I thought I might ask her to help with the fundraising events. It might take her out of herself – you know, help her forget her loss.'

'Fay is coping very well with her loss, Mrs Feldman, isn't she, Hetty? Our daughter, bless her, is stronger than she looks.'

'And what of her premonitions, Lou? Is she also coping with them? Has she had any more?'

Lou Abrams frowned. 'Excuse me, Mrs Feldman. I have absolutely no idea what you're talking about.'

'Surely you know that your daughter believes she can see into the future?'

It was just an innocent remark. She hadn't meant anything by it but there was no mistaking the fury it provoked in Hetty Abrams. She glared at Rosa as if daring her to say another word.

'I'm warning you, Mrs Feldman,' she whispered, 'you'd do well not to interfere with matters that don't concern you.'

As Hetty stormed off, followed by Lou and the boy, Rosa stood open-mouthed. 'How rude,' she muttered, and seeing Lionel waiting for her, she trotted towards him, squeezed his hand and linked her arm through his.

'Everything all right, my dear?' he said.

'No, not really. Mrs Abrams was quite sharp with me. In fact, Lionel, she was rather rude.'

'I see, and is it possible that you said something to upset her?'

'I suppose she might have taken a little remark of mine the wrong way.'

'Then perhaps it wouldn't hurt to pay her a visit and apologise.'

Fay arrived back from work at quarter to two. Her mother was in a foul mood. She could hear her voice coming from the kitchen.

'You want potatoes? Grow them yourself. One hour I queued yesterday. One whole hour and what did I get? Three pounds. Three pounds of potatoes for a family of four. How far do you think that's going to go, Lou? I'll tell you how far. Nowhere.'

Fay groaned and went straight up to her room. Poor Dad, she thought. How does he put up with it? Moments later she heard the front door close and, looking out of her bedroom window, saw her mother march down the front path, slamming the gate behind her.

Her father was sitting in the kitchen reading the newspaper. He smiled. 'It's all right, darling. You're quite safe. She's gone to Cricklewood. She won't be back for an hour or so.'

'What's wrong with her, Dad?'

He sighed. 'It's not her fault. Your mother suffers with her nerves.'

It was always the same. Something would set her off, some little unimportant thing and her father would make excuses for her. Her nerves. She couldn't help it. She didn't mean to be unkind. Best ignore it. She'll snap out of it soon.

Fay poured herself a cup of tea and sat next to him. 'Where's Jack?'

'Out running. He's training hard and Joe thinks he shows promise.'

'And have you heard about the Italians, Dad? Miss Greenwood was telling me about it this morning. They've joined forces with the Germans.'

He nodded. 'I was just reading about it, but don't worry. Your father's joined the Local Defence Volunteers. So, now we'll definitely win this war.' He folded his newspaper. 'We had a rather strange conversation with Mrs Feldman this morning. She asked why you weren't in shul.'

'I hope you told her to mind her own business. What else did she say?'

'She seemed to think that you needed taking out of yourself. She suggested that you might enjoy getting involved with some of her fundraising events.'

'Really? What on earth gave her that idea? I can't think of anything I'd enjoy less.'

'That's what I thought,' he said. 'Listen, *buballah*. I've no idea what made her say it but I'm afraid she really upset your mother. She said you've been having premonitions.'

Fay stared at him. 'She said what?'

'She said you had premonitions.'

For a moment, she was tempted to tell him everything. How, as a child, she worried about being burnt at the stake, like Joan of Arc; how frightened she'd been when she started seeing things before they happened, and how her mother had yelled at her and told her she was a wicked, unnatural child. And how furious she was with herself for telling Mrs Feldman, of all people. Instead, Fay shrugged.

'Don't listen to her, Dad,' she said. 'Everyone knows that Mrs Feldman is a *yakhne*. An interfering busybody.'

He nodded and changed the subject. 'How's business in the shop? Has it picked up at all?'

'No, we're still terribly quiet. Miss Greenwood got hold of some khaki wool from somewhere or other. We spend most of our time knitting socks for the troops and talking about films.'

'You haven't been to the cinema for a long time, have you? Not since...' He stopped and looked at her, apologetically.

She smiled. 'You're right, Dad. I haven't been for ages. Maybe I'll see what's on next week.'

With a few hours of daylight left, she decided to go for a walk.

Apart from anything else she didn't fancy being at home when her mother came home. She had a slice of toast with just the thinnest scraping of margarine and a generous layer of lemon curd, put on her warm coat and walked down to the park in Childs Hill. Couples strolled in the winter sunshine, girls holding hands with young men in uniform, women pushing prams while high above their heads the sky was littered with barrage balloons. Impossible to ignore with their thick steel cables fixed to the ground, the balloons were there to counter low-level attacks. The ornate metal gates and the old iron railings that once surrounded the park had been ripped out and handed over to factories to turn them into weapons. The once lovely lawn had been removed to make way for allotments. Perhaps it would look better once it was planted out with vegetables, but to Fay the bare, exposed earth looked like a mass grave.

Keeping to the path, she found an empty bench. Tipping her face up to the sun, she closed her eyes for a moment, then reached into her jacket pocket, took out a packet of Player's Weights and a box of matches and lit a cigarette.

'Got a light, miss?' A slim-hipped sailor, who looked not a day over seventeen, stood smiling at her. He took a cigarette from behind his ear and put it between his lips. There were two other boys with him. Both sailors, smooth-cheeked, bright-eyed boys, they stood watching as Fay handed him her box of matches and told him he could keep them. The boy thanked her and lit his cigarette.

'Cheerio, miss,' they said.

'Have a good war,' she whispered, as she watched them strolling along the path, laughing and chatting, boys barely old enough to shave, and she thanked God that her brother was too young to join them.

The sun had begun to disappear behind the houses and Fay was about to leave when, without warning, she began trembling. Aware of the startled stares of curious passers-by, she tried to control it but she couldn't stop. Her teeth chattered. Her whole body was shaking. She clenched her jaw and wrapped her arms across her chest, her eyes tightly closed. Never before had a vision announced itself with such violence. She waited until she was able to move and with her legs barely able to support her, she stumbled home.

Chapter 5

She could taste the choking dust. It filled her lungs. She could still hear the drone of planes overhead, the wail of sirens, of anti-aircraft shells exploding, the sound of bombs whistling through the air. Kneeling on the floor beside her bed, Fay prayed that she was wrong. That what she'd seen would never happen. The threat of a German invasion might be on their minds but until now everyone went about their business largely unhindered. They'd even begun to call it a phoney war. But for how much longer? She didn't know, and seeing again those terrible scenes, buildings flattened, ripped apart, open like dolls' houses, curtains hanging in shreds, Fay buried her face in her hands. When the door opened and Hetty bustled in, she didn't have the energy to raise her head.

'What's wrong with you?'

'Nothing's wrong. Leave me alone, Mum. I'm praying.'

'Praying? What do you mean, you're praying? You're not praying. Look at me. I'm talking to you. What on earth were you thinking of?'

'I don't know what you mean and I really wish you'd leave me alone.'

'I'll leave you alone when you've explained why you told Mrs Feldman you have visions.'

Fay sighed. 'I told Mrs Feldman that Bernard wasn't coming back. That's all. Does it really matter what I said to her?'

'Does it matter? Of course it matters.'

Suddenly it was all too much. Her mother's shrill voice. The dreadful vision. The pretence. The secrets. The everyday battle to live like other people did. She began to cry.

'Fay, what is it? Tell me. Is it Bernard?'

Fay shook her head.

'Well if it's not him I'd like to know what else has upset you.'

'No you wouldn't. Believe me, Mum, you don't want to know. So I won't waste my breath.'

Her mother stared at her. Her expression hardened. She backed towards the door, her hands covering her ears. 'No,' she shrieked. 'You're right. I don't want to know. Not another word. This has got to stop. Do you hear me? I'm not listening. It's not natural. You. You're not natural.'

Fay shuddered as the door slammed. She waited until she could her mother thumping around downstairs, then she dragged her chair across to the wardrobe. Standing on tiptoe, she felt for the exercise book she kept hidden there. Taking a pencil from her bedside table she opened the book, filled in the date at the top of the page and wrote a full account of this, her latest premonition. When she finished, she turned back to the first page and began reading the entry she'd made when she'd seen her beloved grandfather lying on the snow-covered pavement, moaning in pain, through the years to the time when, petrified, she'd described Bernard's death; the handwriting changing in style from the careful, narrow script of an eight-year-old girl to the neat, rounded letters of an adult. The format remained the same. At the end of each entry Fay had left a space and in the line below she'd written, *This happened on* – and here she'd filled in the date – *just as I saw it.*

'Dear God,' she whispered. 'Help me lift this curse and let me be normal.'

Outside Caxton Hall, the queue shuffled forward. Fay stared at the poster, "An Evening of Clairvoyance with Renowned Medium, Miss Alice Bartlett", and told herself it could do no harm. Even supposing there was such a thing as life after death, did she really care? A message from Bernard? Well, that would be nice but what good would it do? Twice she almost turned back. Her visions, they were the only thing on Fay's mind, her visions and her mother's refusal to accept them. Almost at the front of the queue, she decided she might as well see it through and at least she could tell Lady Langbourne that she'd given it a try.

She found a seat three rows from the front. All around her, people chattered excitedly as if they were at the opening night of a new play. Had she heard the sound of an orchestra warming up, it would not have seemed out of place. In the middle of the stage was a chair and table. A man approached the stage, lit a white candle and placed it on the table next to a jug of water. As if this was a signal, backs straightened and the room fell silent. The lights dimmed and a plump, matronly woman appeared from behind the curtains and walked slowly to the centre of the stage. Unremarkable in appearance except for the long, dark blue cape she wore draped over her shoulders, she acknowledged the applause with a gentle smile, raised her arms and bowed her head in a pose that made Fay think of the crucifixion. She caught herself playing with the beads of her scarf as if it was a rosary and silently said the Shema. 'Hear, O Israel, the Lord thy God, the Lord is One.'

Miss Bartlett stepped towards the edge of the stage. Speaking in a clear, sweet voice, she addressed the audience.

'Ladies and gentlemen, the work of a medium is not bound by any single religion. It embraces them all, and this evening I hope to bring evidence to the bereaved that man survives the state called death, and to offer spiritual healing to those suffering from "dis-ease", whether in mind, body or spirit.'

Her peculiar pronunciation of the word "disease" struck a chord with Fay, as it must have done with everyone in that room. They were all there for something. Dis-ease. Spoken like that it covered everything. Grief, loneliness, anxiety and fear, and Fay felt all of those things. She wasn't sure how much longer she could go on behaving as if everything was fine.

Miss Bartlett moved across the stage and sat at the table. Fay watched her place the tips of her fingers on the edge of the table and look out at the sea of expectant faces.

'Before we begin,' she said, 'I must explain that my success is entirely dependent on the goodwill of my guides. Let us hope that they are prepared to cooperate this evening. Otherwise I fear I shall have nothing to tell you.'

She closed her eyes and tipped her head back, and in the moment that followed all that could be heard in the room was the sound of her slow, rhythmic exhalations. No one stirred.

When she opened her eyes, Alice Bartlett was smiling and from her seat near the front, Fay distinctly heard her whisper, 'Thank you, Grey Wolf.'

The sneaking cynicism she'd felt while she'd been queuing outside returned, and once again Fay asked herself what she was doing there. But when Miss Bartlett got going, giving message after message – a name here, a date there, the accuracy of each message confirmed by tearful nods or whispered thanks – she found herself sitting a little straighter in her chair. She stretched her spine upwards as if by making herself more visible, she might attract Grey Wolf's attention.

'You. The young woman with the green scarf.' Fay's heart missed a beat. Miss Bartlett was pointing at her. 'Violets. Yes, violets. He brings you violets. A little posy for your coat.'

That's all she said. Just that. He brings you violets. And with barely a pause she'd moved on to someone else. Fumbling in her handbag, Fay pulled out a hanky. Small and edged with pretty lace, it was a present from Rita and quite useless for mopping up the sudden flood of tears. In seconds it was reduced to a sopping wet ball. Someone patted her shoulder. The man sitting next to her offered her his handkerchief. She mumbled her thanks and sniffed into it until the tears subsided. She heard him whisper that she could keep it, so she blew her nose loudly and thanked him again.

Whether she wanted to believe that life really was eternal; that man survived the state of death, there was no doubt in Fay's mind that the violets were from Bernard. Had it brought her comfort as Lady Langbourne had said it would? Did she even need that kind of comfort? If the visions stopped she could cope with anything, but the tension in her shoulders was already growing stronger. Her head tingled as if an army of ants were marching through the roots of her hair and she was beginning to feel more dis-ease than she could handle. Had she sat at the back of the hall instead of taking a seat so close to the stage, she could have slipped out without drawing attention to herself. She couldn't believe it was happening again. It was less than week since the last vision but she recognised the signs and, with every second that passed, she become more and more detached from her surroundings.

Perhaps if she focused on Miss Bartlett, on what she was saying, she could delay the full onslaught of the vision until she was somewhere more convenient, but Miss Bartlett's voice already sounded muffled as if she were a long distance away, and Fay was struggling to hear anything over the noises in her head. The frightful sounds got louder and louder. Nearer and nearer. She pushed her chair back and tried to stand. That was the last thing she remembered.

Chapter 6

Someone was holding a glass to her lips, urging her to drink. Fay opened her eyes. She thought at first that she was in hospital. A grey blanket had been draped over her and a girl in a St. John's Ambulance uniform was holding her hand, but then she saw that she was lying, not on a bed, but on a brown chesterfield sofa, and high above her head hung a huge chandelier.

'Where am I?' she whispered.

Miss Bartlett was sitting beside her. 'You gave us quite a turn, dear. You fainted so we brought you in here.'

'I'm sorry,' she said. 'I should have had something to eat. I came straight from work.'

The girl in the St. John's Ambulance uniform insisted on taking her temperature and feeling her pulse before she was satisfied that there was no need to call a doctor. She brought Fay a cup of tea and two custard cream biscuits and advised her to pay a visit to her own doctor as soon as she could.

'Just to be on the safe side,' she said.

When she'd gone Miss Bartlett leaned forward and peered anxiously into her eyes. 'You're not...with child, are you, dear?' she whispered.

Fay shook her head. 'No, Miss Bartlett. I'm definitely not pregnant.'

'Perhaps it was the message I gave you. It sometimes takes people in unexpected ways. I mean, hearing from the dear departed. Especially those that haven't experienced it before. It can be a bit of a shock.'

'You're probably right. I suppose it was the message that did it.'

'And you're quite sure you're all right? We can't have you passing out on the bus, can we?'

Fay's visions had never caused her to faint before. They'd frightened her. They'd upset her, but this was the first time she'd passed out. She swung her legs to the floor and slipped her arms into her coat.

'You've been very kind, Miss Bartlett, but I'm absolutely fine now.'

At the door she hesitated, fingering the beads on her scarf. She was aware that Miss Bartlett was watching her and suddenly she was overwhelmed by the need to talk to someone. She needed help, and hadn't Miss Bartlett said she might heal dis-ease, and hadn't the visions become unbearable? An unbearable dis-ease? Fay took a deep breath.

'I know I've already caused enough trouble for one evening but I wonder if I might talk to you. Not about my loss. It's something else. Something that I've never told anyone before.'

Miss Bartlett looked at her wristwatch. 'Well, dear, I'm afraid we have to be out of this room in ten minutes. My hotel is just round the corner. Shall we go there and talk? My driver can drop you off somewhere before the trains and buses stop running. Perhaps we can get you a sandwich. You still look rather pale.'

With Miss Bartlett's arm tucked through hers, they walked together along the darkened streets, stepping round sandbags piled against the walls of buildings, not a chink of light showing through their blacked-out windows. Miss Bartlett asked her name and where she lived. Apart from that, nothing more was said until they reached the hotel. Fay was grateful for those moments of private thought. She'd been guarding her secret for so many years, protecting herself from ridicule, that the very idea of sharing it felt quite unnatural. Unnatural. That's what her mother called her. An unnatural child. And now she was about to open up to a stranger, and despite her kindness, she still wondered if she was doing the right thing; if Miss Bartlett was the right person; if she'd regret talking to her as she'd regretted speaking to her mother and to Mrs Feldman.

Barely noticing her surroundings she allowed Miss Bartlett to lead her to a quiet corner in the hotel lounge. A pot of tea and a plate of sandwiches arrived on a silver tray and Miss Bartlett insisted that she try to eat a little something. Fay obediently nibbled a cucumber sandwich, a dainty triangle with the crusts removed.

'I'm sorry for being such a dreadful nuisance.'

'Miss Abrams, I've spent the last thirty years trying to ease suffering. In another life perhaps I might have been a nurse and a mother but I'm neither. So, just tell me what's troubling you and I'll do my best to help.'

'I'm not sure you can, Miss Bartlett. Yours is a genuine talent. You use it to help others. I have visions. I know what's going to happen but whatever I see I can't prevent it from happening. It's not a gift like yours. It's a curse.'

'Prophecy is not a curse, Miss Abrams. It only becomes a curse when you're afraid to use it.'

Fay met her gaze. 'Excuse me, I don't think you understand. I witnessed my fiancé's death. I saw him fall to the ground with a bullet through his chest. I heard the sounds of battle. I smelt gunfire and blood. I felt the rain on my face and the mud beneath my feet, just as if I was there watching it happen and I was helpless to stop it. I knew how he would die. Had I warned him he wouldn't have believed me. So, how is that a gift? How could I possibly have prevented that from happening?'

'The curse of Cassandra. You know the legend of Cassandra?'

Fay shook her head.

'Well, Cassandra had the gift of prophecy. She foresaw the destruction of Troy. She warned the Trojans but no one listened. No one believed her. They said she was insane.'

'Then she has my sympathy,' said Fay. 'I've being seeing things since I was eight years old. I've recorded every incident in a notebook and kept it hidden away and once, when I was foolish enough to tell someone what I've seen, I was called an unnatural, wicked child and I was told that I should beg for God's forgiveness. So, perhaps you'll forgive me too, because I honestly fail to understand how my visions are in any way a gift.'

Miss Bartlett frowned. 'I've upset you, Miss Abrams. That wasn't my intention.'

'And I'm sorry for my rudeness,' said Fay. 'You see, I'm trying to be strong but this latest…' Her voice faltered as her eyes filled with tears again.

'You had another vision? That's why you fainted?'

Fay nodded. 'It's never happened before. I mean, I've never fainted and the visions seem to be getting more frequent so I'm afraid I rather lost my nerve and what I saw tonight… Well, it was so terrible that I pray with all my heart that it doesn't happen.'

'My dear girl, you're trembling.' She reached across the table and covered Fay's hands with hers. 'But perhaps you should stop tugging at those pretty beads on your scarf before they scatter all over the floor.'

'My scarf? Actually it was a gift from a friend of yours. Lady Langbourne. It was she who suggested I came to see you.'

'You know Lady Langbourne?'

'Not well, but she's a customer in the hat shop where I work. She gave me the scarf when she'd heard about my fiancé.'

'Then doesn't it seem highly possible that when you most needed help, you were led here tonight? It certainly looks that way to me. Have you heard the expression, "when the student is ready, the master will appear"?' She smiled gently. 'Not that I consider myself a master, but why don't you just tell me what you saw and then we can decide what to do next. Perhaps you'd like to telephone your parents first and let them know where you are?'

Fay shook her head. Then she took a deep breath and, when she finally began to speak, the words came out in an unstoppable torrent, like a river breaking its banks.

'I can't bear it anymore. These premonitions, they plague me. And I don't understand. Why me? Why do I have to know?' Aware that she'd spoken louder than she'd intended, Fay lowered her voice to a whisper. 'I watched them die, Miss Bartlett. I heard their shouts and screams. They were thrashing about in the water and there was this awful smell and it burnt my throat and my eyes were stinging. I couldn't breathe. The sea was covered with oil. A thick blanket of sticky oil, and those poor people…it was suffocating them. They were drowning in it. In the oil and the sea. Clinging to bits of debris.' Fay closed her eyes. 'And then there was the roar of an engine and I saw a plane flying low over the sea. Heading straight towards them…those poor people, and there was this terrible noise. I can still hear it now. The plane started firing on them. It machine-gunned them as they thrashed about in the water.'

She tried to hide her face. Miss Bartlett stroked her hair, shielding her from the curious glances of the people at the next table, and when Fay lifted her head, she saw that Miss Bartlett's eyes were filled with tears.

'And the name of this ship? Do you know what it's called?'

Fay shuddered and covered her eyes with her hands.

'Can I get you anything, madam?'

The waiter asked if everything was all right and she heard Miss Bartlett telling him that the young lady had just had a bit of a shock and could he please bring two large brandies. When the brandy arrived, she sipped it slowly, feeling the warmth spread through her throat and her chest.

'There's more,' she whispered. 'I might as well tell you. I saw something else. Not this evening. It was a few days ago. I was in the park and I had another vision.'

She described what she'd seen. Homes ripped apart by bombs. Scenes of utter devastation.

'Dear God, not again,' said Miss Bartlett. 'I still have nightmares about the Great War. The Zeppelins…' Her voice faltered. 'You must warn someone. Someone in authority.'

'And what makes you think they'd believe me? A shop girl making a nuisance of herself. That's what they'd say, and anyway, it's not as if it will come as a surprise. We all know what the blackout's for. And those horrible shelters? Miss Bartlett, everyone knows we might be attacked any day now. I can't see the point of issuing a warning. We're as ready as we'll ever be, aren't we?'

'Perhaps more shelters could be provided. More precautions

taken. I could speak to Lady Langbourne. Her husband is a prominent member in the House of Lords. She trusts me and I'm certain she'd listen.'

'I'm not sure that's a good idea. I don't regret telling you. Not for a moment. In fact, it's been a relief, but I feel very uneasy about anyone else knowing about my visions, especially when I can't see what good it will do.'

Miss Bartlett reached across the table and caught hold of Fay's hand. 'But you must see that it would be quite wrong to do nothing.'

Fay sighed. 'The thing is, I'm almost as fearful of becoming another Cassandra as I am of my visions. I've kept quiet about them until now for that very reason.'

'Listen, dear, Lady Langbourne understands better than most what it feels like to have one's beliefs challenged. She'll sympathise. She'll want to help. Will you let me speak to her?'

Fay thought for a moment, then nodded.

'Good. I shall give you my telephone number and if you need to talk to me, you can call me whenever you want. Now, if you wait here for a moment I'll go and find my driver. He'll see you home safe and sound.'

Five minutes later, resting her head against the soft leather upholstery of Miss Bartlett's car as it moved silently through the streets, Fay's fingers strayed to the beads on her scarf. Lady Langbourne had been so kind to her and now she couldn't rid herself of the feeling that she was about to abuse that kindness. Her cheeks grew hot with embarrassment. The visions were her problem. They'd always been her problem and it was wrong to burden anyone else with them, especially someone like Lady Langbourne. What would she think of her? How could she face her again? By the time the car reached Cricklewood, Fay was certain that she had just made another mistake.

Chapter 7

Mary Langbourne replaced the receiver and resting her elbows on the desk, stared through the open window at the garden of her London home. They had breakfasted together; Lord Langbourne with his head buried behind his newspaper, while she, with a practised eye, dealt with the day's correspondence: invitations to be politely refused or accepted, long letters from friends abroad to be read later at her leisure and the usual requests to mention this pressing matter or another to her husband.

At half past nine, he folded his newspaper, dropped an absent-minded kiss on top of her head and announced that he had important business that required his immediate attention. Barely had the front door closed behind him when the telephone rang and the housekeeper entered the room. Miss Alice Bartlett wished to speak to her most urgently.

What Miss Bartlett had to say left Mary Langbourne feeling somewhat depressed. Kind, gentle Alice had been so good to her and she often wondered how she would have got through that terrible time without her help, but to speak to Lord Langbourne about a shop girl's visions, however accurate they were, well, it was asking too much. Not because Miss Abrams was a Jewess, although that alone would make him even less inclined to listen. No, the reason she hesitated to speak to him was simply because he had made it very clear that he did not, and never had, shared her faith in Miss Bartlett. Lord Langbourne had no time for things he could neither see nor touch, and when Mary had tried to tell him that their daughter spoke to her and that seeing Miss Bartlett eased her awful grief, she had been deeply hurt by his thoughtless mockery. Even now, after all these years, she still found it hard to forgive him. He hadn't listened then. He certainly wouldn't listen now, but Miss Bartlett had practically begged her to use her influence on Lord Langbourne.

'We must do something, Mary,' she'd said. 'We must warn someone so at least they can be prepared.'

She sighed. She had been in such a gay mood before Miss Bartlett's call. It had quite ruined her morning. She glanced at the clock. In two hours she was to meet Edwina for lunch. Edwina's enthusiasm for her beloved St. John's Ambulance Brigade was so delightfully infectious that Mary had promised to support the campaign. She'd planned to wear her new hat, and had been wondering if Edwina would turn up in uniform. It would be so like her, and it simply wouldn't do to allow the telephone conversation to spoil the rest of the day. She refused to dwell on it. Instead, she rang the bell for Elsie and told the girl to run a bath for her and to set out her grey frock with the sequinned collar.

Lying in the warm, scented water, Mary Langbourne closed her eyes. It would be wrong, she decided, to do nothing about Miss Abrams. After all, one did hear of such things: people having premonitions of disasters. And if one had prior knowledge then perhaps one could take action and prevent it from happening. But who to approach? Were it not for his closed mind and his refusal to take anything his wife said seriously, Lord Langbourne's position in the House of Lords would make him the ideal choice. And now that she'd had time to reflect she could quite understand and even forgive Miss Bartlett for taking advantage of the bond they shared. They moved in such different circles and she doubted that Miss Bartlett had many connections with persons of status. She could always mention the matter to Edwina, but then again, perhaps not. There were other people in positions of authority with whom she had more than a passing acquaintance. Surely, she thought, there must be someone among them to whom she could speak. Someone in the

Admiralty, or perhaps the Home Office. All she had to do was pass on the information.

'There may be nothing in it,' she would say. 'It may be nothing more than the wild imaginings of an hysterical young woman but I thought you should know. Just in case.'

Her debt to Miss Bartlett settled, it would be up to someone else to decide what action to take. Mary smiled, stepped out of her bath, wrapped herself in a soft towelling robe and began to dress for her date with Edwina.

Outside Selfridges' staff entrance Fay waited for Rita to finish work. On their half-days off they spent the afternoon together. If the weather was fine they had tea in Hyde Park and on rainy afternoons they went to the cinema. The habit had fallen by the wayside since Bernard's death. Rita was not in the mood and felt she should spend as much time as possible with her mother, but Fay managed to persuade her that it might do her good; that the fresh air and a change of scenery might lift her spirits and she rather hoped it would do the same for her.

When Rita appeared, Fay noticed that she hadn't bothered to change out of her uniform and she'd pulled her hat down too far as if she wanted to hide her face. Fay gave her a hug and kissed her cheek and the two girls walked up to Marble Arch. They strolled, arm in arm, along Rotten Row and stopped for a pot of tea and a cheese sandwich. They sat watching the parade of nannies wheeling their precious little charges in their expensive coach-built prams. Fay was tempted to tell Rita about Bernard's message; the violets he'd sent from 'the other side', but the Ebsteins were more religious than Fay's family and she wasn't sure how she'd take it, so she said nothing. She asked how her parents were bearing up. Rita complained that Fay had neglected to visit them recently. She could have told her the reason she'd been staying away, but she said nothing. The moment they set eyes on her, Mr and Mrs Ebstein burst into floods of tears and she'd begun to think that her visits did more harm than good.

'It seems to me,' said Rita, 'that you've recovered remarkably quickly. It makes me wonder if you really loved my brother.'

'Rita, that's an awful thing to say. You know I loved him. I miss him dreadfully.'

'Well, you don't exactly look as if you're pining away. I mean, all that lipstick for example, and your hat.'

'What about my hat? For goodness' sake, Rita, what do you expect? I'm getting on with life the best way I can.'

Rita sniffed. 'It's easy for you. You've always been much tougher than me. Even when you were a little girl, you never cried.'

Fay shook her head. 'You're wrong, Rita. I cried a lot. I still cry, and if I am tough it's because I've ruddy well had to be.'

'Why? Go on. Tell me what's so blooming difficult about your life.'

Fay wasn't about to explain. She shrugged. 'You wouldn't believe me if I told you. Come on, Rita. We both need cheering up, don't we? Let's see what's going on at Speakers' Corner.'

Unsure if chattering about nothing in particular would relieve the tension between them or if Rita would see that as yet another sign of Fay's lack of feeling, she told her what happened to Jack.

'There were two of them. Rotten sods gave him a thick lip and a black eye.'

'Poor Jack,' said Rita. 'He must have been so scared.'

'He'll be okay. He's taken up boxing.'

Rita was horrified. 'Boxing? Whose bright idea was that?'

'Mine. Why? What's wrong with it?'

'It's a dreadful idea, Fay. Jack's not like you. He's a sweet, gentle boy.'

Fay gave up. They walked to Speakers' Corner in silence and joined the crowd who had gathered to listen to a wildly gesticulating man denouncing the evils of religion. Whether it was his own personal distrust of all religions or the hecklers shouting insults at him, the man was certainly angry about something. After fifteen minutes had passed, Rita began to walk away. Fay followed her.

'You,' shouted the man.

Fay turned. He was pointing straight at her.

'Yes, you. Do you care nothing for your fellow man?'

Fay was startled. The crowd were watching, waiting to see if she would rise to the bait.

'Are you not aware what barbaric persecution is carried out in the name of religion?'

Reluctant though she was to draw attention to herself, Fay was unable to resist the urge to reply. 'Actually, sir, I'm only too well aware but I suspect that standing on a soapbox and shouting about it won't really help your cause.'

A shiver ran down her spine as, above the laugher, she heard him say, 'But it's better than doing nothing, young lady.'

Chapter 8

When a week went by without bumping into Rita at the bus stop, Fay began to suspect that her friend was avoiding her. The atmosphere at home was dreadful. Her mother refused to speak to her. They avoided being in the same room together. She didn't want to fall out with Rita as well, and though temperamental friends were the last thing she needed, Fay telephoned her and invited her to go to the pictures.

'They're showing *The Man in the Iron Mask* at the Queen's. We haven't been to the cinema together for ages. Why don't we go on Thursday night?' she said.

Rita was too busy. She had better things to do. She wasn't in the mood. Fay probably could have talked her round if she'd tried but she wasn't in the mood either.

'Suit yourself,' she said. 'I'll go on my own.'

She asked her father. 'Your mother would enjoy that,' he said.

Knowing full well that she wouldn't, Fay shrugged. 'Ask her if you like but I thought it would be nice if it was just you and me.'

She didn't know what excuse her mother made, nor did she ask, but on Thursday evening she and her father walked down to the Broadway together and joined the queue outside the Queen's. By the time they were shown to their seats the support film had already started. A particularly daft film starring Tommy Trinder, which made them both laugh. Next was a cartoon in glorious Technicolor. When the house lights came on her father dug a bar of chocolate out of his coat pocket.

'Let's enjoy it while we can. They'll be rationing it before long. You mark my words,' he said.

The main feature began. It was billed as a romance grander than life itself. Fay settled back in her seat, ready to lose herself, to forget her visions, her concerns about whether she'd offended Lady Langbourne, Rita's sulky behaviour, her mother, everything except the romance of the story unfolding on the screen. But something was wrong. A feeling of unease that was impossible to ignore. Somehow she managed to concentrate on the film, but her enjoyment of it was spoilt by a strange feeling in the pit of her stomach. The film ended. The credits rolled. There was a short pause. The screen filled with British Pathé's crowing cockerel and the newsreel began.

The Allied Forces' retreat had been reported on the wireless. Winston Churchill called the event a colossal military disaster. Now, watching the exhausted men disembark from the ships, the audience cheered and applauded, but moments later they were stunned into silence. French families were being gunned down by the Germans as they fled from their homes, and a dog with its tail between its legs stood shivering and shaking with fear.

'Those poor people,' whispered her father. 'God help us all if the Germans reach these shores.'

But Fay barely heard him. The caption "Dreadful Loss at Sea" flashed up on the screen. Then the picture of a stricken ship, its upturned hull lined with men, appeared and even before she heard the name of the doomed ship, she saw people thrashing about in the blanket of oil; heard their cries as the machine guns fired at them. But none of this appeared on the screen. Nothing was said except that the ship, the cruise liner *Lancastria*, commandeered to carry troops, was sunk off the French port of Saint-Nazaire and it was not yet known how many lives were lost. The newsreader didn't mention that among the passengers were civilian refugees, women and children, or that the ship was carrying more than five thousand people. But Fay knew. The newsreel had been heavily censored. The truth would have done irreparable damage to morale. That much she understood, but she was unable to prevent the sound that escaped her lips.

He father reached for her hand. 'Fay? Are you all right?' he whispered.

She nodded. 'Can we go now? Please.'

Standing outside the cinema, he put his arm around her waist. 'There's nothing uglier than war. Bernard was a good man and I know how hard it must be for you.'

She could have told him that it wasn't about Bernard. It would have been so easy to tell him everything, but in that moment it seemed kinder to let him believe that he understood why she was upset.

'I'll get over it, Dad. I'm just glad that's Jack's too young,' she murmured.

'And your father's too old,' he said.

As they walked up Childs Hill, the light of her father's torch shining on the pavement in front of them, he chatted about Jack's progress at the gym. She guessed that he was trying to take her mind off the newsreel.

'Your brother might have muscles like knots in cotton but according to Joe he's got the makings of a little champion.'

'He's already a champion,' said Fay, but all the way home that other vision, the one that hadn't yet happened, kept playing itself out in her mind. Ten months into the war and Anderson shelters had been erected in back gardens. Brick-built shelters with concrete roofs stood in school playgrounds. Windows were criss-crossed with tape. The country was already prepared for what was coming. Did they need to be told by a shop girl what was going to happen? Fay began to wish that she'd never met Miss Bartlett.

At home, she went straight up to her room. Apart from the exercise book she used to record her visions, she had been keeping a diary for as long as she could remember. Thoughts, feelings, snatches of conversations, they were all there but recently she'd neglected it. There was some catching up to do and she was making good progress when her father knocked on the door. He sat on the bed and cleared his throat.

'Fay, you and your mother. You think I don't notice? So come on, tell me what happened.'

'It's nothing, Dad. You know what's she like. Always making a big drama of everything.'

'Look, darling, I know she can be difficult but please try and make peace with your mother. For my sake.'

Fay sighed. 'All right, Dad, but not right now.'

'I don't care when you do it. As long as you talk to her and sort it out. I feel like I'm living in the middle of a war zone.'

'What does Mum say about it?'

He shrugged. 'Nothing. She says nothing's wrong.'

'I can't promise it will do any good but I'll try, Dad.'

'Good girl,' he said, and he kissed her and left her sitting there with her pencil in her hand, wondering if a truce could ever be reached.

Chapter 9

Dressed in her favourite navy blue crêpe de Chine evening dress, Lady Mary Langbourne stood on the terrace of Edwina's Park Lane home with a glass of champagne in her hand, the sun on her face and the warm scent of jasmine in the air.

'You look marvellous, darling,' Edwina murmured. 'Such a pity Gerald couldn't be here.'

Mary raised an eyebrow and gave an imperceptible shrug. 'I'm rather glad he's not here.'

The purpose of Edwina's little party was to forge personal alliances between the various sections of the Civil Defence departments. Representatives from the Red Cross and Edwina's precious St. John's Ambulance Brigade were there alongside Fire Auxiliaries and senior personnel from the Emergency Hospital Service. Mary already knew that among the names on Edwina's carefully chosen guest list were one or two departmental heads from the Home Office, and that evening she was determined to keep the promise she'd made to Alice Bartlett. She was going to speak to someone about the girl from the hat shop.

Had her husband been with her she would have thought twice about raising the subject in case he overheard and made some caustic remark. Gerald could be so boorish. One of the reasons she was fond of Edwina was the way she stood up to him. Recalling the occasion when Edwina had announced, in a clear voice, that she failed to understand what made Gerald imagine his opinion was more valid than anyone else's, Mary took a sip of champagne and smiled to herself.

'It's going awfully well, darling,' she said. 'Everyone seems to be having a simply marvellous time.'

Edwina glanced across the lawn. Her guests stood in little groups, clutching their drinks and talking quietly to each other. 'I'd be happier if they did a bit more mingling. That's what they're here for. I wonder, would you be an angel and rescue poor Dickie? No, don't turn round. He's over there with that awful little man from the Home Office.'

'Frobisher?'

'Yes, that's him. Such an unpleasant man. He always makes me think of Uriah Heep.'

Mary laughed. She knew exactly what Edwina meant. Gerald disliked him too, which, now she came to think of it, made Arnold Frobisher ideal for her purpose. Taking a deep breath she strode across to where he stood. He had his back to her and, over his shoulder, she could see Edwina's husband with a look of utter boredom on his face.

'Dickie, darling, you simply must circulate.'

Frobisher turned and looked at her. His high domed head shone with beads of perspiration, and, remembering how damp his hand had felt when they'd first been introduced, Mary was anxious not repeat the experience.

Flashing him a dazzling smile she said, 'Mr Frobisher, I didn't realise it was you. Forgive me for interrupting.'

Clearly grateful for her timely arrival, Edwina's husband kissed her cheek and said, 'Mary, you look divine and you're absolutely right. I've taken up far too much of Mr Frobisher's time. Will you excuse me? I simply must mingle before my wife accuses me of neglecting our other guests.' As he slipped away, he bowed his head slightly in Mary's direction and rolled his eyes.

'Mr Frobisher,' she said, 'such a lovely evening. Perhaps a trifle warm, though. Shall we sit over there in the shade?'

Arnold Frobisher pulled a white handkerchief from his pocket and dabbed his face. 'I confess, Lady Langbourne, it is rather too warm for me.'

He followed as she led the way to a spot under the trees. She placed her glass on the table and invited him to sit beside her. 'You don't have a drink.' She caught the attention of a waiter. 'What will you have, Mr Frobisher? Champagne? A nice, refreshing glass of lemonade?'

'Thank you. Lemonade would be most acceptable, Lady Langbourne.'

'I must say this reception is a simply marvellous idea, don't you agree?'

'Indeed it is, and it's an honour to be invited but I'm not sure that I have much to contribute.'

'Come now, Mr Frobisher, you're being modest. You have a great deal to contribute. You are more than qualified to be here this evening as is everyone involved with the protection of British civilians.'

Frobisher bowed his head and with his shoulders hunched, he rubbed his hands together. 'You're very kind, Lady Langbourne, but these other guests have volunteered to put their own lives on the line whereas my work with the Home Office has more to do with matters of national security.'

She glanced over to where Edwina was talking to an animated group of laughing guests. Among the group, Mary spotted the tall, distinguished figure of Sir Thomas Poulton. She wished she could join them, instead of having to speak to this odious little man.

She forced herself to smile. 'And without your vigilance where would we all be? It's you who must be ever alert to unseen dangers. I'm quite sure that you leave no stone unturned.' She paused and took a sip from her glass. 'So, Mr Frobisher, if I told you that I'd heard something to do with the bombing of civilians, you would want to know?'

'Indeed I would. Even the most harmless rumour or whispered suggestion must be thoroughly investigated. And if I say so myself, I am very thorough, on that you can depend.'

'Well, this is a bit more than a whispered suggestion. It concerns an acquaintance of mine. This young woman has premonitions, visions, call it what you will.'

Frobisher raised an eyebrow and gave what Mary could only describe as a condescending smirk.

'Mr Frobisher,' she said, 'I suggest that you would do well to listen very carefully to what I have to say.'

'Lady Langbourne, I assure you that you have my full attention.'

'Then you'll be as concerned as I am that this young woman sees ordinary homes soon reduced to rubble by German bombs.'

'Well, at the risk of alarming you, Lady Langbourne, this young woman, this fortune teller, is probably right. After all, isn't that the very reason for this gathering? So that everything is in place for just such a disaster?'

Mary curled her hands into tight little fists. Her nails dug into her palms. 'Fortune teller? I wouldn't call someone who described, in minute detail, the sinking of the *Lancastria*, a week before it actually happened, a fortune teller, would you, Mr Frobisher?'

His expression changed. He glanced over his shoulder and drew his chair closer to hers. 'If what you say is true, Lady Langbourne, and who am I to doubt you, what you have just told me is most disturbing. Most disturbing indeed.'

'In what way is it disturbing?'

'That would depend a great deal on the level of detail. As a lady in your position will be aware, news of British losses is invariably censored to some degree. One wouldn't wish to compromise the nation's morale.'

'As I've already told you, the young woman's description was extremely detailed and much of it was not revealed in our newspapers or newsreels, nor on the wireless.'

She couldn't fail to notice that he was becoming visibly anxious, and Mary began to take pleasure in his discomfort. 'More than five thousand passengers. Not two thousand, as was reported. Many of them civilian refugees. Woman and children as well as our troops. They were machine-gunned as they struggled to stay afloat in a filthy blanket of thick, black oil. There, is that enough detail for you, Mr Frobisher?'

'I've offended you, Lady Langbourne. I will, of course, have to study the reports thoroughly but if the details of your friend's account are verified then I will owe you my eternal gratitude for bringing the matter to my attention.'

'In that case I don't think there's anything more to be said except perhaps to repeat that the young woman is merely an acquaintance. I couldn't, in all honesty, describe her as a friend.'

Mary picked up her beaded handbag from the table, but before she could get to her feet, he reached out and touched her arm. Feeling his clammy hand on her bare skin, she had to fight the urge to recoil in disgust.

'I trust you've spoken to no one else about this matter?' he whispered.

She shook her head. 'Absolutely not. Not a word.'

He removed his hand from her arm. 'Then would you be gracious enough to let me know the name of this young woman?'

'I only know her as Miss Abrams.'

'She's a Jew?'

Mary frowned. 'Miss Abrams is an intelligent, well-mannered young woman with a most attractive personality, and yes, since you ask, she is Jewish.' Her irritation, which Mary was certain would have been perfectly apparent to anyone else, appeared to go unnoticed by him.

'And your connection with this Jewess is…?

'My connection, Mr Frobisher? The millinery shop in Mayfair where Miss Abrams is employed as a salesgirl. Now, you will excuse me? I simply must speak to our hostess.'

He stood and bowed awkwardly. 'It's been an honour speaking with you, Lady Langbourne. I am most obliged to you and I shall look forward with pleasure to our next meeting.'

As she moved quickly away out of the shadow of the trees towards the terrace, Mary lifted her face towards the sun, breathed in its warmth, composed herself and, sighing with relief, walked across the lawn to join Edwina and Sir Thomas.

Chapter 10

On her way home from work, Fay had just passed the shelter on the corner of Holden Avenue when she heard the wail of sirens. She stood still and gazed up at the sky, listening for the drone of distant planes. Seeing nothing, hearing no sound of engines, Fay ignored the siren and carried on walking. She arrived home to find her brother sitting at the kitchen table. He was reading a comic.

'Why aren't you in the shelter?' she said.

He looked up and smiled. 'Why aren't you?'

There'd already been two false alarms. Trial runs. They had spent a miserable three and half hours huddled together in their Anderson shelter at the bottom of the garden before the all-clear sounded. Nothing happened. No enemy planes flew overhead. No bombs dropped.

'One day it will be the real thing,' she said. 'Perhaps we ought to go down to the shelter.'

'You can if you like,' said Jack. 'I can't hear any planes. Can you?'

'That's not the point, is it? So, where's our dear mother?'

He grinned and pointed to the hall. 'In the cupboard under the stairs,' he whispered.

Fay tapped on the cupboard door. 'You all right in there, Mum?'

'There's an air raid on,' said her mother.

'Then why aren't you in the shelter?'

'It smells in there.'

'What of?'

'Rotten vegetables. There's no room for you in here. Go down to the shelter. Your brother's in there on his own.'

Fay looked at Jack. He held a finger to his lips and Fay closed the kitchen door so her mother couldn't hear them whispering together.

'You know, Jack, we've been lucky so far. It's been troop ships and military targets taking the hits but things could change overnight. I don't want to frighten you but we shouldn't take unnecessary risks.'

Jack shrugged. 'If your number's up, then that's it,' he said.

She laughed. 'Where did you hear that?'

'In here,' he said, pointing to his comic. 'It's what Rockfist Rogan always says.'

Ten minutes later the all-clear sounded. The cupboard door creaked open and her mother appeared in the kitchen.

'Mum, you've got cobwebs in your hair,' said Jack.

'Never mind the cobwebs. Get that kettle on. My nerves are all shot to pieces.'

While Fay made tea, Jack began asking questions about the last war. She could tell her mother wasn't in the mood. Jack didn't seem to notice. She heard him ask about the Zeppelins.

'Isn't it enough it's all happening again?' said her mother. 'Talk about something nice for a change.'

'Mum,' said Jack, 'how old were you when your father died in action?'

'What kind of question is that? I was the same age as you are now.'

'And was he a hero? Did he win any medals?'

'Your grandfather was killed in battle. That's all you need to know. Now, can we please talk about something else?'

It was Fay who changed the subject.

'Tell us about your mother,' she said. 'You never talk about her. I don't even know what she looked like. You must have a photograph of her somewhere.'

Her mother's cup clattered against the saucer. She stared at Fay.

'No,' she said. 'There are no photographs of your grandmother. None.'

'All right, Mum,' said Fay. 'If you don't want to talk about her, that's fine with me.'

'She died when you were three.'

'I know. That's why I don't remember anything about her. I just wondered what she was like, that's all.'

Her mother's lips tightened. 'What she was like? You really want to know? She was like you. More's the pity.'

Before she time to retaliate, Jack pushed back his chair and stood with his hand on her shoulder.

'There's nothing wrong with Fay. She's kind and brave and funny and she doesn't say nasty things about anyone.'

'It's all right, Jack,' said Fay. 'Why don't you take your comic upstairs? I need to have a quiet word with Mum.'

Fay waited until the door closed behind him. 'Okay, let's have it. Come on, spit it out. Get it off your chest once and for all.'

The chair scraped against the floor as her mother pushed it back and got to her feet. Moving quickly, Fay stood in front of her.

'No, you don't. You're not going anywhere till you tell me what this is all about.'

'You know very well what it's about.'

'My visions? Is that it? You think I enjoy them? I was eight years old, Mother. A frightened little girl and what did you do? Did you try and comfort me? No, you shook me so hard my teeth rattled. You said I was wicked. You told me I was an unnatural child. And I believed you. I honestly thought that I was evil and you refused to talk to me. Can't you see how cruel that was?'

Her mother's face crumpled. She sank back on the chair. 'You don't understand. You don't know what it feels like to suffer like I've done. Living with fear every day.'

Fay almost laughed in her face. 'Do you know what, Mum? You wear martyrdom as if it was a badge of honour. You, with your long-suffering sighs and your sour expression. You're lucky that you've got such a kind-hearted husband and to tell you the truth, it's a miracle that Jack is so good-natured. Fear of what? What have you got to be scared of? Come on. I'm listening.'

Before she could answer, the back door opened and Fay's father walked into the room. He was wearing a khaki uniform, and in his hand was a rifle. He was smiling. Fay saw the smile fade as he looked from his wife back to his daughter.

'What's going on?' he said.

'Nothing, Dad. We're just having a nice chat about the old days, aren't we, Mother?' Without meaning to, Fay managed to make the word 'mother' sound like an insult.

'Hetty?' Resting the rifle against the wall, he put his arm round his wife's shoulders.

She brushed it away. 'I haven't had time to make supper. There was an air raid.'

'I know. Just a trial run. That's all. Nothing to worry about. I'll pick up some fish and chips if you like.'

'Don't get skate, Lou. I don't like it. I'll have haddock,' said her mother, and she walked out of the room.

As the door closed behind her, Fay's father picked up his rifle, clicked his heels, stood to attention and saluted. 'Yes, sir. Right away, sir,' he said.

'You look smashing, Dad. Really smart. Is that gun loaded?'

'No, we've got the rifles but no ammunition yet. Still, it looks good, doesn't it?' He took off his cap, breathed hard on its badge and gave it a quick polish with his handkerchief. 'So, tell me, have you ironed things out with your mother?'

'Not sure, Dad. The air raids make her nervous, so it's difficult to say.'

He nodded. 'Poor Hetty. Anyway, darling, at least you tried.'

She didn't know what had woken her. The house was quiet. She looked at the clock. It was ten past two. As she lay there waiting to go back to sleep, her mother's barbed comment began to take on a new significance. Fay threw back the covers and tiptoed downstairs. She closed the living room door quietly behind her. The room was in complete darkness, blackout curtains pulled tightly across the windows, as she felt for the light switch. In the sideboard drawer she searched under starched napkins and tablecloths until she found what she was looking for. The album was inside a box, wrapped in tissue paper. She couldn't remember the last time she'd seen it. Certainly not in the last ten years or so.

She sat at the table and began looking at the photographs. There were her parents on their wedding day, her mother looking small and dainty, smiling shyly into the camera, her father with his arm around her waist. Her parents at the seaside, at the zoo, in the park. Her mother holding a baby, and underneath the picture, in her father's careful copperplate writing, she read, *Hetty and Fay*. Fay on a swing. Fay in a party dress. Hetty in 1928, slightly plumper and with a shadow of the sour expression which would become almost permanent over the years, holding another baby, Fay's brother Jack. There were fewer photographs after that. Fay and Jack together. None of her mother. She turned the pages back to the beginning and studied the pictures again.

There was one photograph that saddened Fay. It had been taken in a studio on her third birthday. Her hair was in curls. She wore a short, white dress and white socks and shoes. She was standing on an upholstered stool. Her mother, trim ankles showing beneath a silk gown, stood beside her, one arm around Fay's waist. They were holding hands and lying on the stool was Fay's doll, Martha. She still had that doll. It sat on her bedside table, a little grubbier than it had once been, but the same doll that her parents had bought for her third birthday. As she studied her mother's face, Fay had to fight back the tears. The gentle, loving expression in her eyes. That look of motherly pride. The way things were before the visions began.

Quickly, she closed the album and reminded herself what she was actually looking for: photographs of her grandparents. She was sure there were one or two, formal studio portraits, stiff, posed, unsmiling shots. Under a sheet of tissue paper at the bottom of the box she found a manila envelope. She tipped its contents on to the table. There were two sepia pictures of her father's parents, mounted on thick card with the name and address of the photographer printed in loopy script across the bottom. Written on the back in faded pencil were her grandparents' names and the date, *Lubov and Vitaly Abramovich, 1908*. Fay smiled as she studied the pictures. Her grandparents, no doubt aware of how suspicious the English were of foreigners, had wisely changed their name to Abrams, perhaps not realising that any Jewish-sounding surname would most certainly arouse the same suspicion.

She was disappointed. She'd hoped to find a photograph of her mother's parents. It wasn't until she was replacing the album in the drawer that she found the photo of Zofia. Fay's heart thumped violently against her ribs. Dressed in the same clothes, the same scarf covering her hair was the woman she'd seen leaning over Jack's cradle. Her mother's mother. And when Jack was born Zofia Kroll had already been dead five years.

'I saw you, Grandma,' she whispered. 'You were there, weren't you?' Fay stared at her grandmother's face, at her sad, haunted eyes. 'Am I really like you? Did you have visions, too?'

Chapter 11

As Rosa Feldman trotted down Hendon Lane she heard the boom of anti-aircraft guns. She ignored the sound. She'd grown used to it. The guns were being tested in case of air raids. "Be Prepared." "Careless Talk Costs Lives." New slogans were popping up all the time. She shuddered as she remembered the number of times Lionel had raised the subject of an Anderson shelter.

'In our garden? In our beautiful garden? Over my dead body,' she had said. And he had raised an eyebrow, in that annoying way of his and said, 'Quite possibly, my dear. Quite possibly.'

"Dig for Victory", her least favourite slogan, meant Lionel's vegetables took priority over her flower beds, but she'd refused to let him dig up her precious roses. Before she left the house that afternoon, she'd cut five yellow ones and a few sprigs of lavender for the rabbi. She knew how much he appreciated those homely touches. At the synagogue, she tapped on his door. There was no answer so she arranged the flowers in a vase and left them on his desk.

At the back of the building was the poky little room where the synagogue's benevolent fund archives were kept. Frowning at the sight of the dusty shelves, Rosa tied a scarf around her hair and covered her dress with an old pinafore. The shelves were filled with an untidy mass of papers and forms, ancient box files with illegible labels, manila envelopes stuffed to bursting, receipts and cash books which looked as if they might, at some time, been subjected to water damage.

Bringing order to the archives was something she'd been meaning to tackle for months. Rosa rolled up her sleeves and made a start, one shelf at a time. First she sorted everything by date, then alphabetically – 1910 to 1914 in one neatly labelled box file, 1915 to 1918 in another.

She had got as far as 1926 when she stopped for a break. Her throat was dry and her hands were grubby. In the kitchen she washed her hands, poured herself a glass of water and wondered if she should call it a day or carry on for a bit longer. It seemed a pity to stop now that she was in her stride. Another hour and she could have the job finished. Deciding that she would at least clean the shelves before she left, Rosa added a handful of soap flakes to a bucket of warm water and carried it across the hall. Standing on a chair she began wiping the grimy surface of the top shelf. It was then that she spotted an envelope wedged between the shelf and the wall.

'Damn and blast,' she muttered as she climbed down from the chair. She dried her hands on her overall and emptied the contents of the envelope on to the desk. Discovering to her annoyance that the contents dealt with a case dated 1915, Rosa reopened the relevant box, checked the name and was about to file the papers in the correct alphabetical order when her attention was caught by a familiar signature. Rosa's father-in-law had been treasurer of the synagogue, and there in his meticulous script, he had apparently authorised the payment of five guineas to one Esther Kroll, aged fifteen. Her circumstances were described as being worthy of the support and benevolence of the fund, her father being deceased and her mother, Zofia Kroll, recently… Here the word was so faded that Rosa couldn't quite make it out. Incapacitated? Is that what it said? She held the thin, yellowing page up to the window. Incarcerated. That was the word. Poor Zofia Kroll had been incarcerated.

Of all the worthy causes that the synagogue had supported over the years, Rosa had not expected to find one quite like this. It aroused her curiosity and she wondered if her father-in-law might recall the case. It was a long time ago but, even at eighty, the old man was still as sharp as a pin.

Rosa's shoulders ached. Her eyes were beginning to feel quite sore from all the dust and she was longing for a nice warm bath. She quickly filed Zofia Kroll's papers away and feeling rather pleased with herself, hurried along the corridor to the front door. On her way out, she bumped into the Abrams boy.

'Oh! Jack, you gave me quite a start,' she said. 'On your way to your Torah lessons?'

'Yes, Mrs Feldman. The rabbi's expecting me.'

Rosa stood in front of the door. 'How's your sister? I haven't seen her in shul recently.'

The boy shuffled his feet. 'Well, she doesn't get home till late and sometimes she has to work on Saturday mornings.'

'And your parents, are they both well?'

He told her they were fine and before she could say anything else, he squeezed past her and into the synagogue. 'Excuse me, Mrs Feldman. Don't want to keep the rabbi waiting.'

Nice boy, she thought. Polite. Not like his mother or that peculiar sister of his.

She was walking along Heathfield Park when it dawned on her that, in all her years as a member of the shul, she couldn't remember a single occasion when Jack's mother attended any of the social events. Mrs Abrams made no effort at all to be part of the community. In fact, now Rosa thought of it, Hetty Abrams actively discouraged attempts to befriend her. It wasn't until she reached the corner that the thought struck her. Wasn't the name 'Hetty' a shortened version of Esther? She wished she'd thought of it before, and that the boy hadn't been in quite such a hurry.

As soon as she arrived home, she hurried into the kitchen and flung open the back door. Lionel was at the far end of the garden doing something to a row of bamboo canes. She frowned. Lionel's pale, sinewy arms were bare. He was wearing an old, greying vest, fit only for dusters. His bony knees were barely covered by a pair of baggy khaki shorts, and on his head was a knotted handkerchief.

'Come inside, Lionel. I want to talk to you. And for goodness' sake, take that thing off your head. What will the neighbours think?'

Lionel smiled and waved. 'Coming, my love,' he said, trundling his wheelbarrow down the path.

She waited until he'd wiped his feet and removed his gardening gloves. 'Lionel, would you say that Hetty Abrams was about the same age as me?' Seeing the confused expression on his face, she said, 'Don't worry, dear, it's not a trick question. Just tell me what you think.'

'In that case, my love, I would say that Hetty Abrams is several years older than you.'

Satisfied with his reply, Rosa reckoned that the mere fact that she was young enough to have a twelve-year-old son must mean that she wasn't as old as she looked.

'The reason I asked,' she said, 'is that while I was tidying up the benevolent fund's archives I found something very interesting. It was something that happened when your father was treasurer. I recognised his handwriting. Anyway, it seems that in 1915 the synagogue was looking after a girl whose mother had been imprisoned.' Lionel had his back to her. She was certain he hadn't been listening to her. 'Lionel, did you hear what I just said?'

'Yes, dear. You said you found something interesting.'

'The girl's mother was imprisoned, Lionel. Incarcerated. And to tell you the truth, I've a very strong suspicion that the girl is none other than Hetty Abrams.'

Lionel turned and looked at her. 'And exactly how have you come to that conclusion, my love?'

She smiled. 'Just a feeling. Call it feminine intuition.'

'Then I urge you, for your own sake, to keep your suspicions to yourself.'

'All I'm saying is that it shouldn't be that difficult to find out if it's true.'

Lionel frowned. In two strides, he had crossed the kitchen to where Rosa stood and was gripping her shoulders so tightly that for one dreadful moment she actually thought he was going to shake her.

'Now, you just listen to me,' he said. 'For once in your life keep your nose out of other people's affairs. I mean it, Rosa. Stop interfering in matters that don't concern you.'

She was astonished. She stared up at him. Still gripping her shoulders and staring straight into her eyes, he lowered his voice.

'I'm telling you for your own good. Whatever you think you found in those archives, it's confidential. It's nothing to do with you. Do you hear me, Rosa? It's none of your business.'

Without waiting for her to respond, he walked out of the room. She heard him go upstairs. He closed the bathroom door rather louder than necessary and for a moment Rosa wondered if he was right. It was unlike him to express his opinion so forcibly. But doing nothing would be against everything she believed in. She couldn't help caring about other people. Hers was a caring nature, and if her suspicions were right, Hetty deserved her sympathy. After all, just because someone didn't ask for friendship or understanding it didn't necessarily mean that they didn't need it.

It was the telephone call from one of her ladies that gave Rosa the excuse she was looking for. She was sorry to let Rosa down but her family's safety must come first. She was taking her children to the country. They were getting as far away from London as they could. If Lionel was right, not about what she had found in the archives but what he'd said about owing Hetty Abrams an apology, Rosa had two legitimate reasons to pay a visit to the Abrams house. Three, if she counted the bundle of runner beans she cut from the garden before she left the house.

She would apologise even though she didn't believe she'd said anything that warranted an apology. If Fay was at home she could ask if she'd given any more thought to joining the Ladies' Guild. She might even persuade Hetty to join, too, and if she could gently guide the conversation towards the last war and to Hetty's childhood, perhaps she might get lucky and satisfy her curiosity about Zofia Kroll.

It was their boy who opened the door. Rosa asked if his mother was at home. Before he had the chance to reply, Hetty Abrams appeared.

'I thought I recognised that voice,' she said.

For one awful moment Rosa thought she was going to shut the door in her face. 'Ah, Mrs Abrams,' she said. 'I'm sorry to arrive unannounced. If it's not convenient I can call back another time but I was hoping to have a few words with you.'

'I suppose you'd better come in then, Mrs Feldman.'

Rosa followed her into the front room. Not as tasteful as her own living room, it was, nevertheless, nicely furnished, surfaces well-polished and the mantelpiece free from clutter.

'Lovely room,' said Rosa, wondering if Hetty would offer her something to drink. It was a warm day and it had been a long walk. Rosa felt hot and sticky and Hetty had still not invited her to sit down.

'This won't take long, will it, Mrs Feldman? I am rather busy.'

'I would have telephoned first but I couldn't find your number. Would you mind if I sat down for a moment?'

Hetty shrugged. 'Help yourself,' she said, pointing to an armchair.

They sat facing each other, either side of the fireplace. Rosa smoothed her skirt over her knees and managed to force a smile. 'Mrs Abrams, I think I may owe you an apology. You were quite right. Your daughter's premonitions are none of my business and it was wrong of me to mention them.'

'And is that all you wanted to say?'

For God's sake, thought Rosa, I've apologised. What more do you want?

'I wonder, may I trouble you for a drink? It's such a warm day.'

Hetty got up and opened the door. 'Jack, bring Mrs Feldman a glass of water, please.'

She would have much preferred a cup of tea, but when Jack appeared with a glass of water, she thanked him. 'Such a nice boy,' she murmured. Then giving him the bundle of runner beans, she said, 'Perhaps you'd like to put these in the kitchen, Jack.' She looked at Hetty. 'From our garden, Mrs Abrams. I thought you might like them.'

'Thank you. Now if there's nothing else...'

'Well, actually I was hoping to persuade you and Fay to join the Ladies' Guild. I've already lost my best helper this morning and, with things the way they are now, I expect an exodus from London might happen quite soon. You see, the trouble is, if the Guild loses any more ladies it's going to leave me in a bit of a pickle.'

'I see. Well, I'll mention it to Fay.'

'What about you, Mrs Abrams? Would you be interested? I really need all the help I can get.'

'I'll think about it.'

'Good. Now, while I'm here there is something else. I know you've lived in this area for a long time. I was wondering if you remember my father-in-law, Morris Feldman. Perhaps your mother knew him. I understand that he was once the treasurer of our benevolent society.'

Hetty was staring straight into Rosa's eyes, lips tightened and eyes narrowed. Rosa knew immediately that she'd touched a raw nerve. A second later Hetty had risen from her chair and was looking down at her.

'Thank you for the beans, Mrs Feldman. Do finish your drink before you go.'

It was all so neatly executed that Rosa found herself outside in the street before she had time to say another word. It was a long walk back to her house and it was still uncomfortably warm, but she had no regrets. She had apologised. She had made an effort, which was more than could be said for Hetty Abrams, and most satisfying of all, if Hetty's reaction was anything to go by, Rosa's suspicions had been confirmed. Perhaps she might never discover what awful crime Zofia had committed, but for the time being Rosa was content.

Chapter 12

On Sunday morning came the gloomy news that during the night, Luftwaffe bomber crews had dropped their bombs on the City of London. Fay listened as the solemn voice of the newsreader announced that from Aldgate to West Ham, factories and shops were on fire and homes had been destroyed. It was believed that the target had been oil tanks at Rochester and Thames Haven but the bombers had overshot the target.

'So it might have been an accident,' said Jack.

Her father frowned. 'Maybe, but you know what's going to happen now? The RAF will retaliate. Mark my words, our boys are going to bomb Berlin and no one's going to pretend that was an accident.'

'And so it begins,' murmured Fay.

'I'll take a stroll down to the newsagents later,' said her father, 'and see what the papers are saying. But from now on we all stick to the rules. Don't take chances. God alone knows what's coming next. By the way, Hetty, I found a bundle of fresh runner beans in the slop bucket. Did you mean to throw them away?'

Her mother was standing by the kitchen door, staring out at the Anderson shelter. 'Mrs Feldman gave them to me. I didn't want them.'

'Why ever not? Lionel probably just grew more than they could use. Anyway, what happened to waste not, want not?'

'I told you, Lou. I don't want them. Now, can we please forget the ruddy beans? I've got more important things on my mind.'

They all turned and looked at her. 'Like what, for instance?' said Fay.

'Like waking up one morning and finding German troops marching up our street.'

'That won't happen, Hetty,' said her father.

'It might,' said Jack. 'My friend at the gym says the Germans are so advanced that they've invented bullets that shoot round corners.'

Her father smiled. 'And you believe that, do you?'

Jack shrugged.

'Whatever kind of bullets they've got, we'd better start stocking the Anderson up with provisions,' said her mother. 'Fay, you can help me make a list. Make sure I don't forget anything. You're good at that.'

Not absolutely sure whether her mother was having a dig at her or whether she simply meant what she said, Fay watched as she opened the pantry door.

'Come on. What are you waiting for? Find a pencil and let's make a start.'

Fay glanced at her father. He smiled and winked. 'Your mother's right. We need spare batteries for the torch,' he said.

'Write that down, Fay,' said her mother.

By the time the list was finished, Fay knew that what she'd said in anger to her mother had struck a nerve. She had the feeling that her mother had been doing some serious thinking and wondered if she dare raise the matter of her visions again when they were next alone. More than anything, Fay wanted to know everything she could discover about her grandmother, but perhaps it was best to take things one step at a time. At least they were being civil to each other. It was a start, enough to be getting on with.

On her way to work the next morning, Fay was a few yards from the bus stop when she saw Rita walking ahead of her. She caught up with her and asked her where she'd been.

'I've been looking out for you every morning. I was beginning to think you were avoiding me,' she said.

'Of course I wasn't avoiding you. They changed my shift, that's all. I've been going in a bit earlier.'

As they waited for the bus, Rita told her that on Saturday night all the windows in her cousin's house had been blown out and part of the roof collapsed.

'They moved in with us yesterday. Just for the time being,' she said. 'My aunt and uncle and Howard. You remember my cousin Howard? It's a bit of a squash but we'll manage somehow, and Mum's so busy that it's taken her mind off Bernard.'

Rita looked different. Her hair was pulled up at the sides and rolled into curls on top of her head. Fay was sure it was a few shades lighter than usual and the summer frock she was wearing was definitely new. She was more cheerful, and so much more like her old self that she wondered what had caused the transformation. By the time the bus reached Marble Arch, she'd managed to worm it out of her. Rita had taken a shine to a young man in the accounts department.

'He's ever such a nice chap,' she said, as they walked, arm in arm, along Oxford Street. 'His name is Danny. He's taking me out this evening straight after work.'

Outside Selfridges, Fay gave her a hug and told her she looked lovely. 'Have a good time and don't do anything I wouldn't do.'

As she crossed the road to Bond Street she felt a twinge of envy. Rita's young man was an accountant. His was a reserved occupation. Unless things changed, he was safe. He wouldn't be called up. Bernard could have avoided conscription too. He was a tailor. They needed tailors for the manufacture of uniforms but he'd made his choice and joined the army. If he'd stayed at home they'd probably be making plans for their wedding now. Fay pushed the thought to the back of her mind. It wasn't helpful to think about what might have been.

When she arrived at the shop she found the normally calm Miss Greenwood quite agitated about the attack on the City.

'I'm miles from there but I could smell the buildings burning.' On Sunday morning she'd looked out of her window and seen a plume of black smoke in the sky. She'd watched it turn red. 'It was quite dreadful,' she said. 'Such worrying times.'

'I think we'll just have to get used to it, Miss Greenwood. It's bound to get worse before it's all over.'

'It seems to me, dear, that considering how serious things have become, you're remarkably calm.'

'I can assure you I'm not the least bit calm. I'm as nervous as the next person but I do try not to worry about the things I can't change. Bashert. It's a Yiddish word, Miss Greenwood. It means "something that's meant to be".'

'Bashert?' said Miss Greenwood.

It sounded so peculiar hearing that word on Miss Greenwood's lips that Fay couldn't help laughing.

'Did I pronounce it right?'

'Perfectly,' said Fay.

It was when she was rearranging the window display, concentrating on draping coloured scarves around the necks of the dummies, that Fay became aware that someone was watching her. Glancing up, she saw a man in a dark suit and a trilby hat. He was standing on the other side of the road. As soon as he saw she was looking in his direction, he turned his face towards the building behind him. When she looked up again, the man had gone.

She tried to put it out of her mind. At lunchtime, she went into the kitchen at the back of the shop. There was an account of the bombing raid on the city in Miss Greenwood's newspaper. Fay began reading it. She heard the telephone ring. She heard Miss Greenwood answer it. Moments later she appeared in the doorway looking rather puzzled.

'I've just had the most peculiar conversation, dear,' she said. 'I really don't know what to make of it. Someone wanted to know how long you'd worked here.'

Fay stared at her. 'Who wanted to know?'

'Someone from the Home Office. He asked all sorts of questions. Did I know if you were born in this country? Did you answer an advertisement or come from the Labour Exchange?'

'And what did you tell him?'

'I told him what I knew. I tried to be helpful but I must say I am at a loss to understand why the Home Office is so interested in you. He even asked if you spoke any other languages and whether I knew you were a Jew.'

'Did he, indeed? I shouldn't worry, Miss Greenwood. They've obviously mistaken me for someone else. Perhaps they think I'm a dangerous spy.'

Miss Greenwood frowned. 'I don't want to alarm you, dear, but for your own sake, I would advise you not to say things like that. Not even in jest. Let's hope you're right. Let's hope they've mistaken you for somebody else. Because quite frankly, I would rather not have another telephone conversation like that again. So let's say no more about it.'

If Miss Greenwood had known about the man who'd been watching her, it would probably have thrown her into a state of anxiety. Fay chose not to mention it. There was only one explanation for the Home Office's sudden interest in her. They'd heard about her visions and either they were taking them seriously or they suspected her motives. Whatever the reason, Fay knew she had no one to blame but herself. She had a horrible feeling that she'd started something she'd live to regret. Shrugging it off as bashert was no comfort, and several times that day Fay caught herself glancing across the road to where the man had been standing. When the shop closed and she was walking towards Marble Arch, she walked quickly, turning her head every now and then to see if she was being followed.

Passing the Cumberland she almost collided with a woman who'd bustled out of the hotel and come to an abrupt stop on the pavement in front of her. Fay mumbled an apology.

'Miss Abrams, is that you?'

She turned. The woman smiled. It was Alice Bartlett, the last person she wanted to bump into. Fay hadn't forgotten her kindness but it was more than a month since she'd collapsed at Caxton Hall. Since then there'd been no more visions. And now, just as she'd begun to hope that she'd had the last one, the Home Office had taken an interest in her and here was Miss Bartlett insisting that Fay join her for a light supper. She didn't want to appear rude but it was with mixed feelings that she allowed herself to be led inside the hotel.

'I've been in town since yesterday,' said Miss Bartlett. 'Such a marvellous hotel. I was just going for a little walk in the park but I'd much rather spend some time with you, dear. Shall we have a glass of sherry before we go in to eat?'

They sat in a corner of the bar. She listened politely while Miss Bartlett told her about a visit she'd taken that morning to the British Museum. She planned another trip to London in a fortnight.

'I'm coming up by train. Perhaps we could meet somewhere. You still have my telephone number, don't you?'

'Yes, I have it somewhere,' said Fay.

Miss Bartlett took a sip of sherry and leaning closer, she whispered, 'Tell me, dear, have you had any more visions?'

She shook her head. 'No, no more since I last saw you. I'd like to think that they've stopped now.'

'Really? I understand how you feel but I doubt that they'd stop just like that.'

Fay frowned. 'Why not? I don't want to have visions. I never wanted them. I want to be normal. Ordinary. Like everyone else.'

'But you're not like everyone else, Miss Abrams. You can never be ordinary, no matter how much you'd like to be.'

Wishing she'd gone straight home, she couldn't hide her irritation. She stared hard at Miss Bartlett. 'I don't mean to be rude. I hope you'll forgive me but I deeply regret having spoken to you about my visions in the first place. I don't feel comfortable about it. It was a mistake.'

'Of course it wasn't a mistake. You needed help and I was happy to give it.'

Fay slid her glass away and took out a cigarette. A waiter appeared from nowhere and lit it for her. As soon as he'd disappeared, she leant forward and speaking very quietly, she said, 'But you haven't helped me, Miss Bartlett. You were very kind and I know you meant well but you haven't helped me at all. In fact, I'd go so far as to say that it's quite possible that, without realising it, you have actually made life rather difficult for me.'

Miss Bartlett looked puzzled. 'I really don't understand. In what way difficult?'

'Let's just say that I seem to have attracted unwelcome attention which, to be honest, is making me rather nervous.'

A broad-shouldered man was standing a few feet behind Miss Bartlett. Fay couldn't see his face. His head was turned away from her. He was holding a dark trilby hat. Her heart lurched and Miss Bartlett turned to see who she was looking at.

'Is that someone you know, dear?' she whispered.

As she spoke, a beautifully dressed woman glided past their table. The man turned. He smiled and Fay watched him bend his head and kiss the woman's upturned face. They walked, arm in arm, towards the restaurant.

Fay looked at Miss Bartlett. 'Sorry, you were saying?'

'I asked if that was someone you knew, dear.'

She shook her head. 'No. I thought it was but I was mistaken.' She stubbed her cigarette out and grabbed her jacket. 'Would you mind terribly if I don't join you for a meal? I seem to have lost my appetite.'

Without waiting for a reply, she got to her feet and stumbled towards the door.

Chapter 13

Broad-shouldered men in dark suits and trilby hats seemed to be lurking everywhere. Fay tried to tell herself that she was worrying unnecessarily. Assuming Lady Langbourne had spoken to her husband, a man in his position would be quite within his rights to make enquiries about the girl in the hat shop who claimed to see into the future. The country was at war and anything out of the ordinary was bound to be treated with suspicion. I should have followed my instincts, she thought. I should have kept shtum.

On her half-day off she persuaded Jack to go to the pictures with her. Jack was not keen. The film was called *The Bluebird* and he was convinced that he wouldn't enjoy it.

'It sounds soppy,' he said.

'It's got Shirley Temple in it,' said Fay.

Jack pulled a face. 'That's what I mean. It sounds soppy.'

A soppy film was just what she needed. Something with a happy ending. When she promised to buy him an ice cream, Jack relented. It was a particularly warm afternoon. Fay was wearing a thin summer frock and a new pair of sandals. Ten minutes away from the cinema, the wail of sirens began.

'What shall we do?' said Jack. 'Carry on or make for the shelter?'

Without answering, she grabbed his hand and joined the sudden rush of people dashing towards the shelter on the corner of Holden Avenue. Unused since it had been hurriedly erected, the cement floor was covered in rainwater. The long stone benches that lined the sides were cold, damp and gritty. Within minutes the shelter was packed. The sirens wailed. Babies cried. The place stank of wet plaster and urine.

No one said much and when they did they spoke in whispers. They'd been there for half an hour or so when a man began complaining about the construction of the shelter. His voice was loud and angry.

'Useless. Bloody useless,' he said. 'We ought to be underground. Not stuck in here.' A young woman, trying to pacify two frightened children, asked him politely to be quiet. He took no notice. 'You'll see. I'm right. These surface shelters are only good for one thing. They might protect us from shrapnel but I'm telling you if a bomb falls on it the whole thing will collapse and kill us all. Useless. Bloody useless.'

Before she could stop him, Jack pushed through the crowd and made his way to where the man was leaning against the wall. 'Excuse me, sir,' he said, 'do you mind keeping your opinion to yourself? No one wants to listen to you and if you don't shut up right now, you are going to find yourself outside in the street. Do you understand?'

Fay was astonished. People cheered. Someone shook Jack's hand. She saw a woman blow him a kiss and as he walked back to where she was standing, people pushed forward to pat him on the back.

'Well done, Jack,' she whispered. 'I'm really proud of you.'

Seconds later came the distant drone of planes. The air filled with the deafening explosion of guns and far away the terrifying sounds of bombs, dropping one after another, like the hollow boom of huge drums. People were praying. Then above the noise a woman began to sing, and as her voice grew steadily stronger, others joined in.

'"There'll be bluebirds over the White Cliffs of Dover…"'

It was more than two hours before the all-clear sounded. As she stumbled out of the dank, filthy shelter, Fay blinked and saw columns of black smoke rising in the distance.

'Some poor blighters copped it,' she heard someone say.

She reached for Jack's hand and asked him if he was all right.

'I need a wee,' he whispered.

She laughed. 'You'll just have to wait, won't you?'

They found their mother in the cupboard under the stairs.

'Mum, you can come out now. Didn't you hear the all-clear?' said Fay.

'I did but my legs are so stiff I can hardly move. Did you get as far as the cinema?'

Fay grabbed her arm and hauled her to her feet. 'No, we were stuck in that shelter near Holden Avenue.'

'Shame, really,' said Jack. 'I was looking forward to that film.'

'Liar,' said Fay. 'So, did you hear the bombs, Mum?' Her mother nodded. 'Someone in the shelter thought they landed south of the river. Woolwich. Somewhere like that. I suppose it will be in the papers.'

'Your father will know.'

'Where is he?'

Her mother glanced up at the clock. 'He got called out. He'll be back soon.'

They were sitting round the kitchen table when the back door opened. Her father stood there, his hair grey with dust.

'Everyone present and correct?' he said. 'Run me a bath, Jack. There's a good boy.' He sank on to a chair. Her mother helped him pull his boots off. She poured tea and urged him to take a sandwich. 'Don't fuss, Hetty. I'll eat when I've cleaned up a bit.'

Three hours had passed since the all-clear. Fay was upstairs in her room when the sirens began wailing. Not again, she thought, and running downstairs, found her father pulling his boots back on. He ordered them all into the Anderson shelter. He was about to leave when he turned and holding out his arms, gave each of them a hug.

'Look after each other, won't you?' he said.

Her mother filled two flasks for them, soup in one and tea in the other. She cut thick slices of bread, spread them with margarine, wrapped them in greaseproof paper, then shut herself in the cupboard under the stairs.

The air in the Anderson wasn't great but it was sweeter than the communal shelter where they'd spent the afternoon. The plank of wood that served as a shelf was filled with tins and packets. When Jack switched his torch on, Fay could see evaporated milk, peaches and salmon and sardines. There were biscuits, a few magazines, comics for Jack and some odds and ends of cutlery and crockery. Piled high with blankets and heavy wool coats, the mattress looked comfortable enough but she shuddered when she spotted the enamel buckets and the squares cut from newspaper which her mother had thoughtfully threaded on to a length of string and hung from a nail. Fay sat on the bed and wrapped a blanket over her legs.

'We might as well make ourselves comfortable. God alone knows how long we'll be here,' she said.

The noise outside grew louder and louder. Nearby, a dog howled and each time the huge anti-aircraft guns fired the ground vibrated around them, above them, under their feet. Sleep was impossible. They sat huddled together, wondering if they'd live through the night. Fay kept thinking about her father. He was out there somewhere in the middle of it and though she hadn't thought of it at the time, his words before he'd left had sounded like a final farewell. If Jack was thinking the same, he didn't show it. He was thrilled by the whole thing and throughout the night kept up a running commentary. It was irritating but Fay couldn't have wished for a more cheerful companion.

At dawn they were still waiting to hear the all-clear. The smell, a mixture of fire and gunpowder, filled the Anderson. Her eyes stung. She longed for a bath even if she was only allowed a few inches of water. That was what she was thinking about, a nice warm bath, when she noticed that the skin on her neck and shoulders had begun to tingle. The sensation grew. It got stronger and stronger. Not now, she thought. Please God, not now. The last thing she remembered before the vision started was the sound of Jack's voice. He was calling her name. She was vaguely aware of the anxiety in his voice but it wasn't until the vision had played itself out that she was finally able to speak.

'Sorry, Jack,' she whispered. 'I didn't mean to scare you.'

'I thought you were going to faint or something,' he said.

Even in that dim light she could see how pale his face had become.

'I'm okay. It's probably a migraine. Nothing unusual. Girls often have headaches at certain times of the month.'

He looked embarrassed but when the all-clear sounded and they staggered, stiff and weary, out of the shelter and into the house, he poured her a glass of water, found two aspirins and stood over her while she swallowed them.

She slept until noon. When she woke she was confused and miserable. She'd so wanted to believe that there'd be no more visions. But this time she even knew when it would happen. How she knew, she couldn't say. If it had been a film there might have been a page from a calendar, a date ringed in thick, black crayon. But in Fay's vision there'd been no calendar, no date ringed in crayon, only the certain knowledge that what she'd seen would happen in a few days. If she could find the courage to forget what they'd think of her, to make them listen, to make them believe her, she'd warn them. The Home Office and those men in dark suits. Instead she did what she'd been doing since she was eight years old. She wrote an account of what she'd seen in her secret exercise book, and since she already knew the date it would happen, she included that as well.

Chapter 14

There was nothing Fay could do to blot out the dreadful image of Oxford Street in flames. She could only pray that she was wrong, but why should this vision be any different to all the others? She'd seen it, and in just under a week it would happen. The next morning she was relieved when there was no sign of Rita at the bus stop. It would have been impossible to behave as if nothing was wrong. Rita would have known she was hiding something.

All around her, passengers, red-eyed from exhaustion, cheerfully exchanged stories. Several times the bus was forced to take alternative routes to avoid craters in the street or fires from burning gas mains but it was not until she was walking along Oxford Street, busy and bustling with people, that the terrible images of her vision really hit her. She pictured it as it would look in a few days. Buildings ablaze. Pavements littered with broken glass and chunks of masonry. Selfridges, John Lewis, Bourne & Hollingsworth and Peter Robinson, the street's most famous department stores, reduced to windowless, burning shells, and the beautiful houses in the squares behind the stores horribly damaged. Nerves on edge, she snapped at Miss Greenwood, then apologised and blamed her behaviour on lack of sleep.

'We're all tired but we must put our feelings aside and carry on as best we can,' said Miss Greenwood.

Fay couldn't think straight. For all the purpose they served, she wondered if her visions were nothing more than punishment for something she'd done in a previous life. By mid-afternoon her mind had begun to clear. If she did nothing else at least she could make sure that Rita kept away from Oxford Street on the night of the raid. She'd invite her to go the pictures, somewhere local, and if Rita didn't fancy that she'd think of something else. What else could she do? If she told anyone they wouldn't believe her. Short of walking around the West End with a sandwich board draped over her shoulders – "Prepare to meet thy doom, the end of the world is nigh" – there was nothing else.

She could warn Lady Langbourne. In fact, the more she thought about it, the more she realised how dreadful she would feel if she did nothing and the house in Portman Square was destroyed, especially if her ladyship was inside it. But Fay could hardly claim to be on familiar terms with one of the wealthiest women in London. The warning would have to come from someone else. There was nothing for it. Though she would rather not involve Miss Bartlett, there was no other way. Miss Bartlett would believe her. She would have to issue the warning on Fay's behalf.

On her way home from work, she stopped at a telephone box. Miss Bartlett was not at home. That evening, rather than risk being overheard, she made an excuse and went to the telephone box at the corner of her road. She lit a cigarette and waited for Miss Bartlett to answer the phone. It rang for almost a minute before she hung up. Miss Bartlett was obviously not there. She pressed Button B. The coins rattled back into the tray. She picked them up, fed a couple of pennies into the slot and phoned Rita. There she had more success, but not without a price.

'Tuesday night?' said Rita. 'No, I'm not doing anything.'

'Let's go to the pictures then. Somewhere local. Golders Green?'

'Okay. I'll tell you what. My cousin, Howard, is still here. Why don't we make it a foursome? It will be fun, and you haven't met Danny yet. You remember Howard, don't you?'

Fay groaned. Yes, she remembered Howard all right. Rita's cousin had an opinion about everything. She doubted an evening in his company would be much fun. Still, it was done now.

She'd been home less than an hour when the sirens began wailing. Another night in the Anderson.

*

The next day she had still not managed to contact Miss Bartlett. She was convinced she was being watched. Her nerves were in shreds. She tried to put it down to lack of sleep but having three visions in as many months hadn't helped much. They left her feeling so drained. If someone invented a pill that would get rid of visions as easily as a couple of aspirins cured a headache, Fay would demand they be given a knighthood. She had even begun to consider talking it through with a psychiatrist. Rosh Hashanah and Yom Kippur were only a few weeks away. She wondered if God would be more ready to listen to her prayers if she turned up at shul in a new hat and managed, for once, not to break the fast. Normally, whenever she began to feel sorry for herself she only had to think of her mother's long-suffering sighs and the thinly-veiled reference to dark, unspoken miseries and that was usually enough to snap her out of her mood. Now, no matter how hard she tried, she struggled to even raise a smile.

Guessing that Miss Bartlett was away, perhaps doing a tour of demonstrations, there was only one way to let Lady Langbourne know what was about to happen. Fay would have to write her a note and deliver it herself. So, with only a few days to go the note had been written and rewritten several times before she was satisfied. The trouble was, no matter how it was worded, she could find no way of making it sound sincere and believable. Even the word 'vision' sounded pathetic. Substituting "premonition" for "vision" was only marginally better. In the end she wrote three or four lines saying that since her premonitions had been so accurate in the past, it would be wrong not to warn Lady Langbourne that she believed there would be a bombing raid on the area surrounding Oxford Street on the night of the 17th of September.

During her lunch break, with the note in her handbag, Fay stood at the corner of Orchard Street. From there she could see across Portman Square to the Langbournes' house. A limousine was just pulling up. The chauffeur stepped out of the car and stood waiting on the pavement. Fay pulled the narrow brim of her hat down as far as it would go and waited. Minutes passed and still she didn't move. She watched as the front door opened. The chauffeur removed his cap and tucked it under his arm and there was Lady Langbourne, standing at the top of the steps wearing a blue floral dress and white gloves. Fay's face grew hotter and the urge to walk away was difficult to resist. Waiting until the car turned left into Upper Berkeley Street, she hurried across the square and up the steps to the front door.

The warning would have been much more appropriate had it come from Miss Bartlett, and the moment Fay dropped the note into the letterbox, she wished she could have reached a hand inside and retrieved it before it was found. It was too late now. Her note had been delivered. As she walked back towards the shop, the thought suddenly occurred to her that since Lady Langbourne was not at home, it might not be too late after all. She could walk back to Portman Square, ring the doorbell and tell the maid that it had been delivered by mistake. It took only seconds to dismiss the idea as unworthy and cowardly.

It was up to her ladyship now. Whether her message was believed or dismissed as nonsense, at least Fay knew she had done the right thing. Like the man in Hyde Park said, it was better than doing nothing. By the time she arrived back at the shop she felt a little more cheerful.

Chapter 15

Mary Langbourne and her husband lunched together in the garden. She had been hoping that he might pay her some attention for a change. The table was well set. A bottle of fine wine had been opened. Cook had prepared an excellent lunch and Gerald was ignoring her. She watched him reading through his correspondence. He opened the last envelope in the pile, took out the pages and giving them only the briefest scan, muttered an oath under his breath and tossed the pages aside.

'Just who do these damned people think they are?' he growled. 'That's what I'd like to know.'

Mary dabbed her mouth with a napkin. 'Is it something I could deal with, darling?'

He scowled. 'I should think you have more pressing matters with which to occupy yourself.'

She wanted to tell him that he was wrong. She had no pressing matters with which to occupy herself. The Langbournes' London home, under the watchful eye of their housekeeper, practically ran itself with barely any supervision from Mary. Moresby Hall, the great, rambling estate in Suffolk, which her husband inherited from his father, was in the capable hands of the estate manager. The retinue of staff they employed understood exactly what was expected of them.

Edwina had her precious ambulance brigade to keep her occupied. One would think there was something useful Mary could do to help the war effort, but on the odd occasion when she'd mentioned to Gerald that she was serious about finding an outlet for her restless energy, the idea had been met with dismissive scorn.

Parliamentary business, which occupied so much of his time, was not something he ever discussed with her. She knew that recently he'd been involved with obtaining royal assent to a new Act and that it had all been done in a mad rush, but it had been Edwina, not Gerald, who'd told her what it was about and why it had gone through in such a hurry.

'It's all to do with the safety of the realm,' she said. 'The Treachery Act. Such a damned silly name and, as far as I can tell, its sole purpose is to provide efficient means of dealing with alien saboteurs. I suppose it had to be done. At times like these, all foreigners must be treated with suspicion.'

Considering how many of the great and good still had strong family ties to Germany, Mary wondered whether sufficient thought had been given to clearly defining what was meant by "a foreigner". Had she enjoyed an argument she might even have challenged Gerald to explain, if only to prove that she had an opinion on the subject, but of course she said nothing.

Gerald's knife and fork clattered against his plate. He rose from the table and collected his correspondence together. Mary looked up at him and smiled.

'I shall be dining at my club tonight,' he announced.

As he passed behind her chair, he touched her shoulder. Mary said nothing. She heard the front door close behind him and when the girl cleared away the dishes, Mary got up and stood in the doorway of her husband's study. Had he been there she wouldn't have dreamt of walking into the room and removing the crumpled pages from his waste paper basket. She hesitated, thought about it for a second or two, smoothed the pages and took them into the living room.

If she was to find something useful to do with her time she would jolly well have to take the initiative herself, and since it was clear that those discarded pages contained nothing of any interest to him, Mary sat at the table and began reading. Even before she'd finished, she had already begun to think this might be exactly what she'd been looking for. She read the letter again. It was a simple request for the Government's support for better shelters for the people in the East End. One suitable site had already been identified. The letter, signed on behalf of the Stepney Tenants' Defence League, had attached to it a petition, several pages long, containing over five hundred signatures. It seemed a most reasonable request and yet her husband was not prepared to lift a finger to help.

The East End of London with its docks and factories was always going to be the prime target for the German bombers, but the matter of shelters was not something to which she'd given much thought. After all, Moresby Hall would provide the Langbournes with a safe haven should the bombings ever become a problem, and despite the obvious horror of her country being at war, so far, it had been little more than an inconvenience. There was still the usual round of parties. They still dined at the best restaurants and, tucked safely away, twenty feet or so beneath the streets of London, she and her friends still danced in their favourite nightclubs. Should one feel guilty about enjoying a privileged life? No, she thought, that would be silly, but the tenants of Stepney's Defence League certainly needed someone to champion their cause. Mary rang for her driver.

'Bring the car to the front of the house in ten minutes. I wish to take a tour of Stepney,' she said.

'Are you sure, madam? I understand that the area has suffered a great deal of damage.'

'So I've heard, but we're going there anyway.' Mary glanced again at the letter. 'Do you think you could find your way to the Fruit and Wool Exchange? I believe it's somewhere in Spitalfields,' she said, and folding the letter neatly, she slipped it into her handbag.

Three hours later Mary arrived back at Portman Square, feeling positively grubby. She had a long, hot soak in the bath and even before she'd climbed out and wrapped herself in a soft robe, she was no longer certain that championing the cause of the poor people of Stepney was something she really wanted to do. She sympathised with their plight. It would have been heartless not to. She'd met the person who'd written the letter and obtained all those signatures; a little man with huge plans for turning the vault under the Fruit and Wool Exchange into a shelter, but there was so much work involved. It was altogether too exhausting. It was all very well wanting to do something for the war effort but one had to enjoy it. Otherwise, what was the point?

She was sipping a gin and tonic when the maid tapped gently on the door. 'Good evening, madam,' she said. 'This letter arrived for you while you were out. It was delivered by hand.'

She didn't recognise the handwriting. The envelope was of poor quality and certainly not from anyone she knew. She guessed it was most likely an account for provisions, something that should have been addressed to the housekeeper, but it was marked *For the personal attention of Lady Langbourne*. She opened it, read the note twice and sat for a moment, not knowing quite what to make of it. Her first thought was that the girl had no business delivering notes to her house. She meant well, Mary was sure of that, and the fact that her predictions had so far been accurate meant that her warning was simply impossible to ignore. Persuading Gerald to leave London for Moresby Hall at a moment's notice would be difficult enough but doing so without explaining why would be almost impossible. With little hope of convincing him, Mary began to feel extremely anxious.

Chapter 16

Business at the hat shop was slow. Fay had knitted enough khaki socks to keep an entire regiment of foot soldiers happy. With nothing to distract her, as the day of the Oxford Street bombing grew closer, Fay's anxiety increased. Each time a car pulled up outside the shop, she feared it might be Lady Langbourne, demanding an explanation. Miss Greenwood would be mortified. Apart from knowing nothing about Fay's visions, popping personal messages through the door of valued customers was not the kind of behaviour she expected from her salesgirl.

At midday a car came to a stop outside the shop. A slim young man stepped out and removed several boxes from the back seat. Fay recognised him and, glad of the distraction, she opened the door for him. For a split second Fay was reminded of Clark Gable. Whether it was the dark hair or the thin moustache, there was no denying it. She hadn't noticed before but Sam Cassell was a good-looking fellow.

He had a nice smile, too. 'Good morning, Miss Abrams. I hope you're well.'

'Quite well, thank you,' she said.

'Ah, Mr Cassell, I'm sorry,' said Miss Greenwood, 'we're not placing any new orders at the moment.' But Mr Cassell had already begun opening boxes and laying his hats out on the counter.

'I think you may change your mind when you take a closer look at our latest models,' he said.

Without being asked, Fay began trying them on.

'Aren't they just a little bit plain?' said Miss Greenwood. 'I must say they look awfully nice on you, Miss Abrams, but are they really suitable for our clientele?'

It wasn't the most tactful thing to do, but before she could stop herself, Fay turned to Miss Greenwood and whispered, 'What clientele?'

Miss Greenwood frowned, but when Mr Cassell suggested that, if they agreed to take the samples, they could have them sale or return, to her surprise, Miss Greenwood agreed.

'I suppose it's worth a try,' she said. 'Perhaps you could rearrange the window, Miss Abrams, and see what happens.'

Mr Cassell took his empty boxes. Fay opened the door for him. He winked at her, a slow, rather saucy wink, and as he drove away he waved and blew her a kiss.

'Cheeky young devil,' said Miss Greenwood. 'Awfully good-looking though. Quite the charmer. He's obviously taken a shine to you, dear.'

'He's a salesman, Miss Greenwood. It's his job to be charming.'

By lunchtime, the elaborately trimmed hats had been taken from the window and the window freshly dressed with Mr Cassell's simple styles. Fay suggested that the prices be displayed. At first, Miss Greenwood resisted.

'Isn't that just a little bit vulgar?' she said. 'Clientele like ours...'

Before she could finish, Fay looked at her and raised an eyebrow. 'Clientele like ours are not buying new hats but there are still plenty of women who want to look nice, even if they do have to keep an eye on the pennies.'

Miss Greenwood sighed. 'I suppose you're right, dear. We must learn to adapt.'

That afternoon, with public transport timetables no longer reliable, the shop was closed a little earlier than usual. Fay said goodnight and paused outside for a moment to admire her window display. She noticed a car glide slowly past her and stop a few yards ahead of her. She was almost level with it when a man stepped out of the car and stood right in front of her. She gave him a half-smile, expecting him to step aside.

'Miss Abrams? Miss Fay Abrams?'

She nodded. He touched her elbow. Fay looked down at his hand and frowned.

'Would you mind coming with me?' he said.

'What for? Who are you? What do you want?'

He didn't reply. Without removing his hand from her arm, he reached inside his jacket with his other hand and pulled out an identification card bearing the portcullis symbol of Westminster Palace. If this was meant to reassure her, he was mistaken.

'Would you kindly let go of my arm?' she said.

'I'm sorry, miss, but I must insist you accompany me.'

'And I must insist you let go of my arm.'

For a split second, a look of confusion crossed his face. He let go of her arm and opened the car door. 'Please, miss, do you mind getting into the car?'

'Of course I mind. What is this? Are you arresting me?'

'No, miss, nothing like that, but it would be better if you agreed to accompany me without making this more difficult than necessary.'

What did he mean? Was he suggesting that he would resort to strong-arm tactics if she refused? Hoping that Miss Greenwood would see what was going on and rush forward and intervene, she glanced back towards the shop. The shop door remained closed.

'Will this take long?' she said.

'I shouldn't think so, miss.'

With one last look back at the shop, Fay got into the car. The man climbed in beside her, tapped the driver on the shoulder and the car moved off in the direction of Bond Street.

Again, she asked what he wanted. His response was polite but unhelpful.

'I assure you there is no need to be alarmed.'

'Really? You don't think it's alarming to be forced into a stranger's car? I can assure you that it is. Extremely alarming.'

'I'm sorry, miss. I'm just doing my job.'

Nothing more was said. The man sat beside her, looking straight ahead. She could smell Brylcreem and tobacco. She would have liked a cigarette. She had a packet in her bag but she sat stiffly upright and concentrated on the route the car was taking. At Marble Arch the driver headed towards Bayswater, turned right, then left, along streets that were quite unfamiliar to her. She didn't know where she was being taken but she understood why it was happening and there was no doubt in her mind that she'd brought it on herself. Her decision to do the right thing had backfired. It was as simple as that.

At the gates of a narrow, grey building, the car came to a halt. Outside, the late afternoon sun was still warm. Inside, the air was cold. There was a faint whiff of bleach and disinfectant. A single window at the top of the stairs provided the only source of light and as she was led along a long, gloomy corridor, the sharp sound of her heels clattered on the stone floor. At the end of the corridor Fay was ushered into a dingy room. There were no windows. Facing her, behind a desk, sat two men. On the desk were a telephone, a stack of manila files, sheets of foolscap paper and an overflowing ashtray. The men looked up when she entered the room. The elder man stood.

'Take a seat, Miss Abrams. My clerk will be taking notes,' he said. 'I hope you have no objection.'

Ignoring his invitation to sit down, Fay stared at him. 'Would you mind telling me who you are?' she said. It was with some satisfaction that she noticed the slight raising of his eyebrow and the momentary loss of composure on his plump, pink face.

'I represent the Home Office.'

'I see. And what does the Home Office want with me?'

'Please, Miss Abrams. Do sit down. Perhaps you'd like a glass of water before we begin?'

Determined to remain calm, Fay reminded herself that she'd done nothing wrong. She shrugged, sat back in the chair and opened her bag. 'I hope this won't take long. Mind if I smoke?' she said.

Without waiting for his permission, she took out a cigarette, lit it and reached across the table for the ashtray.

Despite assurances that it was only an informal interview, that he was simply making enquiries, investigating claims, had a few questions he wished to ask, there was no doubt in Fay's mind that what followed was a full-blown interrogation.

He began by asking if she understood why the Home Office had taken the precaution of interviewing her.

'Not really,' she said. She hadn't meant to sound quite so disinterested and wondered later if her apparently offhand manner had been misinterpreted as deliberately uncooperative but, once the questions began, she found herself continuing in the same vein.

'What connections do you have with Germany?'

'None.'

'What other languages do you speak?'

'None.'

'Which other countries have you visited?'

'None.'

'Where did your information about the *Lancastria* come from?'

'I saw it happen.'

'How?'

'In a vision. I have visions. I see things before they happen.'

'Premonitions?'

'No. They are more than premonitions. These are visions. Accurate. Detailed. As if I was there.'

'So, perhaps you imagine you're another Nostradamus?'

'No, I don't imagine anything of the sort.'

'Your family originate from Germany?'

'No, they don't. My grandparents fled from Russia and Poland to escape religious persecution.'

'You're Jewish?'

'Yes.'

'Are you a member of the Communist Party?'

'No.'

'What political organisations do you belong to?'

'None.'

'Do you have anything more you wish to say about where your information comes from?'

'No. I've already told you.'

'You have visions?'

'Yes, that's right.'

'Miss Abrams, perhaps you fail to fully understand the position in which this leaves me.'

She leant forward and stubbed her cigarette out in the ashtray. 'I'm sorry,' she said. 'What else can I say? I'm telling the truth. I see things before they happen. I wish I didn't. But that's just how it is.'

He sighed and shook his head.

'All right, Miss Abrams. That will be all. For now.'

Five minutes later she was alone in the back of the car, being driven by the same driver who'd picked her up outside the shop.

'Shall I drop you back at Farm Street, miss?' he said.

'No, thank you. The bus stop at the top of Edgware Road, please. I'm going straight home. I'm late for supper.'

Sitting upstairs on the bus, Fay lit another cigarette and wondered how else she might have handled the situation. She had given a good account of herself. She had kept her nerve, but would it have been better if she'd been a little more cooperative? Could she have made more effort to convince her inquisitor that she was telling the truth? No point, she thought. He dealt in facts, hard, tangible facts. Visions were no more believable to him than tales of fairies at the bottom of the garden.

Recalling that he had mentioned the *Lancastria* but had said nothing about Oxford Street, it dawned on her that the contents of her note to Lady Langbourne had not reached the ears of the Home Office. Should she have said something? Had there had been an appropriate moment during the interview when she could have casually slipped it into the conversation?

'By the way, you might like to know that Oxford Street is going to cop it on Tuesday night. Perhaps you might want to issue a warning and keep people away from the area.'

What would he have done? Laughed at her? Kept her in that dismal room, asking more questions for which she could give no satisfactory answers? It was bad enough being dragged off the street and questioned like a common criminal. Why make it worse for herself? But by the time the bus pulled up at Cricklewood Broadway, Fay was no longer certain that she'd been right not to volunteer any more information. Perhaps she would have left herself open to ridicule, but would that have mattered if lives were saved? She kept thinking about the man at Speakers' Corner. His words were beginning to haunt her.

She was halfway up Childs Hill when the sirens sounded. An air raid warden yelled at her to get off the streets. She carried on walking. He yelled again and pointed towards the shelter on the corner of Holden Avenue. She ignored him, and as the sirens grew louder she began to run. When she reached the house, she paused at the front door, touched her fingers to her lips, rested her fingers on the mezuzah and repeated the prayer inscribed on its tiny scroll.

'May God protect my going out and coming in, now and forever,' she whispered.

Fay had recited that same little prayer so many times, but never had its meaning moved her as it did in that moment.

Chapter 17

On Sunday morning Mary Langbourne rose at the usual time and, as she came downstairs, was surprised to hear her husband talking loudly in his study. At first she thought he was speaking to someone on the telephone but then she heard another voice and realised he was not alone. In the morning room the maid brought her a cup of coffee and two slices of toast.

'Has Lord Langbourne had breakfast yet?'

'No, madam. He has a visitor. A Mr Frobisher from the Home Office. He arrived at eight this morning. Lord Langbourne was expecting him.'

'Really? So early? On a Sunday?'

'Yes, madam. His lordship is rather agitated.'

Was it possible, she thought, that Gerald's visitor had taken it into his head to repeat the conversation they'd had at Edwina's party? Surely not. It would certainly explain his agitation. How furious he would be. How humiliated, that his own wife had discussed what Gerald would consider the wild ramblings of a common little shop girl, with someone like Frobisher.

The voices coming from his study grew louder. A door slammed. Hearing footsteps in the hall, Mary left the room and found herself face to face with Arnold Frobisher. His cheeks were red. His eyes blazed with fury. He bowed his head and murmured a greeting.

'Good morning, Mr Frobisher. Just leaving?' She could hear Gerald barking out instructions on the telephone. 'Unless I'm mistaken, my husband is not terribly happy this morning.'

'There was an incident last night at the Savoy, my lady. A rather unpleasant incident, and I'm sorry to say that Lord Langbourne holds me personally responsible.'

Breathing a sigh of relief, she smiled apologetically. 'Oh dear. That must be awkward for you.'

'It is. Most awkward. Lord Langbourne has just made his opinion of me painfully clear and I'm bound to say it is not only unjustified but quite unreasonable. Not to mention deeply hurtful.'

Knowing how unkind Gerald could be, she realised afterwards that she could have handled the situation differently but in that moment Frobisher's remarks seemed rather too provocative. He had crossed the line and she didn't hesitate to let him know.

'Mr Frobisher, I suggest you keep your grievances, real or imagined, to yourself.'

His face grew redder. Glancing at Gerald's study door, he bent his head a little closer to hers. 'And does that include my opinion of your friendship with the young woman in the hat shop?' Mary felt her whole body stiffen. 'A woman in your position should be more careful with whom she associates.'

Anxious that Gerald shouldn't overhear their conversation, she strode towards the front door, flung it open and wished Frobisher a good day.

At the door he turned. His face was only a few inches from hers. 'I have no wish to offend you, Lady Langbourne. In fact, as I said before, I am most grateful to you for bringing the matter to the attention of my department. Nevertheless, I should warn you that by appearing to support this young woman, you risk damaging your good name.'

She would dearly love to have slapped his face. Instead she repeated, with as much dignity as she could muster, 'Good day, Mr Frobisher.'

Arnold Frobisher extended his hand. Did he really expect her to shake hands with him? She raised an eyebrow and stared at him coldly. To her astonishment, he made no move to leave. He was actually smiling at her. His face was so close to hers she could smell his breath.

'Perhaps you, Lady Langbourne, can accept Miss Abrams' claim to see into the future. Luckily the Home Office is not so naïve.'

'Really? Then perhaps the Home Office will change its mind on Tuesday night when Oxford Street is destroyed.'

She saw him open his mouth but before he could speak, Mary slammed the door in his face just as Gerald came out of his study. She turned and looked at him.

'What's going on?' he said.

'Nothing, darling. I was just seeing Mr Frobisher out.'

Taking his arm, she led him into the morning room. She told the maid to bring him a soft-boiled egg and some toast and coffee. She asked him to explain what had brought Frobisher to the house so early in the morning.'

'The man's a complete idiot. The whole thing was an utter shambles. A straightforward briefing with the Ministry of Information and a few journalists. And what happened? A gang of banner-waving Bolsheviks and Jews stormed into the Savoy and refused to leave. If that smarmy toad had done his job properly it would never have happened. They should have been rounded up weeks ago.'

'How simply dreadful. What did they want?'

'They wanted to disrupt the meeting and, thanks to that incompetent fool, that's exactly what they achieved.'

'Why? I mean, why were they there? Did they have a reason for disrupting the meeting?'

'Reason? Those people don't have to have a reason. They're just a bunch of troublemakers. I wouldn't be the least surprised if the same people who signed that damned petition were behind it.'

Mary's face grew hot. 'Petition, darling? What petition was that?'

'Never mind that. Just take a look at this.' Gerald thrust a sheet of paper in front of her. 'Go on, Mary. Read it.'

It was an extract from an article in the *Daily Worker*. Under the headline "The People Must Act", the article claimed that, "If you live in the Savoy Hotel you are called by telephone when the sirens sound and then tucked into bed by servants in a luxury bomb-proof shelter, but if you live in Paradise Court you may find yourself without a refuge of any kind."

If Gerald looked at her she was sure he would notice that her cheeks were flushed. She bent her head and pretended to reread the article. He was right. She was quite certain now that those people at the Exchange, to whom she'd so cheerfully introduced herself, were responsible for the incident at the Savoy. What, she wondered, had possessed her to become involved without first considering the risk to her reputation and that of her husband? She found herself agreeing with Frobisher. A woman in her position should be more careful with whom she associated, but the fact remained that the girl's warning was impossible to ignore.

So far Mary had been unable to come up with a satisfactory reason for leaving London, but if she was to keep herself and her husband safe that night she had to act straight away. The answer was there, staring her in the face.

'Darling, I do hate to see you under such stress. You really need to do something to take your mind off all this unpleasantness.'

'And just how do you suggest I do that? A holiday? That is out of the question.'

'No, darling. I know you're far too busy to take a holiday. I was thinking of somewhere much closer to home. We so rarely have an evening out together, Gerald. I feel positively neglected. Take me to the Savoy on Tuesday. Do let's go. You're such a marvellous dancer and it will be tremendous fun.'

To her relief, Gerald's face relaxed into a smile. 'Tuesday? Why not? I think that's a splendid idea.'

Chapter 18

Tuesday arrived and Fay could think of nothing she fancied less than an evening at the pictures. She'd had an awful night, barely sleeping a wink. Still awake at three, she'd stood at her bedroom window and, peering down into the dark street below, imagined she'd seen a figure staring back up at her. At work that day, she was nervous and jittery and each time a car slowed down outside the shop she held her breath until it passed by. She couldn't rid herself of the feeling that she was being watched. When she got home all she wanted to do was crawl back into bed.

Her mother told her she didn't look well. Fay dabbed a little rouge on her cheeks, reapplied her lipstick and brushed her hair. Dressed in her best jumper and navy slacks, she was ready just in time before Rita turned up at the door holding hands with a sandy-haired young man.

'This is Danny,' she said. 'And guess what? Uncle Max has lent us his car. Isn't that nice of him?'

Fay followed them out to the car, an old Austin, where Rita's cousin sat waiting for them. He nodded at her and patted the front seat. She slid in beside him. She'd met him several times and taken an instant dislike to him. He was rude. His voice was loud. He was, as Bernard had once said, the kind of Jew that gives Jews a bad name.

As the car chugged up Childs Hill, she reminded herself that the purpose of the trip to the cinema was to keep Rita away from Oxford Street. That was all that really mattered. Howard was an idiot but she could put up with his company for a few hours and maybe, if only for a while, she might even forget what it felt like being interrogated by the Home Office.

She had only been in the car a couple of minutes before Howard managed to annoy her. 'Beats me why any woman wants to look like a man,' he said.

She took a deep breath. 'Perhaps you need to have your eyes tested, Howard.'

She saw him glance sideways at her, his gaze fixing for a second on her breasts. Her jumper had tiny sequins embroidered across the shoulders. It fitted like a glove.

'I meant the trousers,' he muttered.

She ignored him, and turning in her seat she spoke to Rita. 'So, where are we're going?'

'Well, I'd really like to see *It Happened One Night*. It's showing at the Ionic but Howard's not keen on Clark Gable.'

'Oh really! That's a shame, and who would Howard rather see?'

Howard stretched his arm across the back of the seat, his hand almost touching her shoulder. 'A real man,' he said. 'Like James Cagney.'

'Well,' said Fay, 'if I had to choose between James Cagney and Clark Gable I know who I'd rather spend a few hours with.'

Rita laughed. 'Me too,' she said. 'And Danny doesn't mind what film he sees. Do you, Danny?'

Outside the Ionic, Howard pointed at the poster. 'Romantic comedy. Huh! I bet that's going to be a barrel of laughs.'

As they were shown to their seats, Howard squeezed himself along the row without an 'excuse me' or a 'thank you'. Sitting in the dark in the smoky cinema, Fay tried not to think about what was happening in Oxford Street or whether Lady Langbourne had taken any notice of her warning. She was aware of Howard yawning and sighing but it didn't take long before she forgot about him and became absorbed in the film. It wasn't difficult. Mr Gable was the kind of film star that would set any girl's heart fluttering. Despite everything, Fay's mood began to lift and when Rita leant towards her and whispered that Danny thought she looked a lot like Claudette Colbert, Fay grinned and squeezed her hand.

They could have stayed on and watched the newsreel but Howard wanted a drink. He drove with one hand on the wheel while Fay squashed herself against the door to avoid the other hand, which was balanced on the back of the seat only inches from her shoulder. In Hampstead they stopped at Jack Straw's Castle. Neither she nor Rita were used to drinking in pubs so when asked what she wanted, Fay said the first thing that came into her head, port and lemon, because she thought that was what girls were supposed to prefer.

They sat outside around a rickety table, the men with their pints of bitter and Rita and Fay sipping port and lemon served in tall glasses. It was a mild September evening and with the unaccustomed effect of alcohol in her veins, it would have been easy to forget the war until a sudden series of explosions and the thunderous boom of anti-aircraft guns sounded in the distance.

It was Danny who spoke first. 'That's close,' he said, pointing up at the flashes of light in the sky and the beam of searchlights. 'Could well be central London.'

Fay shuddered.

Draining his glass, Howard wiped his mouth with the back of his hand, belched loudly and grinned. 'Who cares?'

'I do,' said Danny, quietly. 'And so should you.'

Rita frowned. 'How can you talk like that, Howard?' She was touching Danny's arm, as if she was holding him back. 'You should be ashamed of yourself. You of all people. You cared when it was your own street being bombed.'

Howard shrugged. 'So what? I'm still here, aren't I?'

Fay could have kept out of it. He wasn't her cousin, thank God, but the words were out of her mouth before she could stop them.

'I've been thinking about that, Howard. Why are you still here? Why haven't you enlisted? A tough geezer like you. I would have thought you'd welcome the chance to show what you're made of.'

She heard Rita gasp and saw the amused look on Danny's face. They were both looking at Howard.

'I've got a bad back,' he said.

She watched as, avoiding their eyes, he took a cigarette and lit it. She glanced at Rita. From the look on her face it was clear that she wasn't about to let him off the hook. Fay waited for the fireworks to begin.

'Since when?' said Rita.

'I've always had a bad back,' he muttered. 'You can ask my mother if you don't believe me.'

'I shall ask her. Don't you worry about that.'

Howard tipped his chin upwards and blew a few smoke rings into the air. 'What do you want from me, Rita?' he said. 'You want me to be like Bernard? A bloomin' hero?'

That did it. In one movement, Rita was on her feet, standing with her face inches from his. 'Don't you dare talk about my brother like that. He could have stayed here and spent the rest of the war making uniforms if he'd wanted to.'

'Then why didn't he?'

Seeing the tears in Rita's eyes, Fay stood up, ready to comfort her, but Danny got there first. Wrapping a protective arm around her, he stepped between her and Howard.

'You want to know why? Probably for the same reason that I've enlisted. I never had the honour of meeting Rita's brother but I'm guessing he loved his country, like I do. It's been good to me and my family and I'd rather fight to defend it than stay at home adding columns of figures in Selfridges.'

A group of elderly men, sitting on a nearby bench, began to clap. One man, an empty sleeve pinned back above his elbow, raised his hat with his good arm and shouted, 'Well said, young fellow. I'd go myself if they'd have me.' His friends laughed.

Had Rita known Danny was going to enlist? There was no sign that the news had taken her by surprise. Rita's face simply shone with pride and knowing how devastated she'd been by the loss of her brother, Fay found herself unexpectedly moved. Maybe patriotism was contagious because, by the time the now-silent Howard dropped her off at her house, she'd already begun wondering whether there weren't more useful things to do than to work in a hat shop.

In the kitchen her mother was busy darning Jack's grey woollen socks.

'Still up?' said Fay. 'I thought you'd be in bed by now.'

'I had a few things to take care of.'

'Well, I'm off to bed. Goodnight, Mum.'

She was at the door when her mother said, 'We told Jack he's going to be evacuated. I'm getting his clothes sorted out.'

'I bet he's not too happy about that,' said Fay.

Her mother shrugged. 'It's not safe in London anymore.'

Before they were shown to their table, Mary and Gerald Langbourne spent an hour in the Savoy bar. Gerald paid her the compliment of noticing her dress. He told her she looked marvellous. They drank pink gins and by the time they were ready for their meal they were both quite merry.

'I must say, darling, this was a jolly good idea. I'm glad I let you talk me into it.'

'I'm just happy to see you looking so relaxed, Gerald. You work too hard. You need to let your hair down now and again.'

When they took their place in the dining room, couples were already dancing. Between courses, Mary and Gerald danced too, something they had not done together for months, and Mary began to suspect that the girl was mistaken but even if it did turn out to be a false alarm, it really didn't matter. It was a treat to spend a jolly evening with her husband. He was rarely at home and even then he was usually preoccupied. Mary was enjoying herself. They had just finished their meal. Gerald had ordered brandy and was about to light a cigar, when the music stopped.

'Ladies and gentlemen,' said the bandleader, 'would everyone like to make their way to the basement? There's an air raid going on.'

With the minimum of fuss and a great deal of good-natured chatter, the hotel staff, helped by the guests, carried tables and chairs and unfinished meals down to the basement shelter. The musicians set themselves up on a makeshift stage. Grateful now that she had taken the girl's warning seriously, Mary and Gerald carried on drinking and dancing until two in the morning but when the band stopped playing, she distinctly heard the muffled rumble of explosions.

Throughout that night, the behaviour of the Savoy's employees was extraordinary. Nothing was too much trouble and Mary was certain that the hotel had rehearsed for just such an event. The kitchen staff rustled up bowls of porridge and cups of hot chocolate before everyone retired for the night. Gerald used his influence to secure one of the better underground rooms with its own bathroom. Bathrobes and soft, white towels were provided. The bed was large and reasonably comfortable. The sheets were freshly laundered. Mary already knew from her encounter with the representatives of Stepney Tenants' League that there were far worse places to spend the night.

Lying in bed together, twenty feet or so below street level, Gerald commented on their good fortune. 'I have to say that I'm very grateful to you, Mary. Had you not been so persuasive, who knows what might have happened?'

She smiled and wondered how he would feel if she told him that it was not her who deserved his gratitude but a young Jewess. All Mary had done was give the girl a small gift, a little scarf that she herself neither wanted nor needed. One couldn't call it a particularly generous act and the girl certainly had nothing to gain by warning her. How bizarre, she thought, as she drifted off to sleep, that Lord and Lady Langbourne might well owe their lives to a shop girl with whom she had exchanged only a few words.

Chapter 19

The moment Fay opened her eyes, her first thought was whether she would find the shop still standing when she arrived at work. Half expecting to receive a telephone call from Miss Greenwood telling her not to come in, when no call came, Fay left the house at the usual time. She had got as far as Holden Road and was surprised to see Jack waiting for her.

'What are you doing here?' she said. 'Why aren't you at school?'

'I've been waiting for you. They're sending me away. Did you know?'

'Not until last night when I got back from the pictures.'

'You've got to talk to them, Fay. I don't want to go.'

'Jack, they only want to keep you safe.'

'But I want to stay here. What's the good of being safe if you're all dead and I'm an orphan?'

'That won't happen,' said Fay.

'All right, it won't happen but something could happen to me, couldn't it? I mean, if they send me away to the country, I could be digging turnips or something and a bull could gore me to death, or I could get mangled by a tractor. You'd be sorry then, wouldn't you?'

At any other time, Fay would have laughed. She would have said something to cheer him up. But not this morning. This morning she had enough on her plate without worrying about her little brother.

'Grow up, Jack,' she muttered. 'You're not the only one with problems. Anyway, being evacuated is not exactly the end of the world, is it?'

'It is to me,' he said.

'Well, you're just going to have to get used to it, aren't you?'

He stared at her. 'Why are you being so horrible?' he said.

'I'm not being horrible. Go to school, Jack. Go on. You'll be late. You'll get into trouble.

'So what? I don't care. I'm already late so I might as well walk with you to the bus stop,' he said.

Fay glanced at her watch. 'Okay,' she said. 'It's up to you but don't say I didn't warn you.'

Just before her bus arrived she opened her purse and gave him two bob.

'What's that for?' he said.

'Whatever you like. Just don't spend it all at once.'

From her seat on the bus, Fay watched him traipse back towards the Broadway, shoulders hunched, hands stuffed deep into his pockets. Poor Jack. She could have been a bit kinder. She hadn't meant to be horrible. Two shillings wasn't going to make up for her lack of sympathy. At least she could have told him how much she'd miss him, and it was true. She would miss him dreadfully. She turned and, looking out of the window, caught a glimpse of him disappearing into the crowd.

The journey into town seemed to take forever. The other passengers looked tired. Everyone looked tired these days but unlike her, they had little idea what awaited them and the nearer the bus got to the West End, the more anxious she became. Long before it reached the top end of Edgware Road, it was obvious to everyone that something terrible had happened.

Huge clouds of billowing black smoke rose into the sky. The air was grey with ash and dust. The smell of charred wood, of burning rubber and engine oil filled her nostrils. It caught the back of her throat and made her cough. As the passengers piled off the bus and rounded the corner into Oxford Street, they stood, shocked into silence by the dreadful scene. Then someone swore.

Fay was the first to move. Slowly at first, her head bent, she started walking, avoiding the piles of rubble and broken glass, but at Marble Arch station, unable to avert her eyes, she began to feel sick. The station entrance had completely disappeared, buried under mounds of bricks and plaster.

She'd had her chance and what had she done? Kept her best friend out of harm's way. Warned Lady Langbourne. She could have done more. She could have spoken up. So what if they'd thought she was mad? At least she could have tried to make them listen. But she hadn't. She'd done nothing, said nothing and now it was too late. As she walked towards Farm Street she tried to look straight ahead, not wanting to see the flames leaping from the buildings on both sides of the street. Farm Street itself seemed to have escaped the bombing. Paulette's hat shop had not been damaged. It was still locked up from the night before, but there was no sign of Miss Greenwood. Fay knew that she used the Underground to travel to work and guessed that the trains into town had been delayed because of what had happened at Marble Arch station. The entrance to the station had made her think of a tomb; a sealed tomb, and the thought made her shudder as she stood outside the shop waiting for Miss Greenwood to turn up.

As she waited, the clamour of noise coming from Oxford Street grew louder. The sounds filled her head: the crackle of fire, the ringing of bells and the frantic shouts as timbers crashed to the ground. She'd known what to expect. She'd seen it all in her vision but nothing had prepared her for the despair she felt that morning. She had been given the chance to save lives and she'd thrown that chance away. For what? To save herself from ridicule? For being what her mother called 'unnatural'?

And then she heard Miss Bartlett's gentle voice in her head. 'Prophecy is not a curse, Miss Abrams. It only becomes a curse when you're afraid to use it.' And try as she might to push those words to the back of her mind, she had the feeling they would haunt her forever.

Mary Langbourne had slept in her underwear. Taking a nightgown to the Savoy when Gerald believed they were just there for dinner would have looked rather odd. So, dressed in the gown she had worn the night before, Mary joined the other guests for a light breakfast while Gerald telephoned their driver to come and pick them up.

'Damned nuisance,' he said. 'The lines are all down. Shall we walk, old girl, or take the Underground?'

Neither sounded particularly appealing but in the end they agreed to walk along The Strand to Charing Cross station and take the train the two short stops to Oxford Circus. Stepping out of the Savoy, the air was so thick with dust and ash that her eyes stung. She covered her mouth with her hand and, keeping her head down, clutched Gerald's arm as they walked towards the station.

The train was packed, the passengers unusually quiet. At Oxford Circus, helped by a station guard, passengers made their way up the station steps, clambering over mounds of debris and plaster. Reaching the top, Mary stood, quite unable to move, as she took in the scene of devastation. Oxford Street, poor, dear Oxford Street was on fire. Flames shot out from the windowless buildings. John Lewis, Selfridges, Peter Robinson's, the great department stores that had been so much part of her life, all ruined in a single night. Fire fighters, their faces blackened with soot, dashed from one building to the next, struggling valiantly to dampen the flames. The street ran with water carrying shattered glass into the gutters. Tears ran down her face as Gerald grabbed her hand, urging her to hurry. Together they edged their way round huge chunks of fallen masonry.

'Oh dear. Oh dear,' she kept saying, over and over again. By the time they reached Portman Square, she was sobbing uncontrollably.

'Come on, old girl,' said Gerald, patting her shoulder, 'pull yourself together. Chin up, old thing. Look, we're home. Safe and sound.'

The top floor windows were gone. Glass littered the road and the front door lay across the pavement, but the house was still standing. Elsie, Mary's maid, was outside. She was holding a broom and staring at a vehicle parked on the opposite side of the street. A grey van, its back doors open.

'Oh, sir, madam. Isn't it terrible?' she said.

The girl's eyes were red and swollen.

Reminding herself that she really should set an example, Mary made a supreme effort to control her emotions. Speaking quietly and as calmly as she could, she told her to leave the clearing up until later.

'We'll take tea now, dear. In the drawing room. And some toast I think.'

As she spoke, two men in the grey uniform of the St. John's Ambulance Brigade appeared from the side of the house, carrying a stretcher covered in a red blanket. Elsie took one look and, covering her face, burst into tears. Mary took hold of the girl's hands and pulled them gently away from her face.

'He's dead, madam. John's dead. The poor, dear man. He was in his flat above the garage. The roof caved in on top of him. He didn't have a chance.'

Mary glanced at Gerald. His chauffeur had been with them for more than ten years and they'd both grown quite fond of him.

'We must notify his parents at once,' she said.

Gerald didn't move. As the two men slid the stretcher into the van, he removed his hat and not until the van had driven away did he follow her into the house.

There were things to be done. Things she must attend to. She had to keep busy. She must send a telegram to John's parents. Edwina would help her. She would know where his body had been taken. She'd know how one went about sending the body back to Moresby. That was where his family lived. Was there something else she should be doing? If the household were going to move to Moresby Hall – leave London while they still could – arrangements must be made but all the telephone lines were down. Still, there was nothing stopping her from writing to the estate manager at the hall. She'd start making lists. Yes, that's what she'd do. She'd make lists. Her hands were trembling and she wondered if she were in shock. Perhaps a drop of brandy in her tea would help. Perhaps she should lie down for a while.

Upstairs, she slipped out of her gown, changed into a day dress, combed her hair and sat for a moment staring at her reflection in her dressing table mirror.

'I must keep busy,' she whispered. 'I must make myself useful.'

*

Fay had been waiting outside the shop for almost an hour. She was thinking about going home when she spotted Miss Greenwood at the far end of Farm Street. Fay waved. Perhaps Miss Greenwood hadn't seen her. She was looking down at the ground as if she were deep in thought. As she got closer, Fay noticed that Miss Greenwood's hat appeared to have slid towards the back of her head. Her hair had escaped in untidy waves and the face beneath was unusually pale, the lips colourless, the skin almost grey. A few feet from the shop she stumbled. Fay rushed forward and took her arm.

'Take the keys, Miss Abrams, before I drop them. I'm sorry, dear. I'm all fingers and thumbs.'

Fay unlocked the door and led Miss Greenwood to a chair. Leaving her sitting there with her head in her hands, she looked around to see if there was any damage. A window had been broken in the toilet. Every surface was covered with a layer of gritty ash. She set to work straight away. She taped a piece of cardboard across the window, swept up the glass, dusted, mopped the floor, then seeing that Miss Greenwood had still not moved, she made a pot of tea. Miss Greenwood's hands were trembling as she tried to lift the cup to her lips. It was then that Fay realised she was crying.

'I'm sorry, dear. I'll be all right in a minute. It's just all too much. I never…in all my life… I'll never forget it…never. I saw them. So many bodies.'

Sitting beside her, Fay held Miss Greenwood's hand and listened with growing horror as she described what she'd seen. At Marble Arch station a team of men had begun clearing the entrance and, as she'd been walking past, they were carrying bodies out and laying them on the pavement.

Fay clutched her stomach. Wave after wave of nausea rose into her throat. Unable to stop herself, she dashed to the toilet and was immediately sick. When she came back, Miss Greenwood had already washed up their cups and was standing by the door with the keys in her hand.

'Are you all right, dear? I'm so sorry. I didn't mean to upset you.'

Fay nodded. She didn't trust herself to speak.

'Let's go home, shall we?' said Miss Greenwood. 'I can't see any point in either of us being here today and I doubt there'll be any business done tomorrow either. We might as well lock up and go home. Come in on Friday. Perhaps things will be better by then.'

Avoiding Oxford Street, they walked together along side streets. At Park Lane she and Miss Greenwood parted company.

It was late afternoon when she arrived home, and even before she put the key in the door Fay knew something was terribly wrong. Her parents were in the living room. Jack stood at the window staring out into the street.

Her mother looked at her. 'What have you done?' she moaned. 'What have you done?'

Chapter 20

'I could tell you when their car pulls up, Fay. Then you could dash out the back door and we could say we haven't seen you.'

Fay tried to smile but her mouth was suddenly so dry her lips stuck to her teeth. 'Thanks, Jack, but I don't think that's a very good idea, do you? Did they say when they were coming back?'

'Not exactly,' said her father. 'They just said they'll be back later. That was about an hour ago.'

'Well, I suppose there's nothing for it. I'll just have to wait.'

Her mother snorted. 'And is that all you've got to say for yourself?'

'Hetty, that's enough. They wouldn't tell us what it was about, darling.' He looked at her and shrugged. 'It's probably nothing. Just a silly mistake.'

She wanted to say something to put his mind at ease but before she could think of anything, Jack turned away from the window. 'They're back,' he whispered. 'They just pulled up outside. What you going to do, Fay?'

'I'm not going to do anything. I just want to get it over and done with. Whatever it is.'

'That's my girl,' said her father.

A moment later, she heard a knock on the door. Her father led two men into the living room. Her mother groaned and muttered something under her breath. Fay glanced at her. Her neck was bent, her face hidden. Her fingers were twisting and pulling at a button on her cardigan. Expecting them to be the same people who'd bundled her into the car, Fay recognised neither of the stony-faced men who stood in the doorway.

The shorter and older of the two addressed her politely. 'Miss Abrams, I apologise for the intrusion but we need you to come with us now.'

Before she could reply her father said, 'Do you mind explaining what this is about?'

'I'm sorry, sir. I'm not in a position to say.'

'All right, but I think we're entitled to know who you are.'

The younger man flashed an identity card at him. She saw the look of bewilderment on her father's face.

'I don't understand,' he said. 'What does the Home Office want with my daughter?'

'I'm not at liberty to say, sir.'

Her father frowned. 'All right. I'll get my coat,' he said, but her mother grabbed his hand and begged him not to go.

'Mrs Abrams is right, sir. We really need to speak to your daughter alone.'

'But where are you taking her? Will this take long?'

'That depends, sir,' he said.

'On what?'

'On whether Miss Abrams is prepared to cooperate.'

'It's all right, Dad,' said Fay. 'Everything will be fine.'

Her parents followed her out into the hall. At the front door she told them not to worry.

'You'll see. I'll be back soon,' she said, but the second she stepped out on to the path, her mother let out a terrible howl. Alarmed, Fay turned and stared at her. Her mother's arms were stretched out towards her. Concerned that she might be about to collapse, Fay hesitated but the men moved quickly, ushering her towards the car. When she looked back at the house she saw her father leading her mother indoors.

Mary was about to cross the road into Hyde Park when her attention was caught by a man with a notebook in his hand. He was standing at the entrance to Marble Arch station. He wore the uniform of an

ARP, and as she grew closer she saw he was completing some kind of report form. She hesitated for a moment before speaking to him, unsure if she actually wanted to hear the details.

'I thought the Underground was supposed to be safe,' she said.

'So did I, madam. Took us all by surprise, I can tell you. It weren't supposed to happen. High explosive. Went straight through the roof, pierced the girders and plunged right down below. The damned thing exploded in the tunnel. Took all the tiles clean off the walls. Trouble is, in an enclosed space like that, the blast effect is magnified.' She really didn't need to know how many people lost their lives. He told her anyway. 'At least forty badly injured. Twenty dead,' he said. 'Terrible, ain't it?'

She didn't stay in the park long. At any other time she would have stopped to admire the colour of the turning leaves but today Moresby Hall was becoming more attractive by the minute. If she remained in London in spite of the danger, as the king and queen had chosen to do, she would feel obliged to make herself useful. The problem remained that she didn't know how. In Moresby, there would be no such problem. Life might be dull but there at least she could escape the ugliness of war. She could almost pretend it wasn't happening.

Back in Portman Square, her maid took her hat and brought her tea. Mary had just settled down when the telephone rang. The girl answered it.

'Madam, it's for you. Mr Frobisher would like to speak to you.'

'Me? Are you sure he doesn't want to speak to Lord Langbourne?'

The girl covered the mouthpiece. 'No, madam. He definitely asked for you.'

Mary sighed. She couldn't imagine what Frobisher had to say. Unless it was to apologise for his appalling behaviour.'

'Yes, Mr Frobisher. What is it? I'm in rather a hurry,' she said.

'Ah! Lady Langbourne. I won't keep you. I just wanted to offer you my own personal gratitude and of course, the gratitude of the Home Office, for providing me with such important new information.'

'New information, Mr Frobisher? And which particular information are you referring to?'

'Why, Lady Langbourne, surely you haven't forgotten our conversation? I believe I mentioned at the time that the Home Office was not so naïve as to believe your friend's claim that she could see into the future.'

Mary's jaw tensed. Her face grew hot. 'I remember it well. Very well indeed.'

'In that case, my lady, you'll understand that, entirely thanks to you, as we speak, your little friend from the hat shop is being brought in for questioning. This time the interview will be conducted properly. I take a personal interest in this matter so I shall be questioning her myself.'

Having no desire to be drawn into further conversation with him, she wished Frobisher a good afternoon and slammed down the receiver.

'Arrogant little prig,' she whispered. Mary was filled with remorse. There was no doubt in her mind that the horrid little man would take great delight in humiliating Miss Abrams and she could well imagine what a dreadful ordeal it would be. Mary thought for moment or two, then she picked up the receiver and dialled Edwina's number.

'What is it, Mary? I'm terribly busy.'

'Anything I can help you with?'

Edwina laughed. 'Not unless you fancy trying to identify the bodies that we dragged out of Marble Arch station.'

Mary shuddered. Whether she left London for the safety of leafy Suffolk or stayed put, she was certain of one thing. The injured, the dead and the dying would have to do without her help.

'Honestly, Edwina, I don't know how you do it. I do so admire you. Tell me, darling, who do we know in the Cabinet?'

'Practically everyone, I should think. Which ministry in particular?'

'I'm not sure. Security, I suppose.'

'Well, of course Herbert Morrison is the Home Secretary. He's in charge of Home Security. Unless you mean MI5, in which case I think Brigadier Harker is your man.'

'Oh! Good lord, no.' Mary laughed. 'Not MI5. It's nothing like that. A minor thing. A mistake. Just an acquaintance of mine in a spot of bother.'

'Then Morrison's probably your man, and speaking of acquaintances, does the name Alice Bartlett strike any chords with you?'

'I may have heard the name somewhere. Why do you ask?'

'Well, I assumed you knew her well. My team have just completed identification. Apparently she had your name in her address book and your private telephone number. I was meaning to call you later. I thought you'd probably want to know.'

It took a second or two before Mary understood what she was saying. After she replaced the receiver, she shed a few private tears for Miss Bartlett and, remembering Frobisher's imperious tone and her own careless indiscretion, several hot, angry tears for herself. Then she wiped her eyes, took a deep breath and demanded to be put through to the Home Office.

Chapter 21

Fay was silent for most of the journey. She could have asked if it had been absolutely necessary to pick her up at her house. She could have said she deeply resented the anxiety caused to her family; that her mother suffered with her nerves, but since her escorts were probably just obeying orders, she knew the responsibility lay elsewhere. And, to be perfectly fair, they did try to put her at ease. They made casual comments about the weather and the blackout. They talked about rationing, and by the time the car arrived at its destination, she had learned that the older man missed having three heaped spoonfuls of sugar in his tea and the other would sell his grandmother for a couple of juicy oranges. From her, they learned nothing.

She had been expecting to be taken to the same building in Bayswater where she'd been interrogated before. Instead she found herself being led down a long, dimly lit tunnel deep below a building somewhere in Whitehall. In places the tunnel widened and she noticed rooms on either side. She heard typewriters clattering and telephones ringing. At the foot of some wooden stairs, the man stopped.

'Up here, miss. Hold on to the rail. It's quite steep.'

She counted seven steps. At the top they turned right and stopped in front of a door. He pushed it open.

'Wait here, miss. Make yourself comfortable.'

Unlike the hard stone of the tunnel, the room was carpeted. She blinked and as her eyes became accustomed to the harsh light, she noticed that the carpet was shabby and threadbare and stained.

The room looked more like an untidy storeroom than an office. Was she really expected to make herself comfortable? How? Where was she supposed to sit? Looking round, she saw a stack of folding chairs. They were leaning against a rusty filing cabinet. Fay took one and sat in the middle of the room, waiting. According to the clock on the wall the time was eight minutes to six. She watched the hands move slowly and on the dot of six the door opened. A man in a brown suit, a folder tucked under his arm, walked briskly towards her and extended his hand.

'Well, Miss Abrams, we meet at last.' His hand was warm and damp. She wished she'd worn her gloves. He dragged a chair over and sat with his knees almost touching hers. 'My name is Frobisher,' he said. 'Arnold Frobisher. Representative of the security department of the Home Office. You are acquainted, are you not, with Lady Langbourne?'

'I am,' she said, searching in her handbag for her cigarettes.

'I'd prefer it if you didn't smoke, Miss Abrams.'

Fay closed the clasp on her handbag and sat with her arms folded across her chest. 'You do know that I've already been questioned once by the Home Office, don't you?' she said.

He pulled a bundle of papers from a folder, tapped them with his finger and frowned. 'Yes, Miss Abrams, I'm well aware that you've been questioned before but I'd like to make it perfectly clear from the start that I shall expect a great deal more cooperation from you than you gave my colleague.'

She would have liked to tell him that his colleague had been a great deal more pleasant. Instead, she frowned. 'Excuse me, Mr Frobisher,' she said, 'but I answered all the questions and I answered them truthfully.'

'Then you won't mind answering them again, will you?'

'Not if you don't mind wasting your department's valuable time.'

'Perhaps you'll have the goodness to let me worry about that, Miss Abrams. Now, let's get straight to the point. Where does your information come from? I can only assume you have contacts with the German military. What information have you passed on to them?'

Fay's eyes narrowed. She took a deep breath and stared at him.

'I don't have any information. I don't know anything. I don't have any contacts in Germany or anywhere else. I have visions, that's all. I've had them since I was eight years old. I wish I didn't have them. It's not comfortable knowing what's going to happen, especially when no one believes me, but I thought someone should know about the raid on Oxford Street. So I warned Lady Langbourne.'

'What made you think she would take your warning seriously?'

There was something about the way he said it that put her on guard. She didn't completely understand why she should feel that way but she considered her reply before she spoke.

'I had no way of knowing whether or not she would take my warning seriously, but Lady Langbourne is in a position of influence and she showed me kindness when my fiancé was killed in action.'

Mr Frobisher referred to his notes. 'Your fiancé. That would be Bernard Ebstein.'

Alarmed by the thoroughness of his investigation, Fay's composure began to crumble. 'My fiancé was in a reserved occupation, Mr Frobisher. He needn't have joined up. It was his choice. He died defending this country.'

'Most noble, indeed. Now, let's get back to your…visions, shall we? What can you tell me? The proposed date for the German invasion, perhaps? Or maybe there's something else you'd care to share.'

'Mr Frobisher, I don't think you understand. I'm not clairvoyant. I can't see into the future just by closing my eyes. I don't know when I'm going to have a vision. It just happens. If I knew anything, anything at all, about a German invasion, I can promise you, I certainly wouldn't keep quiet about it.'

'All right, Miss Abrams. Let's leave that there for the moment. Do you keep a diary?'

Unsure if she'd heard properly, Fay stared at him. 'A diary? You want to know if I keep a diary?'

He nodded.

'What's that got to do with anything?'

'Just answer the question, Miss Abrams.'

'Yes, I keep a diary.'

'Do you have it with you?'

'No, of course not.'

He made a tutting noise with his tongue. 'How disappointing. Perhaps I should send someone back to your house to collect it.'

'Mr Frobisher, do what you want. There's nothing in my diaries that will interest you.'

She watched him rustling through his papers. 'Let's forget your diaries for the moment. Would you like to tell me about your connections to the Communist Party?'

'What connections? I don't give a hoot about politics. I'm not interested.'

'Really? And what about your father?'

'What about him?'

'Come now, Miss Abrams. We already know that he's friendly with Joseph Weissman.'

Fay's face grew hot. She opened her handbag, took out a cigarette and completely ignoring Mr Frobisher's snort of disapproval, she lit it, drew the smoke down into her lungs, then slowly blew it out.

'Leave my father out of it, Mr Frobisher,' she said, glaring at him through a cloud of smoke. 'My father's friendship with Mr Weissman, or anyone else for that matter, has nothing whatever to do with my visions.'

'What about your grandmother? Are you going to tell me that she has nothing to do with them either?'

'My grandmother?' She almost laughed. 'I'm afraid you're barking up the wrong tree, Mr Frobisher. My grandmother's dead. She died seventeen years ago.' She watched him rustling through his papers.

'Zofia Anja Kroll. Born 1881 in Krobia, Poland. Died 1923 in Kilburn.'

She stared at him, trying to think ahead, to understand where his line of questioning was leading.

'Well, Miss Abrams?'

'Well, what, Mr Frobisher? What do you want me to say?'

'Zofia Kroll. She was your grandmother, wasn't she?'

She nodded. 'Yes, but I didn't know her. I don't remember anything about her. I was only three when she died.'

'Perhaps I'm not making myself clear,' he said, and placing his hands palms down on his knees, he tapped his fingers against his legs. 'You see, Miss Abrams, English law has changed very little in the past twenty-five years, which means the same Act under which your grandmother was detained still exists today.'

Fay's heart gave a sudden lurch. She swallowed hard. Looking around for an ashtray and finding none, she pinched the end of her cigarette between her finger and thumb.

'I'm sorry. I don't know what you mean. What are you saying? That my grandmother was arrested? What for? What did she do?'

He smiled. 'Oh dear,' he said. 'You really don't know, do you? Your grandmother was confined for a year under the Witchcraft Act. An archaic Act, I won't deny, but nevertheless one that provided us with the means to keep Mrs Kroll out of the way.'

Fay's eyes began to sting. She blinked and swallowed hard. 'That's barbaric,' she said. 'I don't believe you. My grandmother was not a witch.'

'I didn't say she was, Miss Abrams, but I must tell you that I'm finding it very difficult to believe that your family has never spoken about it. One can only assume that they were too ashamed. The point I'm making is that suspicions are naturally aroused when someone claims to have knowledge that they have no business having. Especially when one's country is at war, and I'm afraid that during the Great War, your grandmother claimed to know rather too much for her own good and for that of the country. Much like you, Miss Abrams.'

Hearing her grandmother's fate from the lips of such an odious man was bad enough. Now he was threatening her with detention, and what's more, he was enjoying it. She wanted to slap him and get out of that place as fast as she could into the clean, fresh air.

'I'd like to leave now, Mr Frobisher, if it's all the same to you,' she said.

'Not so fast, young lady. I haven't finished with you yet. Not by a long shot. I will tell you frankly, any threat to national security is a matter of grave concern to me and my department.'

Fay's jaw was clenched so tightly it was difficult to speak. 'Mr Frobisher. I work in a hat shop. I've worked there since I left school. I have no political allegiance to any organisation. I am not a threat to anyone. And what you have told me about my grandmother has come as a complete surprise to me. I have nothing to tell you. I don't know anything. Now, please, may I leave?'

Before he could reply, the door opened. The man, the elder of her two escorts, nodded in her direction.

Mr Frobisher looked furious. 'I thought I told you I didn't wish to be interrupted.'

The man apologised and, covering his mouth, whispered something in Mr Frobisher's ear. Mr Frobisher stormed out of the room. When he returned, two minutes later, his face red, his arms flapping, he picked up his bundle of papers and, without looking at her, he muttered, 'That will be all for now, Miss Abrams. You can go but you'd do well to remember that you haven't heard the last of this. I shall be watching you closely. Very closely indeed.'

Chapter 22

Her father hugged her. Was she hungry? Did she want tea or would she prefer something stronger? But when Fay followed him into the kitchen her mother wouldn't even look at her. She just sat there, head bent, fiddling with the buttons on her cardigan. Fay glared at her.

'Have you any idea what you've just put me through?' she said. 'You and your secrets. Did I really have to hear it from a stranger?'

Her mother raised her head slowly. Fay saw her eyes dart towards her father.

'Don't look at him, Mother. I'm talking to you.'

Her father frowned. 'Fay, there's no need to be so rude, is there?'

'Look, Dad, being questioned was bad enough but being told things about my own family, things I should have known, was downright humiliating. So, you'll have to forgive me if you think I'm being rude, but you weren't there.'

'Things? What things?' said her father. 'I don't know what you're talking about.'

'Mum knows what I mean. I'm talking about my grandmother.'

They were sitting round the kitchen table, Fay and her father waiting for her mother to say something, but she just sat there, looking down at her hands with her lips pressed tightly together.

'Well, Mum. I'm waiting.'

'So am I,' said her father. 'Will someone please tell me what's going on?'

Fay hesitated for a second. Had she felt any sympathy for her mother she might have waited until they were alone and had it out with her in private. But it was too late now and she had no desire to protect her. So, she took a deep breath and just blurted it out.

'The Home Office think I know more than I should. I have visions, Dad. I see things that haven't happened yet. Mum knows about it. She's always known. And apparently her mother had visions too.'

Her father looked confused. 'Our daughter has visions and you never thought to mention it to me, Hetty?'

'I didn't want to upset you, Lou.'

'But you could discuss it with Mrs Feldman? I wondered what she was talking about. Now I know.'

'It wasn't me, Lou. You honestly think I would tell that woman?'

Her father sighed. 'Hetty, I don't care who you told. I don't understand why you kept it from me. Unless you've forgotten, she's my daughter, too.' When he turned and looked at her, Fay saw at once the pain in his eyes. 'These visions of yours, how long have you been having them?'

'Since I was eight, Dad. Twelve years. And Mum never told you because she's ashamed. She thinks I'm unnatural. She thinks there's something wrong with me, don't you, Mother?'

Her mother's head was bent, her face hidden. She didn't speak. Fay looked at her father. A tiny vein was throbbing near his left temple. Suddenly, he slammed his fist down on to the table. Her mother jumped. Fay saw her hand flutter up to her chest.

'For God's sake, Hetty, say something.'

'Lou, don't.' Her mother was whimpering. 'My nerves…'

'Forget your bloomin' nerves for a minute. What about mine? You're going to explain if I have to sit here all night. I'm listening, Hetty. I'm waiting.'

'You don't understand what it's been like for me, Lou. Neither of you understand. First my mother. Now her. I'm scared, Lou. All the time. I'm so scared.'

'What of? Of me? What am I, some kind of monster? You couldn't tell me that my daughter sees things?'

Watching her, Fay felt an unexpected wave of pity for her mother.

Reaching across the table, she took her hand. 'This can't go on, Mum,' she whispered. 'Look what it's doing to you. Tell him. Tell him everything.'

She wondered how much he already knew. Had he any idea that his own mother-in-law had been in prison? Her mother's eyes were closed. Before she spoke she gave a long, shuddering sigh.

'I lied to you, Lou. My mother... I told you she'd been ill but she wasn't ill. They came to the house and they took her away and I didn't see her again for almost a year. I was only fourteen. I was all alone. I knew people already thought she was peculiar so when they asked me where she was, I said she was having treatment and they believed me and once you tell a lie...well, it's hard to stop.'

'Who took her away, Hetty?'

'The police. They arrested her. They said there were laws against witchcraft and she had to go to prison. She wasn't a witch, Lou. She just...saw things. She tried to warn them about the things she'd seen but you remember how bad her English was. They wanted to stop her. They wanted to shut her up. They said she was damaging morale. She was a threat to national security. And when I met you...I couldn't tell you she'd been in prison. I didn't know if you'd still want me.'

'Hetty, did you really think it would have made a blind bit of difference? All I ever wanted was to take care of you.'

'I know, Lou, and you did take care of me and things were just fine. But then Fay started having visions and it started all over again and when those men turned up today...' She buried her face in her hands.

'You thought the same thing would happen to our daughter? I can see how you must have felt but I'm your husband, Hetty, and right now I feel like I don't know you.'

'I'm so sorry. All I ever wanted was for everything to be normal.'

Fay put her arm around her mother's shoulders. 'You mean you wanted me to be normal. So did I, Mum. I never wanted to have visions and I don't suppose my grandmother did either.'

'What I don't understand,' said her father, 'is how this man from the Home Office knows about your visions.'

'It's a long story, Dad. Can we talk about it later? I'm really tired.'

'All right, it can wait, but just tell me one thing. Will he want to see you again?'

Fay sighed. 'I honestly don't know, Dad. I certainly don't want to see him again.'

She left her parents sitting together in the kitchen. It was late but they still had a lot to talk about and she couldn't wait to crawl into bed. Halfway up the stairs, she heard Jack's bedroom door closing. She guessed he'd been listening. She wondered what he would make of it, but for her it was something of a relief. Everything was out in the open. She was free to speak openly about her visions, at least within the circle of her family.

But what of Mr Frobisher's threats? The way her grandmother had been treated was barbaric, but things were different now, weren't they? Opinions had changed. The same Act might still be there on the statutes but would anyone seriously try using it today? Fay was English. So were her parents. They'd been born in this country. She understood her rights and if it came to it, she could stand up for herself. How different it must have been for her grandmother. A foreigner, an outsider, a widow, separated from her young daughter, she must have been out of her mind with worry.

Frobisher had given Fay a hard time but she'd refused to be bullied and certainly not by the likes of him. Rotten bastard, she thought, and she wondered what on earth he expected to find in her diary. He was in for a big disappointment if he ever got his hands on it, unless he took pleasure in knowing that she'd sold two hats on Tuesday and had an argument with her mother on Wednesday. There was nothing in it to interest him but she couldn't help wondering what he'd make of her exercise book with its accounts of all her visions.

She was flicking through its pages when she heard her father's footsteps on the stairs. Forgetting for a moment that there was no longer any need for secrecy, she slipped the book under her pillow.

'Well,' he said, 'it's been quite a day, hasn't it?'

'You're all right though, aren't you, Dad?'

He shrugged. 'Well, I'm a bit sad but I'll get over it. You don't have to tell me about your visions right now if you don't feel like it, but...'

Fay slid her hand under the pillow. 'Read this, Dad. Perhaps it will help you understand.'

He sat beside her on the bed and read each page, each account of every vision she'd had. When he'd finished there were tears in his eyes.

'Now I feel useless as well as sad,' he said. 'It breaks my heart to know that my girl had to deal with something like this on her own.'

'I got used to it, Dad. I taught myself how to cope.'

'You were eight years old. Weren't you frightened?'

'At first I was. I was scared that I'd be burnt at the stake, like Joan of Arc. I tried to pretend that I was like everyone else, especially around Mum.'

'Your mother handled it badly and frankly I'm surprised at her. She should have known better but I suppose we mustn't be too hard on her. You have such courage. She's not strong like you.'

'Then all I can say is it's a good thing she doesn't have visions, too. Thank God it skipped a generation.'

He smiled. 'Two witches in the family are more than enough, thank you very much. Now, you get some rest. See you in the morning, *buballah*. Sleep well.'

'I can sleep in. I've got the day off tomorrow.'

'Well, in that case, I'll take the day off, too. I'll take you out for lunch. To Blooms. Just the two of us.'

'And what about Mum? Won't she feel a bit left out?'

'Maybe she will, but to tell you the truth, if I hear another word about Mrs Feldman, I don't think I can trust myself. By the way, darling, what made you tell her about your visions?'

Fay shrugged. 'I don't know. It just slipped out. We were talking about Bernard. I told her that I knew he wasn't coming back. I probably said a bit more than I should, but it hardly matters now, does it?'

'Not to me it doesn't.'

'Nor me, but Mum's always worried about what other people think.'

He frowned. 'Let's hope things will be different now.'

Chapter 23

When Jack tapped on her bedroom door Fay was still in a deep sleep. She was in the middle of a dream. She was about to be executed. Her eyes were covered by a blindfold. Something was looped around her neck. She couldn't see what it was but she knew it was Lady Langbourne's scarf and it was getting tighter and tighter and she was trying to tell them that she hadn't done anything wrong. Jack interrupted at precisely the right moment. She opened her eyes and there he was, standing in the doorway, wearing such a solemn expression that she patted her bed and told him to come in. Jack sat beside her and cleared his throat.

'I want you to know that I don't care what you've done,' he said. 'I don't even care how bad it is...' He cleared his throat again. 'I just want you to know that I'm going to stick by you no matter what. They can say what they like but I'm not going anywhere while my sister's in trouble.'

She wanted to hug him but when she reached for him, Jack's body stiffened and she understood. He didn't want assurance from her. It was his turn to do the assuring.

'You heard what we were talking about last night?'

He nodded. 'Not all of it, but I know you're in trouble.'

'The thing about listening at keyholes, Jack, is that you hear bits and pieces and you get the wrong end of the stick.'

'But they think you're a witch,' he said.

Fay smiled. 'See, that's what I meant about eavesdropping. You get it all wrong. Now, you listen to me. Are you listening?'

He nodded. 'Sometimes I see things before they happen. I know things that I shouldn't know and those men...well, they want to find out how I know.'

'So, you're not a witch?'

She shook her head.

'And you're not in trouble?'

'Not really. At least, nothing I can't handle but I appreciate your concern. I'm very lucky to have such a nice brother. Now, shouldn't you be getting ready for school?'

Jack's fingers were resting on the door handle. He hesitated, then turned and looked at her. 'Even if you are a witch, I'm ever so glad you don't laugh like one,' he whispered.

It took a second before she knew what he meant. They'd gone to the pictures to see *Snow White* and he'd been so scared by the wicked stepmother's cackling laugh it had given him nightmares. He couldn't have been more than six or seven but he obviously hadn't forgotten. Remembering her own nightmare, Fay decided against staying in bed any longer in case she drifted back to sleep. She stuffed her feet into her slippers, grabbed her dressing gown from the back of the door and went downstairs for breakfast.

Even allowing for the drama of the previous evening, it was obvious to Fay that the atmosphere in the Abrams household that morning was decidedly odd. Her father was rather too jolly. Her mother kept throwing nervous glances in her direction, smiling whenever their eyes met and then looking away. Only Jack behaved as if nothing had happened, that is, until he left for school. On his way out he stopped behind Fay's chair and patted her shoulder twice in a manner she could only describe as paternal. She tried not to smile. Whether the gesture had gone unnoticed by her parents, Fay wasn't sure, but the moment the front door closed behind him, her father clapped his hands together and grinned.

'Your brother, bless him, made a little speech just before you came downstairs. He announced that he will not be evacuated. We could say what we liked. He didn't care. He won't go and we can't make him.'

'Really? And how do you feel about that?'

Still smiling, her father said, 'Quite honestly, I'm rather proud of him.'

Fay glanced at her mother. 'And how about you, Mum? Are you proud of him, too?'

She shrugged. 'What can I say? He won't listen to anyone.'

'Yes, but are you proud of him?'

Fay saw the look that passed between her parents. Her mother nodded.

'I'm proud of both of you.'

Fay swallowed hard, looked down at her plate and, eyes stinging, sat dabbing crumbs of toast with her finger. When she pushed her chair back and began clearing away the breakfast things, her mother put her hand on her arm.

'Leave that,' she said. 'I'll do it. You can have a bath. Take your time. There's plenty of hot water.'

Before she took her bath, Fay opened the drawer where the photographs were kept and removed two photos, one of her father's parents and the other of Zofia. The card on which the portraits were mounted showed signs of age. The corners were curled and creased but the photographs themselves were undamaged. They hadn't faded. They bore none of the brown speckles she'd seen in some old photos. She slipped them inside an envelope and went upstairs.

Blooms was packed and, as always, it took a few minutes to get used to the wall of sound that greeted them as Fay and her father stepped inside. A waiter led them to a table, cleared the plates, wiped the table with a corner of his apron and invited them to sit down. Her father had once told her that there was something about good food and good company that made Jews excited and that was why they talked so loudly. At the time, she'd wondered whether they would be quite so excited if they were sitting down to a meal prepared by her mother. She'd known it was an unkind thought. Her mother lacked joy, but then Fay hadn't known why and only now was she beginning to understand. Her mother's life had been soured by secrets and she wondered if it was too late for her to really change.

'What was Mum like when you met her?' she said.

Her father sighed. 'Pretty. Not quite seventeen. Dainty. Softly spoken. Terribly shy. I thought she was lovely but it took ages before she trusted me enough to go out on a date.' He smiled. 'You might not believe it but your mother is a good dancer if no one's watching.'

Failing to conjure up an image of her mother dancing, Fay asked about her grandmother, Zofia. What was she like? Did he get on with her? What did his parents think of her?

'Well,' he said, 'what can I tell you? Your grandmother was not an easy person to get to know. Her English wasn't that good. She was rather excitable. And my parents, they didn't have much in common with her. They tried. They really made an effort…at first.'

'So when Mum told you her mother had been in hospital for a long time, did she actually say why?'

He frowned. 'No. I don't think she did.'

'And you never asked?'

He shook his head. 'I think everyone assumed that it was some kind of mental breakdown.'

'Because of her strange behaviour?'

Before he could reply, a man with a wiry grey beard squeezed past their table and wrapped an arm round her father's shoulders.

'Lou Abrams, as I live and breathe,' he bellowed. 'And who is this gorgeous young woman? Don't tell me this is your daughter. Look at her,' he shouted, to no one in particular. 'How come an ugly so-and-so like him can father such a beautiful girl?'

For an awful moment, she thought the man might pinch her cheeks, but he was already moving away between the tables, stopping to talk to everyone he knew. Her father pulled his chair closer and reached for her hand.

'Listen, darling. These visions you've been having…' He glanced over his shoulder. From where she was sitting, Fay had a good view of the whole restaurant. No one was taking any notice of them, and there was such a racket going on, no one could have heard what they were saying. 'These visions,' he murmured, 'how does the Home Office know about them?'

She told him everything. Their heads close, voice lowered, she told him about Miss Bartlett and Lady Langbourne and about being bundled into a back of the car and questioned.

'So yesterday wasn't the first time someone from the Home Office spoke to you?'

'No, but it was a different man yesterday. The first man was quite civil towards me. He just asked a load of questions and then let me go but Mr Frobisher, the man I saw yesterday, he...' She hesitated.

'What, darling? What did he do? Did he hurt you? Threaten you?'

'Not exactly, but he made a point of letting me know that the same Act that was used to imprison my grandmother was still on the statutes and he'd obviously been finding out everything he could about the whole family. He even knew that Joe Weissman is your friend.'

'Joe? What's he got to do with it?'

'I'm not sure. He didn't actually say but he implied that Joe was a member of the Communist Party and that your friendship with him suggests that you might be a member, too. He was trying to intimidate me, Dad, that's all. Just letting me know what a clever little weasel he was.'

'But what is it the Home Office actually want from you? That's what I don't understand. I mean, it's not as if you've been spreading panic among the masses, is it?'

She sighed. 'They don't believe me and I can't honestly blame them. They deal in hard facts. Visions, premonitions, prophecies – it's all the same to them. I might just as well say I saw it in the stars.' Fay leant closer and covered her mouth. 'What they want to know,' she whispered, 'is where I really get my information from. They think I'm a spy, Dad. They think I'm in league with the enemy.'

His grip on her hand tightened. He was frowning. 'Then we've got to convince them that you're not.'

'And how are we going to do that?'

'Can't your friend help? Lady Langbourne? A word in the right ear?'

Fay smiled. 'She's hardly my friend, Dad.'

For a moment, neither of them spoke. 'What can I do?' he said. 'There must be something. Someone I can talk to.'

She shook her head. 'I don't think so, Dad. We'll just have to wait and see what happens.'

'Well, darling, let's pray they don't take it any further.'

'God willing,' she murmured.

They bought two large chunks of *lockshen* kugel – fine noodles baked with raisins and eggs and sprinkled with cinnamon – to take home for Jack and Hetty. In a shop near Aldgate Pump, Fay chose two matching silver frames for the photographs. She'd brought the photos with her to make sure the frames were exactly the right size.

Her father seemed pleased, if not a little puzzled, until she announced as they were leaving the shop, 'It's time they came out of hiding, Dad. They ought to be on show where they can keep an eye on us.'

Chapter 24

The cocktail bar at The Dorchester was almost empty. They had the place to themselves. Mary watched Edwina twirl the stem of her glass between gloved fingers and wondered what was going through her friend's mind.

'Do you think I've been foolish?' she said.

Edwina frowned. 'Of course you've been foolish. I mean, why ever get involved in the first place?'

That was exactly what she'd expected Edwina to ask, and Mary had already prepared her answer.

'Look, darling. I know you don't have much time for people who believe they can speak to the dead or claim to see into the future. I understand that and I respect your opinion, that's why I never told you about Miss Bartlett, but she was wonderfully kind to me when I lost my daughter. So, when she told me just how accurate the girl's predictions were and asked me to pass on a warning to someone in authority…'

'You chose Arnold Frobisher. But why him, darling? Of all people. Why choose Arnold Frobisher?'

It was Mary's turn to frown. 'Well, he was there, Edwina. At your party. He was from the Home Office and at the time it seemed like the perfect opportunity to repay Miss Bartlett's kindness and do what she'd asked me to do.'

Edwina raised an eyebrow. 'And I'm sure he was most grateful.'

Ignoring the sarcasm, she repeated what she could remember of her conversation with Frobisher. 'He suggested that my little friend from the hat shop – that's what he kept calling her – was nothing more than a fortune teller. Quite frankly his manner was more than a little condescending until I told him what Miss Abrams knew about the *Lancastria*...you remember. It was in the news...but the details she was able to provide had never been mentioned. Honestly, darling, you can't imagine how satisfying it was.'

Edwina smiled. 'Oh, I think I can.'

Mary slid the girl's note across the table. 'Read this,' she whispered. 'I received it four days before the attack on Oxford Street.'

She watched Edwina as she read. Edwina folded the note and handed it back to her. 'Don't tell me you showed this to Frobisher?'

Mary shook her head and, feeling her cheeks redden with embarrassment, she described the ugly scene that had taken place in her house on the previous Sunday.

'He made me so angry. He was threatening me, telling me that my association with the wrong people would destroy my reputation and Gerald's. And then he said something about how naïve I was to believe the girl's claims.'

'And what did you say? No, let me guess. "You won't think I'm so naïve on Tuesday night, Mr Frobisher, when Oxford Street takes a hammering?" Am I right?'

'I know. It sounds pathetic, doesn't it? But honestly, darling, I couldn't stop myself.'

Of all the ways Edwina might have reacted, the last thing she expected her to do was to laugh.

'I'm glad you find it amusing, Edwina,' she said.

'But Mary, can't you see? It is amusing. Gerald's made him feel like a worthless idiot. The man is utterly humiliated and if you hadn't added your penny's worth he might have kicked a few tyres on his way home. Punched the wall. Yelled at his wife. But there you are practically rubbing salt in his wounds, telling him to keep his grievances to himself. You provoked him, and now the little man's retaliating.'

Mary had always admired Edwina's unemotional detachment. One could rely on her to approach problems with the minimum of fuss. Today, her friend's cool, rational manner only succeeded in annoying her. Forgetting that she didn't particularly like glacé cherries, she stabbed one with her cocktail stick, popped it into her mouth and shuddered.

'One expects a little more sympathy from one's friends, Edwina,' she said, and immediately recognised that she was behaving like a sulky child.

Edwina appeared not to notice. Leaning across the table she took Mary's hand in hers. 'You made a mistake, darling. You spoke to the wrong man but not everyone in the Home Office has an axe to grind like Frobisher. There are other people who might listen to you.'

'Like who?'

'Well, Thomas Poulton springs to mind.'

'Really? You think he'd be interested?'

'Why shouldn't he be? He knows you. He works closely with Herbert Morrison. What's more, he's quite chummy with our Prime Minister and it's no secret among his circle of friends that Winston has, on occasion, taken the advice of a clairvoyant. I should think Sir Thomas would be most sympathetic. Personally, darling, I would keep out of it but, if it makes you feel better, it can do no harm to put Thomas Poulton in touch with your little friend.'

It did make her feel better. If she could repair the damage she had done to the young woman who may well have saved her life, nothing would make her happier. She'd telephoned the Home Office but she had no way of knowing whether she'd been successful in bringing Frobisher's interrogation to a halt. And though she didn't know him well, whenever she'd spoken to him, Thomas Poulton was always utterly charming. He had been quite flirtatious when they'd met at Edwina's last party. She remembered him taking her hand and holding it for far longer than was strictly necessary. Mary was smiling. Sometimes Edwina could be simply marvellous. Clever Edwina. Such a good friend. One could always rely on her to solve life's little problems.

Holding her empty glass aloft, she said, 'Another cocktail, darling?'

She would have to speak to the girl first. No point mentioning it to Sir Thomas before the girl had agreed to talk to him. She would telephone the hat shop in the morning. No, she thought, a little note would be more appropriate. And then once the girl had agreed, a letter to Sir Thomas explaining how remarkably accurate the girl's visions were. Yes, definitely a letter and perhaps a tiny drop of scent on the inside of the envelope?

Chapter 25

Though she would rather have no visions at all, now that the burden of secrecy had been removed, Fay was ready to accept that they were part of her. It was useless wishing they would stop. Nothing she did would make the slightest difference. She was stuck with them. For now, at least.

Journeying into town on Friday morning, Rita asked what she was thinking about. 'You were miles away,' she said. 'What's the matter?'

'Nothing much, I was just thinking about work. Business is so slow, I'm not sure how much longer Miss Greenwood can keep me on.'

'Plenty of jobs going at Selfridges.'

'I'm sure there are but I wouldn't mind doing something different.'

'Really?' said Rita. 'I don't like change much but then I'm not terribly adventurous, am I?'

'But you've got Danny. You're a lucky girl, Rita. He's a really smashing bloke.'

'I think so, too,' she said. 'By the way, I owe you an apology, Fay. It wasn't one of my better ideas, inviting cousin Howard to make up a foursome. I'd forgotten how loathsome he could be. I'm sure he wasn't always like that.'

'Oh, I think he was,' said Fay, and Rita laughed.

In Oxford Street, buildings still smouldered. Since Wednesday, the pavements had been cleared of glass. Rubble and chunks of plaster had been piled into untidy mounds and teams of workmen were already blocking Selfridges' windows with pieces of timber. In one shop, where the windows and door had once stood, the defiant owner had hung a notice. *More open than usual.*

As they reached the turning near Selfridges' staff entrance, Rita took hold of her hand. 'Listen, Fay. I want to tell you something. I know you miss Bernard as much as I do but I really hope you meet someone nice one day. Honestly, I do.'

Fay was surprised. Only a few weeks earlier Rita had accused her of not really caring about Bernard. What's changed? she thought. It took less than a second to work it out. Rita was in love. She was happy and Fay was glad for her. She gave her a quick hug and kissed her cheek.

'Better go,' she said, glancing at her watch, 'while I've still got a job to go to.'

Miss Greenwood was already there, perched on a stool behind the counter, untangling a ball of khaki-coloured wool.

'I'm not late, am I?' said Fay.

'No, dear. I'm terribly early. I was certain it would take simply ages to travel into work this morning so I allowed rather too much time. The buses were slightly slower than usual but the train wasn't delayed at all. I could have had an extra half-hour in bed if I'd known. Did you enjoy your day off? Do anything special?'

'My father took me out for lunch.'

Miss Greenwood looked wistful. 'How lovely. I did think about taking myself off to the pictures. I do so enjoy watching a film during the day but everything gets so dusty at home if you don't keep on top of it.'

'Don't tell me you spent the day cleaning, Miss Greenwood.'

'That's exactly what I did. Still, it will be nice to go home to a clean, tidy flat.'

Poor Miss Greenwood, she thought. The shop was the centre of her life and Fay wanted more out of life. She wasn't sure what she was looking for. She knew she'd never find a kinder boss but surely there must be something she could do where she could feel more useful.

She was filling the kettle when she heard Miss Greenwood speaking to someone. Thinking it might be a customer, she quickly dried her hands and found Mr Cassell leaning against the counter. Miss Greenwood looked at her and smiled.

'Mr Cassell was just saying that he'd been quite worried about us, Miss Abrams.'

'I heard what happened in Oxford Street, Miss Abrams, so I made a little detour and popped round yesterday to see if you were all right. When I saw that the shop was closed I imagined all sorts of terrible things. I can't tell you how relieved I am to see you, both of you, looking so well.'

'Wasn't that kind of him, my dear? Perhaps Mr Cassell would like a cup of tea.'

'If you're sure it's no trouble. Milk, no sugar, please,' he said.

As she waited for the kettle to boil, Fay stared at herself in the mirror. Her cheeks were quite flushed. Taking her compact from her handbag, she dabbed her face with the powder puff, reapplied her lipstick and combed her hair. She set the tea tray, not with the bone china reserved for special customers, but the everyday set which she and Miss Greenwood used. She didn't want to give him the wrong impression. Though, from the way he'd been looking at her, had she served him tea in a tin mug he wouldn't have noticed. When she came back with the tray, Miss Greenwood was talking about the window display.

'Miss Abrams has such a natural flair. I know I can rely on her judgement.'

'Very nice. Very nice, indeed,' he said, but he wasn't looking at her window display. He was looking straight at Fay. 'I was wondering, Miss Abrams, if I might have your telephone number,' he said.

Fay was flustered. Before she could answer, Miss Greenwood said, 'You can always phone her here at the shop, Mr Cassell. I won't mind in the least.'

He smiled. 'In that case, shall I save myself a phone call and simply ask if Miss Abrams would join me on Sunday? Lunch in the park? A picnic, perhaps, if the weather is fine.'

Fay daren't look at Miss Greenwood. She was quite certain that she was practically holding her breath waiting to hear her response, and she rather resented the position in which she found herself. She was tempted to turn him down.

'Do you mean this Sunday?' she said.

He nodded. 'Yes, if you're not doing anything special. I could meet you at Camden station if you like. Would twelve be all right for you?'

She hesitated. 'Yes, I think that would be all right.'

He gave a little bow. 'Until Sunday then, Miss Abrams. I wish you both a good day and a safe journey home.'

At the door he bowed again and Fay and Miss Greenwood watched him drive away.

'Well,' said Miss Greenwood. 'I told you, didn't I? He's quite smitten and unless I'm very much mistaken you are rather taken with him, too.'

Fay shrugged. 'He's not bad and I wasn't doing anything particular this weekend. I suppose he'll do, Miss Greenwood…until the real thing comes along.'

Some time during the afternoon, Fay was turning yet another khaki-coloured heel when she looked up and saw a dark limousine glide to a stop right outside the shop. The car looked familiar.

Oh please, not again, she thought. Was it too late to dive behind the counter and hide or had she already been seen?

'I do believe that's Lady Langbourne's car,' said Miss Greenwood. 'I'm sure she'll have plenty to say about our new window display. She's not going to like it one bit.'

Fay watched as Lady Langbourne's driver got out of the car. It was not her usual driver. His uniform appeared to be rather too small for him and instead of removing his cap and opening the passenger's door, he strode straight into the shop.

'Letter for Miss Abrams,' he said. 'From Lady Langbourne.'

Embarrassed, Fay took the envelope from his hand. He nodded and left the shop. As soon as he'd gone she read Lady Langbourne's letter, then showed it to Miss Greenwood.

'What does this mean, Miss Abrams?'

Aware of her frown and the sharp edge to her voice, Fay shook her head. 'Honestly, Miss Greenwood. I have absolutely no idea.'

She read it again.

> I would be most grateful for the opportunity to discuss a proposal with you. I shall expect you on Sunday afternoon at quarter past three. I do hope you are free. If you have a prior engagement please be good enough to telephone and let me know.

'Surely her ladyship isn't offering you a job? If that's the case then I have to say that I'm surprised at her. Sending notes to you here at the shop. It's not the way one should go about things. It's not right. Not right at all.'

She could have reassured Miss Greenwood, there and then, that whatever Lady Langbourne wanted to discuss with her it was most definitely not an offer of employment. Instead she said, 'I have no idea what her ladyship wants, Miss Greenwood but I can't possibly see her on Sunday, can I? I already have a prior engagement, so perhaps I should let her know straight away.'

Miss Greenwood gave a little sniff. 'If you wish to use our telephone, that's entirely up to you but perhaps you'd prefer your conversation to be more private. You must do whatever you think best, Miss Abrams. I'm sure I don't mind in the least.'

For the second time that day, Fay found herself resenting the awkward situation in which she'd been put by others and she wondered if Lady Langbourne was always so indiscreet. Miss Greenwood knew nothing about her visions and she had no intention of ever letting her find out. Not wanting her to think she was hiding anything, she went straight to the counter and picked up the receiver. As Miss Greenwood hovered nearby, sniffing and feigning indifference, Fay told Lady Langbourne that she was terribly sorry but she was busy on Sunday. Her ladyship was clearly disappointed.

'I must say, Miss Abrams, it would have been more convenient for me had you been free on Sunday but since you have a prior engagement, would you be good enough to call round to Portman Square on your way home this evening? I promise I shan't keep you long.'

Chapter 26

Fay arrived at Portman Square at a few minutes past six. One of the pearl buttons on her blouse was missing. She had replaced it with a plain white shirt button. So, when the maid offered to take her jacket, she said she preferred to keep it on. Feeling awkward and unprepared, she was shown into a huge drawing room where Lady Langbourne, immaculately dressed in a chiffon gown, sat waiting for her.

'Miss Abrams to see you,' said the maid. 'Will you be wanting tea, madam?'

Lady Langbourne shook her head. 'No, that won't be necessary. Miss Abrams won't be here long.'

Knowing how uncomfortable she would have felt taking tea with her ladyship in that elegant room, Fay was relieved and when Lady Langbourne invited her to take a seat, she sat with her back straight and her hands folded neatly in her lap.

'I see you're wearing the little scarf I gave you, Miss Abrams.'

She had forgotten she was wearing it. She touched its beaded fringe. 'Yes, madam, I wear it all the time.'

'I'm pleased to hear it. Now, I promised I wouldn't keep you long and I'm sure you're anxious to get home, so I'll come straight to the point. First, I must say how much I appreciated your little note. I am indebted to you, Miss Abrams. You may well have saved my life and that of my husband.'

'I'm only glad you weren't harmed, madam.'

Lady Langbourne sighed. 'Sadly, others were not so lucky. Our chauffeur, John, was fatally wounded that night.'

'I am sorry, madam.'

'So am I. He was a good man. Miss Abrams, I owe you an apology. I made a rather foolish mistake and I'm afraid I may be responsible for causing you a great deal of trouble. You see, when I spoke to Mr Frobisher about your visions, my only intention was to make him aware of your gift so he might make use of it. You must believe me. I had no idea he was going to make things so awkward for you.'

'Madam, I didn't think for one moment that you—'

Lady Langbourne held up her hand. 'No, Miss Abrams, allow me to finish. I know he interrogated you and, knowing what I've now learned about Mr Frobisher, I'm quite certain it was a thoroughly unpleasant experience and for that I'm very sorry.'

'He threatened to imprison me, my lady.'

Lady Langbourne's eyes widened. 'How utterly dreadful. Miss Abrams, you must tell me everything he said. Perhaps you would like tea after all?'

Her mouth was very dry, but now she felt sufficiently at ease to ask for a drink. Lady Langbourne rang for her maid.

'Tea? A little brandy?'

'Honestly, madam, water will be just fine.'

The maid returned with a crystal glass on a silver tray. Taking a couple of sips of water, Fay wondered how much she should say. Should she mention what she'd discovered about her grandmother? Should she tell Lady Langbourne about that terrible, archaic Witchcraft Act? Was there any point in hiding anything? If Lady Langbourne was in a position to persuade the Home Office that she was not a threat to national security, then it made sense to tell her everything. Beginning with the moment she was picked up outside the shop, Fay described what had happened, wondering all the while whether she was giving rather more detail than her ladyship needed to hear. But at no time did Lady Langbourne show any sign of impatience. She listened attentively to everything Fay had to say until she described how the interrogation was interrupted.

'There was a telephone call,' she said. 'Mr Frobisher left the room and when he came back he was very angry but he told me I could leave.'

Lady Langbourne smiled. 'My dear Miss Abrams, I can't tell you how pleased I am to hear that. You see, the moment I found out what was going on I telephoned the Home Office and insisted the interview be terminated. I wasn't certain whether they'd taken any notice of me.'

'I'm really grateful to you, madam. I'd begun to wonder if it would ever end.'

'I suppose you must have done. Mr Frobisher is such a horrid little man, isn't he? If I'd known what he was like I can promise you I would have had nothing to do with him. Still, it is not too late to turn the situation around to your advantage. I am not without influence, Miss Abrams, which brings me to the purpose of our little talk. Would you be prepared to reveal your visions to someone else, someone who would be grateful for prior knowledge of any event that might affect the outcome of this terrible war?'

The suggestion was so unexpected that, for a moment, Fay was quite lost for words.

'I'm really not sure. You see, I am not used to being believed and for that reason I've always kept quiet about my visions. It was only because Miss Bartlett insisted it was the right thing to do that I agreed to let her speak to you about them.'

Lady Langbourne's expression changed. She was frowning. She shook her head and sighed.

'Miss Bartlett. Dear Miss Bartlett. Poor lady. Such a kind, caring woman.'

Fay stared at her.

'You don't know? You haven't heard? No, of course, you haven't. Miss Bartlett is dead, my dear. Her body was retrieved from Marble Arch station.'

Fay felt as if she'd been punched in the stomach. The image returned as vivid as ever. The entrance to the station, blocked by rubble. A sealed tomb. Fists clenched, an intense feeling of helplessness swept through her.

'Oh, madam, I can't help thinking that she might still be alive if I'd done more. I had her telephone number. I telephoned her several times. I should have tried harder.'

'And what about the other people in that station? Could you have saved them, too? No, of course you couldn't but if the right person had known about the bombing of Oxford Street it might have been an entirely different picture.'

But the right person hadn't known and now Miss Bartlett was dead. Once again, Fay heard those words in her head.

'Prophecy is not a curse, Miss Abrams. It only becomes a curse when you're afraid to use it.'

For a moment Fay struggled to stop herself from weeping. 'Madam, I don't know what to say,' she stammered. 'This person…if I have another vision, do you think he would believe me?'

'I wouldn't have suggested it had I not been certain he would be entirely sympathetic. I see you are not still convinced, Miss Abrams.'

Fay shook her head. 'I've been questioned twice. Both times I was more or less accused of being in league with the enemy. No one believed that my information came from my visions. I think Mr Frobisher and his colleague both suspect I'm some kind of double agent.'

Lady Langbourne smiled. 'But you and I know better than that and if you spoke to Sir Thomas Poulton I can promise you that he would treat you with far more respect.'

Still, Fay hesitated, torn between protecting herself and doing the right thing. She remembered that afternoon in Hyde Park and the man who'd asked her if she cared nothing for her fellow man. She did care. She cared very much.

'All right, Lady Langbourne. I'll speak to him.'

Whatever the outcome, it had to be better than doing nothing.

Within minutes of Miss Abrams' departure, Mary Langbourne had written her letter to Sir Thomas, dabbed a drop of her favourite scent on the inside of the envelope and given it to the maid to post.

Aware that Gerald could easily turn up while she was talking to Miss Abrams, had he wanted to know what the girl from the hat shop was doing sitting in their drawing room, Mary had an explanation already prepared. The girl was simply taking instructions about remodelling the trimmings on her favourite hats. That would probably have satisfied him. He might even have been secretly pleased to think that his wife was being so frugal but he hadn't turned up and for that she was grateful.

Mary's cheeks felt slightly flushed and she was certain her eyes were sparkling a little more than usual. Yet Sir Thomas was only partly the cause of the excitement that coursed through her veins. To be instrumental in paving the way, encouraging the girl to use her visions for the good of all, gave Mary exactly the purpose she needed. It might not bring the recognition that Edwina enjoyed, but that didn't matter. It was enough that she felt useful. Her mind was made up. She would stay in London. The bombs would not drive her away.

Now she had only to wait until Sir Thomas responded to her little note. It would be up to him to set up a meeting with Miss Abrams. And imagining how grateful he would be once he understood the girl's undoubted gift for prophecy, Mary congratulated herself and rang the bell for tea.

Chapter 27

Even with an army of helpers this was always a challenging time for Rosa. The two most important events in the synagogue's calendar came one after the other with hardly time to take a breath. First there was Rosh Hashanah, the Jewish New Year, followed eight days later by Yom Kippur, the Day of Atonement, the one day when everyone, even those who were never seen inside a synagogue at any other time, turned out in force. Whether they actually fasted for the full twenty-five hours or went home in the middle of the day for a quick snack, Rosa neither knew nor cared. It was enough to know that they were there when the shofar was blown at the end of the day and the second after that sound was heard – that long blast on a hollow ram's horn – they would all troop into the side room expecting to break the fast with a good spread.

For days she had been knocking on doors, telephoning everyone she could think of, pulling out all the stops to obtain promises of help. She'd had no time to think about Zofia Kroll but she was still there in the back of Rosa's mind and she hadn't given up yet. She had even asked her father-in-law if he recalled anything from his days as treasurer of the benevolent society, in particular anything to do with Esther Abrams, but the old man could remember nothing.

That afternoon Rosa was at the synagogue. Polishing the furniture in the entrance hall and keeping all the wooden rails gleaming had always been one of her ladies' jobs but, as if she hadn't got enough to do, that was something else Rosa had taken on. Working methodically, using small circular movements, she began applying polish to the long table outside the rabbi's study. She had just begun to get into a nice rhythm and was wondering if she should treat herself to a new hat for the holidays or whether she could get away with replacing the trimmings on last year's model, when she heard shouting from the street outside. Rosa frowned. A second later, she heard loud laughter, followed by an almighty crash. She ducked and only narrowly missed being struck by a huge stone as it shattered the window behind her.

The study door was flung open.

'Mrs Feldman, my dear lady, are you all right?' said the rabbi.

Before she could reply, the Abrams boy raced past her out into the street. The rabbi found her a chair. He brought her a glass of water and insisted that she remained where she was while he fetched a brush and pan and swept up the broken glass. Stooping under the table which only seconds before she had been happily polishing, the rabbi found the missile. A jagged rock with sharp edges.

'Mrs Feldman, if you had been injured I would never have forgiven myself. You might have been killed. Should I telephone your husband? Do you think someone should check you over?'

Rosa's heartbeat, which had risen alarmingly, was already returning to normal. The attack was random. She knew she hadn't been especially singled out as the target. It wasn't personal but it had shaken her, and the truth was that she didn't feel entirely confident about walking home on her own.

'If you wouldn't mind phoning Lionel, perhaps he could come and pick me up.'

'I'll take you home myself, Mrs Feldman. It's the least I can do. Just give me a moment while I call the glazier.'

She smiled bravely. 'I don't want to be a nuisance, rabbi.'

He patted her hand. 'Not another word. You just sit there and get your breath back.'

When he led her to his car she allowed him to support her by the elbow as if she was still feeling a little fragile, although by then Rosa was almost fully recovered. At the end of the road she spotted the boy running back towards the synagogue. Rabbi Shultz stopped the car. He wound down his window and asked Jack if he was all right. The boy quickly tucked his arms behind his back, but not before Rosa saw the bloodied knuckles he was trying to hide.

'It was those two *mamzers* – begging your pardon, Mrs Feldman – the thugs who had a go at me the other week, rabbi.'

As far as Rosa was concerned describing them as bastards was no better than they deserved. 'They had a go at you, Jack? That's terrible,' she said.

The boy looked embarrassed.

'Did you see where they went, my boy?' said the rabbi.

Jack shook his head. 'No, sir, they gave me the slip.'

His fists were still hidden behind his back. Rosa knew he was lying but there was something about his expression that stopped her from giving him away. Rabbi Shultz was telling the boy he'd be back in ten minutes.

'Carry on reading from where we left off, Jack. I'm just seeing Mrs Feldman gets home safely.'

'You're not hurt, are you, Mrs Feldman?' said Jack.

Rosa shook her head. 'A little shaken, that's all. Nothing to worry about.'

She waved as the car moved off. Jack, she couldn't fail to notice, kept his arms down tightly by his sides and she wondered how on earth he thought he was going to hide his hands from the rabbi's sharp eyes.

Chapter 28

Had she not been so upset about Miss Bartlett, Fay would probably have been looking forward to her date with Sam Cassell. Lady Langbourne was right. Even if she had managed to contact Miss Bartlett she couldn't have saved the other poor souls who'd died with her. But it wasn't them Fay cared about. It was Miss Bartlett. Miss Bartlett who'd insisted her own driver should take her all the way back to Cricklewood when she'd collapsed at Caxton Hall. Miss Bartlett who'd invited her for supper at the Cumberland. Dear, kind Miss Bartlett who'd tried so hard to convince her that the visions were a gift. And now that she was ready to believe her, it was too late. Too late for Miss Bartlett, but maybe not too late for others. Fay had been given the chance to redeem herself. All she had to do was talk to Lady Langbourne's friend.

'I'd rather he didn't telephone me at the shop, madam,' she'd said. 'Miss Greenwood must know nothing about it.' And then, hoping Lady Langbourne wouldn't be offended, she'd added, 'So it might be better if there were no more notes delivered to the shop.'

Now, as she glanced at the clock on her bedside table, she wondered what on earth she was going to say to Sir Thomas. She had nothing to tell him. There'd been no visions since Oxford Street. The air raids went on, night after night. No one had any idea which areas would be targeted next but with Sir Thomas on her side, perhaps she wouldn't have to deal with Frobisher or his nasty threats ever again. She imagined how furious he would be, especially after all the trouble he'd taken to rake up her family's past. Cheered by the thought, Fay lay in bed deciding what she should wear for her date.

Jack was already up and about. She heard him go into the bathroom and a few minutes later heard his footsteps on the landing. Throwing back the covers, she flung on her dressing gown and went downstairs. She filled the kettle and cut a slice of bread. The bread was stale but perfectly fine for toast. She was watching it brown under the grill when Jack appeared, fully dressed and looking rather solemn.

'Going for a run?' she said. He didn't reply. She looked at him. 'Jack, I asked you a question.'

'I heard you.'

'Then why didn't you answer me?'

'All right. If you really want to know. I'm not going for a run. I'm going to the gym.'

'It's a bit early, isn't it? It's Sunday. What time does it open?'

He shrugged. 'It will be open by the time I get there. I'm walking.'

'Don't be daft,' she said. 'You can't walk to Aldgate. Do you need some money for the train?'

She watched him splash milk into his cup. 'No,' he said, 'I'm all right I don't need anything. I've got money. I just fancy walking, that's all. You got a problem with that?'

'Okay. There's no need to be so rude. I was only trying to be helpful.'

'Well, don't bother. You can't help me. No one can.'

She stared at him. 'Try me,' she said. 'Come on. Sit down. What's wrong? Are you in trouble?'

He laughed. There was something about that laugh that wasn't right. She'd never seen him like that before. She got up and shut the kitchen door.

'Okay,' she whispered. 'It's just you and me, *boychik*. What's going on?'

He dragged a chair over and sat down. She couldn't see his face.

'Jack, look at me. Whatever it is, we can sort it out.'

'All right. But you're not going to like it. I think I killed someone, Fay. The police will find out it was me. I'll have to go to court and then they're going to lock me up and hang me.'

'They can't hang you. You're twelve years old. Now, tell me what happened. From the beginning.'

'It was those boys. You know. The goyim who beat me up. There was a fight. The big one, it was him. He threw the first punch. So, I hit him. He went down and whacked his head on the pavement. His friend was there. He saw it all. He can identify me.'

'Hold on a minute, Jack. What makes you think he's dead?'

'I went back later. There was loads of blood on the ground where he hit his head.'

'That doesn't prove anything, does it? When did this happen?'

'The other day. I was at shul with the rabbi and they threw this rock through the window. It just missed Mrs Feldman. So I chased after them. I wasn't going to fight them. Mr Weissman always says, "Save your fists for inside the ring." So, I just warned them. I told them what would happen if they ever came near the synagogue again. Then I walked away but then one of them started throwing stones. I went back. He threw a punch. I moved out of the way. Then he threw another punch so I hit him.'

She smiled. 'Good for you. He was asking for it, wasn't he, and I promise you we'd have heard by now if the bugger was dead. So you can stop worrying. No one's going to lock you up, Jack. I promise you.'

'They locked our grandmother up, didn't they? And she didn't do anything bad, and they want to lock you up just for seeing things.'

Grabbing his hands, she squeezed them tightly. 'I want you to listen very carefully. Are you listening?' He nodded. 'No one's going to lock me up. Do you understand? Nothing bad is going to happen to me.'

'But those men…'

'You can forget about them. I'll have you know that your sister is a very important person. I have friends in high places now. Lords and ladies who want to know about my visions.'

'Really? Lords and ladies?'

'Really,' she said, 'and I'm going to help them win the war. Now, are you still sure you want to walk to Aldgate?'

Jack grinned. 'Lend us a couple of bob, Fay, and I'll go by train.'

'I thought you said you had enough money.'

'I was fibbing. I spent it on comics.'

The door opened. Their mother stood there in her dressing gown.

'What's going on? Why's everyone up so early this morning?' she said.

'Don't know, Mum,' said Fay. 'Must be 'cause it's such a nice day.'

Jack winked at her and went back to his room.

Her mother opened the back door and looked out into the garden. 'So, are you doing anything special today?' she said.

'Yes, I'm going for a picnic. In Regents Park.'

'That's nice. With Rita?'

'No, actually, I've got a date.'

'A date? What do you mean? With a man?'

Fay smiled. 'Yes, of course with a man. He's someone I met at work. A salesman.'

Her mother frowned. Fay knew exactly what was coming next.

'It's not a year since Bernard died and you're going out on dates already? It's not right, Fay. What will people think?'

'Why don't you stop worrying about what other people think, Mum? It's none of their business, is it?'

'But people talk, Fay. You know what they're like.'

'Then let them talk and just be glad for me.'

Her mother studied her for a moment and nodded. 'I am glad for you. It's just a bit soon, that's all. What time are you meeting this man of yours?'

Fay laughed. 'Don't get carried away, Mum. It's only our first date.'

She took her time getting ready. She'd washed her hair the night before, pinning it into curls and covering it with a silk scarf. After her bath, she dressed, applied a little more make-up than she would normally wear for work and brushed her hair until her arm ached and her hair shone. The green frock showed off her narrow waist and when she looked at her reflection, she was pleased with what she saw. Thinking it might get chilly later on, she draped a blue cardigan around her shoulders and went back downstairs.

Her father was sitting at the kitchen table reading his newspaper. He looked up, smiled and gave a long whistle.

'Your mother tells me you're meeting a young man. Is he nice?'

'Of course he's nice, Dad. I wouldn't be going out with him if he wasn't.'

'Well, you look lovely, dear. Really lovely.'

Her mother was doing something at the sink. She dried her hands, looked at Fay and, without saying anything, twirled a finger in the air. Fay, hand on hip, turned slowly. Her mother nodded.

'Too much lipstick if you ask me but apart from that you'll do. Not sure about that cardigan though. You know what they say. Blue and green should never be seen.'

Her father laughed. 'Nonsense, Hetty. Blue and green make the boys keen.'

On the journey into town, she managed to push Miss Bartlett to the back of her mind. It felt strange to be going on a date. Bernard had been her first real boyfriend. They had been together since she was fifteen. She was out of practice and, by the time the train pulled into Camden Town station, she began to wonder if her mother had been right all along. Perhaps it was a bit soon to be seeing someone new. Especially someone like Sam with his confident, well-practised charm, but it wasn't long before she realised that Sam Cassell was every bit as nervous as she was. He was waiting for her outside the station. When he saw her, he smiled and told her she looked very pretty.

'I've made us a picnic,' he said. 'Nothing very grand, I'm afraid. Just some bridge rolls. Do you like cheese? Cheese and tomato? I didn't know if you preferred coffee to tea, so I've made a flask of both. There's a bottle of ginger beer as well. It's probably lukewarm by now but it should be all right.'

They entered the park through York Gate. The sun shone and, feeling its warmth on her back, as they strolled up the main avenue towards the zoo, Fay was glad she'd accepted his invitation. They found a bench outside the high fence where, on her last visit, she remembered seeing giraffes peering over the top.

'Do you have any brothers and sisters?' he said.

'Just the one,' said Fay. 'My brother, Jack. He'll be thirteen next year. His bar mitzvah's coming up soon but I think he's harbouring ambitions to become Cricklewood's first Jewish boxing champion.'

Sam laughed. 'There are far worse ambitions.'

'What's yours?' she said.

He thought for a moment. 'I'm not sure. I've always fancied getting into retail. A little hat shop or maybe a bookshop. Nothing too grand but it's hard to think about anything beyond this war, isn't it?'

'Will you be signing up?'

He shrugged. 'We've just been contracted to manufacture caps for the army but Dad's not as young as he was. I'm not sure how long he could carry on without me.'

Fay thought about Mr Ebstein, struggling to keep the business going without Bernard there to help him.

'If my brother was old enough, he'd be a pilot, like Rockfist Rogan. That's his hero.'

'Mine too when I was his age. I've kept all my old comics. Perhaps he'd like to have them.'

Fay laughed. 'He'd love you forever,' she said.

Sam spread a clean handkerchief on the bench and offered her a sandwich. 'This is my favourite spot in the park,' he said.

'Mine, too,' she said. 'But I miss the giraffes. Where have they gone?'

'Whipsnade Zoo. They're probably having the time of their lives right now, making friends with the other evacuees.'

Relaxed and comfortable in Sam's company, though she hadn't

meant to talk about Bernard, it felt perfectly natural to tell him that she'd been engaged. He took her hand and gently stroked her wrist with his thumb. He wanted to know how long they'd been engaged; how long they'd known each other before Bernard had died.

'Such a waste,' he said. 'It makes me so angry. You'd think the bloody Germans would have learned their lesson by now. They didn't win last time and they won't win this time either.' He let go of her hand. 'My brother-in-law's missing in action. My poor sister is out of her mind with worry.'

They were both silent for a moment. She wished she could turn the clock back so that they were still talking about daft things like the giraffes or Rockfist Rogan, and she began to wonder what it would feel like to be kissed by him. There hadn't been anyone apart from Bernard. But he was gone and even his own sister wanted her to meet someone new. The war had changed everything. There was no right or wrong time. There was only now. Without thinking, she turned and, reaching up, put her hands gently on either side of his face. He was looking at her when she leant forward and kissed him.

Chapter 29

Rosa did not need reminding that her last visit had gone badly. She had approached the subject of the benevolent fund in a particularly clumsy manner and though no apology was due, she was not comfortable knowing that she managed to upset Hetty again. The truth was, Rosa was simply desperate for volunteers. She had asked everyone she could think of. Hetty was her last hope.

Had she let her know she was going to call round that morning, Rosa might have suspected that Hetty had actually troubled to dress for the occasion. When she opened the door, Rosa noticed immediately how different she looked, and it definitely wasn't her imagination. Hetty Abrams was relaxed and almost pleasant.

'Apologies for turning up unannounced, Mrs Abrams. Lionel picked some peas for you. I do hope you can make use of them. I haven't caught you at an inopportune moment, have I? You weren't going somewhere, were you?'

'No, Mrs Feldman. I'm not going anywhere. Do come in.'

Rosa followed her into the lounge. 'We'll be seeing you in shul for the holidays?'

'Yes, I'll be there. I suppose it's about the holidays that you're here. I guessed you might ask me.'

'I'm so short of volunteers, this year, Mrs Abrams. You won't have to do much. A cake. A few sandwiches. I know it's not easy with so many things on ration but if everyone does their bit I'd like to think we can still break the fast in style.'

Hetty was fiddling with her wedding ring. 'Well, Mrs Feldman,' she said, 'my family would tell you I'm not the world's best cook but I do a nice chopped liver and my gefilte fish is not bad, if that would help.'

Rosa couldn't believe what she was hearing. Since when had Hetty Abrams been so accommodating? So friendly. So...nice.

'Well, if you're sure it's not too much trouble that would be marvellous. Do let me know if you need any onions, won't you? Lionel's grown some real beauties.'

Hetty leant forward in her chair and thinking that she was about to bring the conversation to a close, Rosa picked up her handbag.

'Perhaps you'd like a cup of tea before you go?' said Hetty.

Rosa said she would love a cup and, when Hetty left the room, Rosa wandered over to the mantelpiece. Next to the clock were two photographs in silver frames. They certainly hadn't been there on her last visit. The photos were old. In one, the man with his arm around a smiling young woman bore such a strong resemblance to Lou Abrams, she was certain that the photograph was of his parents. The other, she guessed, must be of Hetty's mother. She studied the woman's face closely. Zofia Kroll, she thought. So this is what you looked like. Not at all like your daughter, are you? More like your granddaughter, only not quite so attractive.

It was then that Rosa noticed the envelope. Propped up against the clock and embossed with the blue portcullis of Westminster, it was addressed to Miss Frances Abrams. Rosa glanced quickly over her shoulder, picked up the envelope and saw that it had not yet been opened. What, she wondered, could Westminster possibly have to say to a girl like Fay Abrams? So curious was she that had the envelope been open, she might have been tempted to find out but hearing the clatter of tea things and Hetty's footsteps in the hall, Rosa quickly replaced the envelope and returned to her seat.

'What a pretty tea set, Mrs Abrams,' she said. 'Such a dainty pattern. Is it new?'

'No, not new at all. It belonged to Lou's mother.'

Rosa smiled. 'So, it's an heirloom. I am honoured.'

Hetty didn't return the smile. In fact, Rosa detected a certain iciness in her steady gaze. 'Well, don't be, Mrs Feldman,' she said. 'I use them all the time.'

Puzzled by Hetty's change of mood, Rosa found herself floundering for something to say, anything that might restore the atmosphere and lighten the moment.

'I've been meaning to say what a wonderful boy your son is. Such lovely manners. He's a credit to you, Mrs Abrams. A real credit.'

A slight nod of the head signalled Hetty's acceptance of the compliment, but that was all. She didn't say anything. Rosa was still floundering.

'And of course, Fay has really blossomed into a most attractive young woman. How is she, by the way?'

'She's fine. Still blossoming.'

She should have changed the subject; left it like that, but there was something about Hetty's expression that made Rosa say just a little more than was strictly necessary. 'I've always thought she's such an interesting character, and so unusual.'

'Unusual, Mrs Feldman? In what way is she unusual?'

Again, there was that icy stare. Rosa had been so careful to avoid any unpleasantness. She hadn't asked any personal questions. It had all been going so well. Until she'd mentioned Hetty's bloomin' tea set.

'Well, I suppose what I meant to say is that she's...'

'She's what, Mrs Feldman, Strange? A bit odd? Is that what you were going to say?'

Her face was growing hotter by the minute. She had the feeling that Hetty might even be playing with her. Placing her hand against her chest, she shook her head.

'Mrs Abrams, on my life, I thought no such thing. I know that your daughter has premonitions, if that's what you're talking about. She told me so herself. And I will say that I was somewhat taken aback at the time but surely that's what makes her so special. So unusual. As I said before, Fay is a very interesting young woman.'

If she hadn't been sure before, she had no doubt now. Hetty, far from being angry, was actually taking pleasure in Rosa's discomfort.

'Why, Mrs Feldman, you've gone quite pink,' she said, and to her astonishment, Hetty laughed. She just had time to notice how Hetty's face, normally so sour and miserable-looking, was in that moment quite transformed, before Hetty produced a handkerchief from her pocket and waved it helplessly, as if she was fanning herself. 'Do forgive me. It's just that it's such a relief.'

Rosa folded her hands in her lap. Her back straight, she stared at her, uncertain whether to smile. If the joke was on her, it was better if she adopted a dignified pose. Mild confusion. In that moment, that was the expression that came most readily to her. She continued to stare. She said nothing. She was waiting for an explanation.

'You see, I've wasted an awful lot of time worrying about what people think. What they might say. Things I have no control over. And all that worrying, well, it's not good for you, is it? Don't get me wrong, Mrs Feldman. I'm not going to start discussing my family affairs with anyone. Not even you. That's not my way. It's just that I'm learning not to care quite so much what anyone thinks anymore. And like I said before, it's such a relief.'

'Good,' said Rosa. 'I'm very pleased for you.'

Shifting forward in her seat, Hetty smiled. 'I knew you'd understand,' she said.

Rosa reached for her handbag. 'Thank you for the tea, Mrs Abrams.'

'Oh, do call me Esther. Or Hetty if you like. My friends call me Hetty.'

Wondering if the peculiar woman actually had any friends, Rosa got to her feet and followed her into the hall.

'So...Hetty,' she said. 'I can count on you to do something for our little spread?'

'Of course you can. Depend on it, Rosa. I won't let you down. And do thank Mr Feldman for the peas.'

At the gate, she turned. Hetty was standing at the front door. Rosa waved. Whatever had brought about the spectacular change in her behaviour, it was a huge improvement. My new friend, Hetty Abrams, she thought, and still somewhat bemused, she smiled to herself as she walked down the hill towards the Broadway.

Chapter 30

By half past eleven Fay had already made a couple of sales. Business seemed to be picking up. Miss Greenwood should have been happy but there wasn't a single smile from her the entire morning. Fay knew what was bothering her and to jolly her out of her mood, she decided that a little white lie was do the trick.

'That note,' she said, 'Lady Langbourne's mysterious proposal? You'll never guess what it was about. A collection box for one of her charities. She wanted to know if I could put it in the synagogue.'

'Did she indeed? Is that all? Couldn't she have asked you that on the telephone?'

'That's what I thought,' said Fay.

'Well, I must say it was an extraordinary way to go about things. I mean, sending her chauffeur round with a note? Was that really necessary?'

'I really don't know. Perhaps people like Lady Langbourne do things differently to the rest of us, Miss Greenwood.'

It was during their lunch break that Miss Greenwood, now completely thawed and back to her usual self, asked Fay about her date with Mr Cassell. They were sitting in the kitchen at the back of the shop. The "closed" sign was in the window. Fay had made a pot of tea and she and Miss Greenwood were sharing a sandwich.

'Do tell me, my dear. I've been longing to know. Did you enjoy your picnic on Sunday? Did you have a nice time?'

'Very nice. We had a lovely day.'

'And will you be seeing each other again?'

'Oh yes, I'm quite sure we will.'

'Good. I'm pleased to hear it. He's a very nice, young man.'

'I kissed him, Miss Greenwood,' she whispered.

'You didn't! My goodness. What must he think of you?'

Fay smiled. 'I think he liked it.'

'Miss Abrams, you really mustn't give him the wrong impression. You don't want him to think you're too forward, now, do you?'

'It was only a kiss, Miss Greenwood.'

But it was more than that. She hadn't wanted to think about Miss Bartlett or her visions and she hadn't wanted Sam to think about his brother-in-law or his poor, anxious sister. So she'd kissed him. And after he'd got over the surprise, he had kissed her and they'd sat in the park, his arm around her waist and her head on his shoulder, until the sun went down and for a while they were the only two people who mattered.

'You know, dear,' said Miss Greenwood. 'Sometimes I wonder whether I'm just a bit old-fashioned. I've never been very adventurous.' She sighed. 'I don't know. Perhaps I would have had more fun if I'd been more like you.'

Fay turned the "open" sign towards the window and smiled. 'Well, you never know, Miss Greenwood. It's not too late, is it? Didn't you tell me once that no one ever knows what's round the next corner?'

At Selfridges' staff entrance, Rita was just coming out. She waved.

'Good news, Fay,' she said. 'Howard's gone. They've moved back into their old house. I can't tell you how glad I am to see the back of him. My uncle and aunt are perfectly nice people but...'

'Howard is horrible.'

She laughed. 'He is, isn't he? And all that brilliantine. Honestly, it's disgusting. Mum didn't know how to get the grease out of the pillowcases, but fear not. We got advice from an expert. A good rub with crushed aspirin, an overnight soak in white vinegar and lemon juice and hey presto, they've come up like new.'

'And who is this expert?'

'Mrs Feldman, of course. Who else could it be? She telephoned last night. She said she'd been having tea with your mother. I must say I was a bit surprised.'

Fay laughed. 'You must have heard wrong.'

'No, she definitely said that she was at your house yesterday afternoon. Your mother promised to make chopped liver for the do after the fast.'

Fay stopped walking and stared at her. 'I don't believe it. Are you sure?'

'Well, that's what Mrs Feldman said.'

'But my mother can't stand her. What else did she say?'

'She thought my mother might like to make something too. That's why she phoned. Oh, and she thought your tea set was very pretty and you look like your grandmother.'

'She said that? How the hell does she know?'

Rita shrugged. 'Don't ask me. Anyway, according to her, she and your mum had an awfully nice time together.'

Fay simply couldn't imagine a more unlikely scenario and she couldn't wait to get home and find out what was going on. She knew that her mother's behaviour had changed. Anyone could see that. Not that she was cheerful. That would have been too much to hope for, but certainly less miserable, less withdrawn, warmer and, compared to how she had been before the truth had come tumbling out, Hetty Abrams was almost pleasant. But offering to do something for Mrs Feldman? Having tea with her? She might have changed, but surely not that much.

'Rita,' she said, as they got off the bus at Cricklewood, 'are you sure Mrs Feldman said they'd had an awfully nice time?'

Her mother was sitting on a chair near the open door. She had a colander on her lap and she was shelling peas. Fay filled the kettle and dragged a chair over next to her.

'So, what's all this about you and Mrs Feldman? I hear you had a cosy afternoon together.'

'Who told you that?'

'Rita did. She spoke to her last night on the phone.'

Her mother smiled. 'I wouldn't call it cosy. Amusing, perhaps.'

'But you don't like Mrs Feldman, Mum.'

'True enough, but it was still a pleasant afternoon. She's short of volunteers, so I said I'd do something, that's all. For Yom Kippur.'

'Honestly, I can hardly believe what I'm hearing.'

'Why? I know I'm not the best cook in the world but I do a very nice chopped liver, if I say so myself.'

Fay nodded. 'That's true, but I'm still struggling to imagine you and Rosa Feldman nattering away like old friends.'

Her mother's head was bent over the colander but Fay could see she was trying not to smile.

'Well, Mum, come on. Tell me. What did you two talk about?'

'Oh, this and that. You know. Your brother. You. Your visions.'

Fay gasped. 'You're joking. You actually talked to Mrs Feldman? About my visions?'

'Mrs Feldman thinks you're very interesting. Fay. "A very unusual girl" was what she said.'

'And what did you say?'

'I agreed with her. Don't worry. I didn't tell her anything she didn't already know.'

'I'm not worried, not in the least. It's just that... Honestly, Mum, I never thought you'd...'

'Never thought I'd what?'

'Well, speak about it. To anyone. And least of all to her.'

Her mother shrugged. Fay marvelled at the change in her. It was miraculous, and she wondered if her mother had any regrets about the years she'd wasted weighed down by secrets. Fay felt like hugging her. But she didn't just in case it spoilt the moment. Just in case her mother rejected the gesture and disappeared back inside her shell. Instead, she put her hand gently on her shoulder.

'Mum, did Mrs Feldman tell you that she thinks I look like my grandmother?'

She shook her head. 'No, but we were sitting in the living room. She must have seen the photograph.'

'And do I look like my grandmother?'

Her mother put her head on one side and looked at her. 'I suppose you do. By the way, there's a letter for you. It's on the mantelpiece in the other room. It looks official.'

The envelope was leaning against the clock. Fay picked it up and seeing the Westminster crest, guessed it was from Sir Thomas Poulton. That's quick, she thought, and she wondered what Lady Langbourne had told him to make him respond so promptly. She glanced at the photograph of her grandmother. Zofia Kroll. Tall and thin like Fay. Small pointed chin. Large dark eyes. A solemn expression. Perhaps if you smiled, she thought, we might look more alike.

She took the envelope upstairs, slipped off her shoes and propped herself up against her pillows. The letter was typed and the address from where it had been sent was the Home Office. It was not from Sir Thomas. Her shoulders stiffened as she began to read. She read it twice. Fay was biting her lip when she finally stuffed the letter back into its envelope.

Chapter 31

When Sir Thomas telephoned that morning, Mary was surprised to hear from him. She had not expected such a quick response but when he confessed he'd been so intrigued by her letter that he'd simply had to speak to her straight away, she was delighted.

'Do tell me about this friend of yours,' he said.

'Miss Abrams is not exactly a friend, Sir Thomas. I don't know her well but I can promise you she has an extraordinary gift.'

'My dear Mary,' he said when she'd finished describing the accuracy of the girl's visions, 'I should very much like to meet this young woman. I'm glad you told me about her and it would be foolish to dismiss the improbable when it's backed by that kind of evidence.'

'I was certain you would see it that way,' said Mary. 'Sadly, not everyone thinks as we do, Sir Thomas, but I believe that the unexplainable is always worth exploring, don't you?'

'I do,' he said, 'and nothing will give me greater pleasure than exploring it with you, Mary.'

She smiled. 'Really? I shall look forward to that, Sir Thomas. Immensely.'

'So shall I,' he said. 'Perhaps later, after my chat with Miss Abrams? In the meantime, could you ask the young woman to telephone my private secretary? I'll give you his number. Do ask her to call as soon as she can and tell her that I'm looking forward to meeting her.'

It hadn't occurred to Mary that he would see the girl without inviting her to be there, too. In fact she'd rather taken it for granted and she might have been disappointed had it not been for the vague promise that they would meet later. Just the two of them. As she replaced the receiver, Mary glanced at her reflection in the mirror. Her cheeks were quite flushed. Silly creature, she thought, as she smoothed her hair.

It was still early. Not yet eleven. Her dressmaker would be arriving soon and Mary had been wondering if the piece of cream silk she'd bought in Liberty's would be enough for a nightgown and perhaps a little chemise. She was smiling as she sat at her desk and called Edwina.

'You were right, darling,' she said. 'Absolutely right. Sir Thomas was utterly charming and entirely sympathetic. Such an open-minded man. He wants to meet the girl as soon as possible.'

'You've spoken to him? That was quick. You didn't waste much time, did you?'

'Well, it was the least I could do. After what Frobisher put her through, the poor girl deserves a little help. I simply had to do something. Anyway, I just wanted to say that I know you don't have much patience for that sort of thing but I am glad I told you about it. Of course, Gerald mustn't know what I've been up to. It's just between you and me, darling. All right?'

'Whatever you say, Mary, but I do wish you didn't worry quite so much about what Gerald thinks.'

'Edwina. He's my husband. It's only right that I consider his feelings.'

'I'm not suggesting that you ignore his feelings.'

'Then what are you saying?'

'Forget it, Mary, it's none of my business.'

'No, do go on.'

'Well, you know, don't you, that I'm very fond of you. You're very dear to me, Mary, but there are times when I wish you could be…how shall I put it? A little more assertive.'

'Are you saying I lack confidence, Edwina? Because I don't think that's true at all.'

'No, darling, that's not what I'm saying. Oh dear, I wish I hadn't started this.'

Whatever Edwina had to say, Mary had a strong suspicion she wouldn't like it. 'I think you'd better just say what's on your mind, don't you? It's obviously something you've been thinking about for a long time.'

'Don't be cross with me, darling. I just think that Gerald can be a bit overbearing sometimes. And I can't help thinking that you could stand up for yourself just a little more.'

'I do stand up for myself, and not everyone wants to be like you, Edwina.'

'Oh dear, you are cross with me, aren't you? Forget what I said, darling. I'm thoughtless and pig-headed and you're the kindest, sweetest girl in the world. Forgive me?'

'I don't know, Edwina. I'm not sure that I can.'

'Lunch?' said Edwina. 'My treat. On Wednesday?'

They had just finished talking when Elsie tapped on the door and told her the dressmaker had arrived. Upstairs in her dressing room, Mary went through her wardrobe finding items that needed minor repairs while her dressmaker suggested alterations to some of her costumes. A skirt to be shortened. A jacket to be nipped in at the waist. New shoulder pads for her tweed coat. Absorbed in the task, her conversation with Edwina almost forgotten, Mary unfolded the piece of silk and draped it over a chair.

'I thought perhaps a nightgown with a fitted bodice.'

'Beautiful,' murmured the dressmaker. 'I suggest we cut it on the bias to flatter madam's figure.'

'And would there be enough material for a chemise as well?'

'Yes, but dare I say, with a little lace, perhaps in a pale shade of coffee, cami-knickers might be nicer?'

Mary was delighted. Later, after she had gone, Mary took her book into the garden and sat in the shade. She thought she might finish the chapter she was reading before she strolled round to the hat shop and had a word with Miss Abrams. She was glad she was able to do something for the girl.

*

Mary was still reading when the sun disappeared behind a bank of clouds and she noticed a sudden chill in the air. Sighing, she closed her book and looked at her watch. It was quarter to three. She had just decided to change into something warmer when she heard a loud bang coming from somewhere in the house. It sounded as if the front door had been slammed shut with some force. Dropping her book, Mary rushed inside to see what was going on. Elsie was already there, standing in the hall, staring at Gerald. His face was bright red. He was loosening his tie.

'It's all right, Elsie. Everything's fine,' said Mary.

The girl gave her a nervous glance, turned and walked away.

'Darling, what's wrong?' she said, lifting her face to kiss him.

Ignoring the gesture, he pushed past her and, without saying a word, flung the study door open, pointed his finger and indicated that she should step inside. Gerald followed her into the room, closing the door loudly behind him. She watched as he removed his jacket. Perched on one of the uncomfortable chairs he kept especially for visitors while he sat facing her behind his desk, Mary waited for him to speak. He raked his fingers through his hair, tugged at his tie, then placing his hands palms down on his desk, he leant forward and glared at her. She was beginning to feel nervous.

'What is it, Gerald? What's happened?'

'You tell me, Mary,' he said, and reaching for his jacket he drew something out of an inside pocket. 'Just what do you think you're playing at?'

'Please, darling, don't shout. I'm not playing at anything.'

He was holding a piece of paper. She tried to give him a reassuring smile, but her mouth was suddenly dry.

'Well, unless you deliberately set out to humiliate me, I see no excuse for your behaviour.'

She asked to see what he was holding. He said it was none of her business and, with the echo of Edwina's words in her head, when Mary replied she made sure that her voice was clear and firm. She told him that she had absolutely no idea what he was talking about and, unless he explained what she was supposed to have done, he could sit there until he'd calmed down or she was going to her room. His expression changed from fury to surprise.

'I mean it, Gerald,' she said, pushing her chair back. She was standing, looking down at him. 'Now, are you going to tell me what this is all about?'

He asked her to sit down. He asked her quietly. Politely. Mary, her arms folded across her chest, sat staring at him.

'According to this letter,' he said, 'which was delivered to my office this morning, you interrupted an important interrogation. You insisted it be stopped. And what makes it particularly humiliating is that Frobisher complains that, having been prevented from carrying out his duty – the thorough examination of a possible threat to national security – should something catastrophic happen the blame will not lie with him but with me.'

Mary shook her head. 'He really is the most hateful little man. I'm most dreadfully sorry, Gerald. I honestly didn't expect him to react like that.'

'And I fail to understand why you interfered in the first place. What on earth does it have to do with you?'

Realising that she had no choice but to explain her connection to Miss Abrams, Mary told him the whole story.

'Visions? What nonsense. Good lord, Mary, have you any idea how ridiculous that sounds?'

'Really, Gerald. You think it's ridiculous? Just remember that while Frobisher accuses her of being a spy and threatens her with imprisonment, Miss Abrams probably saved our lives. Yours and mine.'

He spoke slowly, pronouncing each word as if he were talking to a disobedient child. 'In future, Mary, I shall expect you to behave with more sense. I will not have my reputation tarnished by my wife's foolish exploits. Is that understood?'

Mary's jaw tightened. Her fingers curled, the nails digging into her palms. There was a slight pause before she rose from her chair. Head high, she walked towards the door.

'Just where do you think you're going? I haven't finished with you yet,' he said.

At the door she turned and looked at him. 'Don't raise your voice to me like that, Gerald. I'm going out. There's something I have to do.'

'Whatever it is, I'm sure it can wait, Mary.'

'No, I don't think it can,' she said, and closing the door quietly behind her, she went upstairs and slipped a jacket over her dress. Moment later, Mary was striding purposefully along Oxford Street towards the hat shop.

Chapter 32

'You haven't had a row with your young man, have you, dear?' said Miss Greenwood. 'Only unless I'm mistaken you seem a little out of sorts today.'

Fay did her best to smile. Out of sorts? she thought. That's one way of putting it. The way she was feeling Miss Greenwood was lucky she'd even turned up for work.

'I'm all right,' she said. 'I just didn't get much sleep, that's all. You know, what with the sirens going on and off all night.'

'So it's not a lovers' tiff. I am glad.'

'Miss Greenwood, I've been on one date with Mr Cassell. You can hardly call us lovers.' Her voice was unnecessarily sharp and immediately she wished she hadn't been so unpleasant. 'I'm just tired, Miss Greenwood. I suppose we're all a bit on edge, aren't we?'

'I suppose we are, but if something is bothering you, dear, you know you can always talk to me.'

For all her kindness, Miss Greenwood was the last person Fay wanted to talk to that day. She might have spoken to her father if only he'd been at home, but she'd hardly seen him. He'd been on LDV duty for five nights on the trot and by the time she got up that morning he'd already left for work. Not that there was much he could do. Mr Frobisher's letter had made his intentions very clear. He was not going to give up. He had only to say the word and Fay could be detained without trial. He was, he promised, keeping a close eye on her every move.

Perhaps Lady Langbourne could use her influence. But how did one go about asking someone like her ladyship for help? It wasn't like knocking on a neighbour's door for a cup of sugar, and as the day wore on Fay's nerves were stretched to their limit. She couldn't think straight. Every car that passed, every figure that stopped on the street outside, every innocent telephone call increased the tension building inside her.

'You really don't look well, dear,' said Miss Greenwood. 'I think you should go straight home to bed.'

But as nervous as she was, Fay actually felt safer inside the shop than out on the street where she could be picked up and carted off to goodness knows where. She would have stayed there all night if she could, huddled down behind the counter where no one could find her.

'I'd rather keep busy, Miss Greenwood,' she said.

'Well, I'm sorry, dear, but I'm not prepared to take responsibility for you coming down with something serious. You will go home right now and you can telephone me in the morning and let me know how you're feeling. If I don't hear from you I shall assume you are still not well.'

Fay tried to argue, but Miss Greenwood was adamant.

'Go on. Off you go and please, dear, do take care of yourself, won't you?'

Unsure which was better, to walk as quickly as she could or to take her time, looking over her shoulder, watching for signs that she was being followed, prepared to dive into the nearest doorway and hide, Fay got as far as the corner of Farm Street when, walking towards her, she saw the familiar figure of Lady Langbourne. Forcing herself to appear calm, Fay smiled pleasantly.

'Lady Langbourne' she said. 'How nice to see you.'

'Well, this is an extraordinary coincidence, Miss Abrams. I was just coming to see you.'

'Me, madam?'

Lady Langbourne smiled. 'Yes, you, Miss Abrams. I have something to tell you. That matter we were discussing? Sir Thomas Poulton? You do remember, don't you?'

Fay nodded. 'Of course I do.'

'Then let's go somewhere quiet where we can talk. I dare say you wouldn't say no to a pot of tea and a little pastry.'

'Lyons is just around the corner, madam. Would that do?'

But Lady Langbourne was already hailing a taxi and, feeling as if she was about to be rescued, Fay was in no position to argue. She hadn't glanced in the mirror since she'd left home that morning and it hadn't occurred to her to powder her nose before she left the shop. Having no idea where Lady Langbourne might take her, she could only hope that it wasn't somewhere where she would feel awkward and out of place.

'It's quite nice in the Cumberland, madam,' she said, as the taxi pulled up beside them. 'I was there with Miss Bartlett quite recently. And it's very near.'

'Ah! Yes, dear Miss Bartlett. Well, I suppose the Cumberland will do as well as any other.'

It seemed to Fay a dreadful extravagance to take a taxi from Oxford Circus to the Cumberland. She could have walked it in less than ten minutes, but how much safer it felt to be whisked there in a taxi. For a few moments at least she could relax without the need to look over her shoulder. And whatever her ladyship had to tell her, Fay was determined to make the most of this unexpected opportunity.

She had Frobisher's letter with her. Apart from its threatening tone, the letter contained a somewhat unkind reference to Lady Langbourne. Her ladyship was going to be very interested when she discovered what he'd said about her, of that Fay was certain. And suddenly it no longer mattered that her nose could do with a dab of powder and that her stockings were darned in at least two places.

As they entered the main lounge, she found herself heading towards the corner where only a week or so earlier she'd sat with Miss Bartlett. It might even have been the same table, but this time it was Lady Langbourne who asked the question.

'Have there been any more visions?'

Fay shook her head. 'No, madam, I'm pleased to say.'

'Nothing? What a shame. I was hoping you'd have something exciting to tell Sir Thomas.'

'I'm sorry to disappoint you, madam, but for me it's something of a relief.'

'But you will still talk to him, won't you? He's most anxious to meet you. That's what I wanted to tell you.' Placing a white card face down on the table, she slid it towards Fay. 'Here is his secretary's telephone number. You must telephone as soon as possible and arrange a meeting.'

'Well, I hope that a meeting with Sir Thomas does nothing to worsen the situation.'

Lady Langbourne frowned. 'Am I right in assuming this means there have been further developments?'

'I'm afraid there have.'

'Frobisher?'

Fay nodded.

'That nasty little man seems determined to make a thorough nuisance of himself. He's written to my husband. Such a rude letter.'

'Oh, madam, I am sorry.'

They were interrupted by the arrival of the waiter. Without asking Fay what she preferred, Lady Langbourne ordered a pot of Earl Grey and a selection of pastries. As soon as he was out of earshot, she moved her chair a little closer.

'Well, Miss Abrams, thanks to Frobisher, my husband knows all about my involvement. He knows I intervened and spoilt Frobisher's plans to interrogate you and Frobisher took great delight in complaining bitterly about my actions. It was spiteful and completely unnecessary.'

Fay murmured an apology. 'I'm sorry. I seem to have caused you a great deal of trouble.' But to her surprise, Lady Langbourne smiled.

'I must confess I would rather that none of this had happened, but I stand by my decision to intervene on your behalf. So, we shall see it through. You and I, Miss Abrams. Now, perhaps you'd like to tell me about these further developments?'

Fay opened her bag. 'This is a letter from Frobisher. It arrived this morning,' she said. 'I think you'd better read it, madam.'

'Am I right in thinking that I am mentioned in this letter?'

'I'm afraid you are.'

'Then perhaps we both deserve a cigarette,' she said.

Fay was relieved. She'd been dying for a cigarette ever since she'd got into the taxi but, with Lady Langbourne sitting beside her, she hadn't been sure if it was the done thing. Lady Langbourne opened a cigarette case and invited her to take one. Not Fay's usual brand. No Player's Weights for her ladyship. These cigarettes were Sobranie Cocktails. Pink and lilac. Fay chose a lilac one and from nowhere a waiter appeared with a lighter.

'All right, Miss Abrams. I suppose we'd better see what the beastly man has to say for himself.'

Fay leant back in her chair, watching Lady Langbourne's face as she read. She could tell from her expression, the way her lips tightened and her eyebrow rose, when she'd reached the bit where Frobisher referred to her as "a person who should know better than to interfere in matters of national security".

'Bloody man. Excuse my French, Miss Abrams, but this is intolerable. As soon as you've finished your tea I suggest you call Sir Thomas' office and arrange to see him.' She pointed to the far wall near the staircase. 'There's a telephone over there, and in the meantime I'll let him know what's been going on and ask what can be done.'

'Lady Langbourne, I really don't want to put you to any more trouble.'

'My dear girl, I've already told you it is I who am responsible for all this nonsense. Not you. Now, not another word. You just leave everything to me.'

Fay smiled. 'I really am most awfully grateful, madam. Mr Frobisher's letter has caused me no end of worry and I dread to think what might happen to me without your help.'

Lady Langbourne narrowed her eyes, tipped her chin upwards and blew out a thin line of smoke. 'To tell you the truth, Miss Abrams,' she said. 'I'm beginning to rather enjoy myself.'

Half an hour later, having made an appointment to see Sir Thomas Poulton the following morning, Fay and Lady Langbourne parted company.

'You have my telephone number, Miss Abrams. Let me know how your meeting goes, won't you? I shall be anxious to hear how you got on.'

Fay assured her that she would and as she walked around the corner to Edgware Road, not once did she glance over her shoulder to check whether she was being followed.

Arriving home earlier than usual, when her mother asked what was wrong, almost out of habit, she was about to come up with an acceptable excuse when it dawned on her that there really was no need for secrets any more.

'I've been having tea at the Cumberland Hotel. They do an awfully nice tea and such delicious little pastries.'

Her mother sniffed. 'I'm sorry I asked.'

'I wasn't joking, Mum. I really was at the Cumberland. That letter, remember? The one that came yesterday? Well, it was from Mr Frobisher. The man who interrogated me. Apparently he hasn't quite finished with me yet.'

Steadying herself with her hand gripping the back of the chair, her mother stared at her. 'He wants to lock you up, doesn't he? Just like your grandmother.'

'Yes, but that won't happen. I've been speaking to Lady Langbourne. That's what I was doing this afternoon and she's put me in touch with a friend of hers, and from what she tells me, Sir Thomas is a very influential man.'

Looking as if she might faint, her mother pulled the chair out and sat gazing up at her. 'Lady Langbourne? Sir Thomas? Who are these people? What have they got to do with you?'

'Lady Langbourne is a friend. Well, a customer actually. She's the one who gave me that scarf. You know, the one with the beads. And Sir Thomas is one of her friends.'

'So, now all of a sudden, my daughter is moving up in the world?'

Fay laughed.

'You'll be too grand to speak to us soon. You're sure they're on your side? I mean, those people, they're not like us. It might be a trick.'

Later, when her father and brother came back from the gym, Fay told them about Frobisher's threats and Lady Langbourne's powerful friend. She chatted freely and openly and it felt wonderful. Normal. The way it should be.

'You saved her life,' said Jack. 'Now she's going to save yours.'

Fay laughed. 'I wouldn't say that but she is grateful and she's determined to put a stop to Frobisher's little plan.'

'And her friend Sir Thomas, he's in a position to help?' said her father.

'I hope so. He seems very keen to meet me.'

Her father smiled. 'I'm so proud of you, darling.'

'Me too,' said Jack.

Her father was still smiling when Fay glanced across at her mother and noticed that the frown, which had almost disappeared from her face over the past few days, had reappeared. Her eyes were unfocused. She was staring off into the distance. For a second or two, she wasn't there. She was somewhere else.

Fay looked at her father. He hadn't appeared to notice; neither had Jack, and when she looked back at her mother, the moment had passed. She seemed to be with them again. But when she saw the way Fay was watching her, her mother shook her head slowly as if warning her not to say anything. You too, Mum, she thought? Was it possible that even now there were things her mother was still not ready to share?

Chapter 33

Fay's appointment with Sir Thomas was at half past eleven. On her way to the station, dressed in her dark grey business suit, she telephoned the shop and told Miss Greenwood she was feeling better but could do with another day at home if that wasn't too inconvenient.

'I'm just pleased you're all right, dear. I've been quite worried about you. By the way, I hope I did the right thing. Mr Cassell called in at the shop yesterday after I sent you home. He was most concerned when I told him you weren't well. He said he wanted to write to you, so I gave him your address. Is that all right?'

'It's fine, Miss Greenwood.'

'I didn't give him your telephone number, dear. I wasn't sure if you wanted him to have it. Anyway, he's going to write to you, and you never know, he might even send you some flowers. I'll see you tomorrow, then. Do look after yourself, won't you?'

That's just what I'm trying to do, she thought. She didn't like telling lies to Miss Greenwood, but what else could she do? She could hardly tell the truth: 'I'm taking the day off, Miss Greenwood, because I'm meeting a gentleman in Westminster to discuss the little matter of my visions. I hope you don't mind.'

No, it was one of those times when a little fib, even a great big one, was the better option and there was no point feeling guilty about it.

The meeting with Sir Thomas was at his office, near St. James' Park. Not wanting to arrive too early, Fay took the train as far as Leicester Square and walked the rest of the way, past Charing Cross towards

Westminster. The rain had held off, which was just as well because she had not thought to bring an umbrella. Her hair had refused to behave that morning so she'd tucked most of it under the small brim of her hat. She was reasonably happy with her appearance. She wasn't particularly nervous but what really bothered her was that here she was, about to meet this important gentleman and she had absolutely nothing to say to him. Nothing that was in any way helpful. If he could do something about Mr Frobisher, as Lady Langbourne seemed to believe, she would be indebted to him but she was beginning to wonder why he should raise a finger to help her when she could offer nothing in return.

Past the Old Admiralty Buildings on one side and Scotland Yard on the other, sandbags piled high against the walls of the buildings, she headed towards Downing Street and the Palace of Westminster. In Whitehall she began to seriously question why she'd imagined that someone like her, a girl from a hat shop, could march into one of these imposing buildings and expect to be even given the time of day. But she reminded herself that when she'd telephoned Sir Thomas' secretary to make the appointment, he had not only been most polite but he'd seemed to be expecting her call.

At the address she had been given, she rang the bell and was shown into what she took to be a waiting room. It smelt of cigars and furniture polish. On a table next to a massive bookcase she saw a few copies of *The Illustrated London News*. She removed her gloves and was about to take a seat when the door opened and a man bounded across the room towards her.

'Miss Abrams,' he said, as he took her hand, 'Thank you so much for coming. I can't tell you how much I've been looking forward to meeting you. I haven't kept you waiting, have I?'

'No, sir, I just arrived.'

'We'll be more comfortable in my room. I'm sure we can rustle up a coffee for you.'

His room was on the first floor, an elegant, high-ceilinged room with huge windows beyond which the lake in St. James' Park could be seen.

'What a beautiful view,' she said.

'I confess it can be a bit of a diversion sometimes. Especially on a fine day. When there's work to be done I sit here,' he said, 'with my back to the windows.'

She smiled and he invited her to take a seat. A woman appeared and set a tray of coffee on a side table.

When she'd gone Fay said, 'To tell you the truth, Sir Thomas, I feel a bit of a fraud. I'm afraid I'm about to waste your time. You see, I have nothing to tell you. No visions. Nothing that will interest you.'

'But it's you I'm interested in, Miss Abrams,' he murmured. Had she been the type, she might have blushed, so intent was his gaze. 'You see, I understand from Lady Langbourne that you have an extraordinary gift.'

Fay shook her head. 'It doesn't feel like much of a gift, Sir Thomas. In fact, sometimes it's a bloomin' nuisance.'

He laughed. 'A bloomin' nuisance? Well, I imagine it could be a bit inconvenient.'

He wanted to know what it felt like. Did the visions appear without warning? How long did they last? Was it like watching a film? Feeling completely at ease, she talked for the first time in her life about what it actually felt like to see things that hadn't yet happened. She described herself as a witness, an unwilling observer, and Sir Thomas was so obviously interested in everything she had to say that her confidence grew.

'The thing is, Mr Frobisher doesn't believe a word of it. He thinks I'm a spy. A threat to national security,' she said.

'Ah! Yes. Frobisher. One can't fault his diligence but I'm afraid Arnold Frobisher does rather lack finesse. A bit of a bull in a china shop. Anyway, Miss Abrams, he won't be troubling you any more. As of tomorrow he's been relocated to another department.'

'That is good news. Well, perhaps not for Mr Frobisher but if it means I can stop worrying about being flung into jail…'

'No one is going to put you in jail, my dear. I can promise you that won't happen.'

She sighed. 'I'm very grateful to you, sir, and I'm sorry I have nothing to tell you.'

'From what you said earlier, I imagine you're relieved there've been no more visions. But I want you to promise me that if you happen to have any more, no matter how insignificant, you'll let me know straight away.' From his wallet, Sir Thomas Poulton produced an embossed card. 'Just telephone me on either of these numbers, my dear.' He smiled. 'Day or night.'

At the door they shook hands. Had he held her hand a little longer than necessary? She was smiling as she walked towards Charing Cross station. Remembering that she'd promised to let Lady Langbourne know how she'd got on, she found a telephone box and opened her purse. Two embossed cards. Two friends in high places. Not exactly a collection, she thought, but impressive nevertheless.

Lady Langbourne sounded pleased to hear from her, and when Fay told her what Sir Thomas had said about Mr Frobisher, she said she was very relieved to hear it.

'I'm delighted that your meeting was successful. Sir Thomas is quite charming, isn't he? I knew you'd get on with him.'

'He was very kind, madam, and I'm very grateful to you for arranging the meeting.'

'It was nothing, Miss Abrams. It was the least I could do. And of course you will let me know if anything happens? I mean, if there are any more visions?'

'Actually, madam, Sir Thomas gave me his card and if I do have another vision I'm to telephone him immediately. Day or night, he said.'

'Oh! Really? He wants you to speak directly to him?'

'Well, that's what he asked me to do.'

'I see. Well, in that case, that's what you must do.'

Oh dear, thought Fay, as she replacedthe receiver, I think I may have put her ladyship's nose slightly out of joint.

She arrived home at three, having stopped off on the way for a sandwich and a glass of lemonade.

'Well, I must say you look very pleased with yourself,' said her mother. 'Was Lord Whatsit nice to you?'

'He's not a lord, Mum. He's a sir. Sir Thomas Poulton. And yes, he was very nice to me. I'm not going to be thrown into jail, and if I have another vision I'm to telephone him straight away.'

'You think you can trust him?'

'Well, I jolly well hope so.'

'They're not like us, you know,' her mother muttered.

'So you keep saying.'

'There's another letter, Fay. It came second post. Don't worry. It's not from the Home Office.'

'How do you know who it's from? I hope you're not opening my letters.'

'I don't need to. Someone's written *S.W.A.L.K.* on the envelope. Sealed with a loving kiss? That's not the Home Office, is it?'

The letter, a single page, was from Sam. He missed her. He hoped she was feeling better. Did she feel up to going to the pictures? *Young Mr Lincoln* was showing at Leicester Square. It had Henry Fonda in it. Did she like Henry Fonda? Would she telephone him if she fancied going during the week? He just wanted to hear her voice so he knew she was okay.

Her mother was standing behind her as Fay put the letter back in its envelope. 'I'm guessing it's from the young man you went out with on Sunday, unless you've got more than one on the go.'

'His name is Sam, Mum. Sam Cassell. He wants to take me to the pictures.'

Her mother stared at her. 'Sam? You mean like Sam Ebstein?'

Fay stared back at her. 'Yes, Mum. Sam as in short for Samuel.'

'Well, you know what that means, don't you? It's a sign, Fay. A good sign. You and this young man? It's meant to be. It's bashert.'

'So, if his name was say, Clark, would that be a bad sign?'

'Not necessarily, but tell me, how many Jewish boys do you know called Clark?'

Fay laughed. Her mother smiled, reached up, touched Fay's cheek and for a moment she recognised the sweet, playful expression on her mother's face. It was the way she looked in the photo, and Fay wished she could hold on to that moment forever.

The sirens sounded while she was changing out of her business suit. Accustomed to the nightly air raids, no one expected a raid at five in the afternoon. Night fell. The air raids began. That was the pattern, but hearing them in broad daylight, when people were out and about, making their way home from work, was terrifying. Especially when Fay remembered that it was about this time that her father usually came home with Jack.

Chapter 34

Rosa was right in the middle of preparing the evening meal when the sirens sounded. No one expected an air raid this early in the day. Most nights there was time to finish their meal and listen to the wireless for a while before it started.

'Damn and blast,' she muttered as she turned off the gas. 'Morris, are you upstairs?'

'It's all right, Rosa. I'm coming down now,' he said.

'You get settled in the shelter,' she said. 'I'll join you in a minute. I'm going to wait here for Lionel.'

Rosa's father-in-law had been staying with them for a month now. He was no trouble and she enjoyed his company.

'I'll wait here with you, Rosa,' he said.

'You'll do no such thing. Go on,' she said, pushing him towards the back door. 'You haven't left a light on in the bathroom, have you?'

'No, why would I put the light on? It's still daylight.'

'All right. Just checking.'

She watched him plod across the garden to the Anderson, carrying what he called his emergency supplies. An old cushion, his heart pills, his cough mixture, spare batteries for his torch and a small bottle of brandy. She waited until he disappeared inside, then went to the dining room and looked out of the window. From there she could see to the end of the street. Where is he? she thought. He'd only gone out for a newspaper. What was he doing? He must know how worried she'd be. Their house was far closer to the newsagents than that dreadful communal shelter. He wouldn't have gone there, would he? There'd be no reason to unless he'd done something stupid like suddenly deciding to take a walk around the park before supper. Had he stopped off to admire the council's newly planted vegetable garden? That would be just the sort of thing he might do. Well, it would serve him right if he had to spend the whole bloomin' night squashed inside that filthy, smelly shelter.

The sirens hadn't stopped wailing. On and on they went. Rosa dashed into the kitchen, filled a shopping basket with some dried provisions, the bread and butter pudding she'd just finished making and the last of the apples. Then she raced round the house closing the blackout curtains and joined Morris in the Anderson.

'Where's Lionel?' he asked as she eased herself down on to the bench beside him.

'Don't ask me. I haven't a clue where he is but I'll tell you this for nothing. He's going to get a piece of my mind when he does turn up.'

The sirens stopped and in the silence that followed they heard the distant drone of aircraft. Closer and closer it came. The boom of gunfire ripped through the air. Rosa covered her ears. She could see Morris' lips moving. He was praying. Then she heard the high-pitched whistle as the bomb plummeted to the ground. The explosion when it landed was deafening. It was several minutes before the corrugated iron frame supporting the earth around their shelter stopped shaking and rattling.

'He's dead,' she wailed. 'I know it. Lionel's dead.'

Her father-in-law, who'd lived through one war, fought on the front line, come home injured and survived the Zeppelins, was crying. They clung to each other and sobbed. She wanted him to say she was wrong. Lionel was safe. He was probably leading a sing-song in that awful shelter. Telling everyone to stay calm. He was like that. A leader among men, in his own quiet way. Silently, she swore to God that if Lionel came home, if he was still alive, she would spend the rest of her days making him happy. She would never be unkind. She would never nag or tell him what to do.

She had no idea how long it was before the all-clear sounded.

Three or four hours. Maybe more, but when she finally crawled out of the shelter, her back was so stiff she couldn't straighten up. As she staggered towards the house, her legs threatened to give way beneath her. With her father-in-law's help Rosa made it into the kitchen. She sank down on to the nearest chair and closed her eyes while she tried to gather her thoughts.

'What am I going to do without him?' she murmured. 'What am I going to do?'

'Listen to me, darling. The first thing you must do is find out if anyone's seen him.'

He was right, of course. There was no point moping. No point just waiting. Not when she could be doing something. On the hall table next to the telephone lay her address book. She opened it, picked up the receiver and listened. Nothing. Her father-in-law had followed her into the hall.

'Lines down?' he said.

She nodded and sat on the stairs. For a moment she felt utterly defeated. There must be something...

'Morris, I'm going out,' she said. 'I'm going to find him.'

He wanted to go with her but she told him he must stay where he was in case anyone turned up with some news. She had just put her jacket on and was about to open the front door when she heard voices outside. Footsteps on the path. Then someone hammered on the front door. Rosa groaned.

'You open it, Morris. I don't think I can bear it,' she said, and buried her face in her hands.

As the door swung open, Lionel, supported between Lou Abrams and his boy, staggered into the hall. His clothes were in tatters. One eye was closed. His jaw hung open. Blood trickled from his mouth. He collapsed on to his knees and in one movement Rosa was beside him, cradling his head in her arms.

It was two hours since the all-clear had sounded. Fay had begun to imagine the worst, but her mother seemed remarkably unconcerned. Fay couldn't believe how calm she was. It wasn't normal. She felt like shaking her just to get a reaction. Surely, she thought, she must be out of her mind with worry. But no. There she was, sitting at the table, tucking into her evening meal. When she finished eating, without comment, she set places for Jack and his father. Then, as if she expected them to turn up at any moment, she covered their meals with upturned plates, placed them in the bottom of the oven to keep warm, switched on the wireless and began darning a pair of Jack's grey socks. Fay couldn't stand it a moment longer. She had to say something.

'Mum, the all-clear sounded ages ago. Aren't you the least bit worried?' she said.

Her mother looked up and frowned. 'No. Why should I be worried? I'd know if something bad had happened.'

'How would you know? You're not clairvoyant. So how could you possibly know unless...'

Fay was staring at her, watching for any little sign that might give the game away. There were none.

Her mother met her gaze and speaking in a clear, firm voice, said, 'I don't have visions if that's what you were thinking. I've never had them. Not a single one. But...' She hesitated.

'But what, Mum?'

'I'm not like you or your grandmother but sometimes...I just know things.'

'What do you mean, you know things? What sort of things?'

'Well, Jack and your father, for instance,' she said. 'I know they're all right. I'd have a feeling if something was wrong. I can't explain but I'd know. I always know.'

'You're not talking about intuition, are you? The kind of feeling that everyone gets now and again?'

'I know what intuition is, thank you very much, and no, it's not intuition.'

'And it's not visions? Or messages from the other side?'

'Don't be ridiculous. I'm telling you, Fay, any minute now, your father and brother will walk through that door ready for a hot meal.'

When the back door opened and her father and Jack stumbled

into the kitchen, her mother put her sewing box on the floor, threw a triumphant glance at Fay and said, 'There you are. Wash your hands. Supper's ready.'

Jack groaned. 'I'm full up, Mum. I couldn't eat another mouthful.'

'Full up? What do you mean, you're full up?'

'What could we do, Hetty?' said her father. 'It was Mrs Feldman. You know what she's like. She insisted on feeding us.'

'She fed you?' said her mother. 'Why would she do that?'

Jack loosened the belt on his trousers. Her father kicked off his shoes without bothering to undo the laces and sank heavily into the chair beside Fay, his legs stretched out in front of him. Her mother was glaring at him.

'For goodness' sake, Hetty, don't start,' he said. 'A couple of yobs jumped on Mr Feldman in the park. They beat him up and left him there. The air raid started. He tried to get to the shelter but he was too badly hurt and when the all-clear sounded we were on our way home and that's when we found him. No bones broken but he's lost a tooth and he's got a massive bruise over his right eye. Mrs Feldman cleaned him up. He'll be all right in a day or so.'

Her mother's concern was genuine. 'Poor Rosa,' she said. 'What a shock she must have had.' But all the time her father had been talking, Fay had been keeping a close eye on Jack. Something was definitely bothering him.

'Mrs Feldman said I'm a hero,' he said. He was speaking very quietly and she couldn't help but notice the look that passed between him and his father. Her mother must have noticed it too.

'What's going on, Lou?' she said.

He closed his eyes. 'Not now, Hetty. I'm too tired. I'll tell you later. Jack, upstairs. Go on. Time you were in bed.'

Fay watched as her mother opened her mouth to speak. Then obviously realising, as Fay did, that now was not a good time, without saying a word she got up, turned the oven off and began filling the kettle.

'Don't bother with tea for me, Hetty,' said her father. 'I'm going upstairs. I need a serious talk with our son.'

As the door closed behind him, Fay looked at her mother. 'Well, Mum. What are those feelings of yours telling you now?'

Her mother ignored her.

Chapter 35

Fay sat on the edge of Jack's bed. 'Why is Dad cross with you?'

Jack sighed. 'Mrs Feldman told him what happened at the synagogue. She didn't mean to get me into trouble. She was just saying that I'd chased after the boys who broke the window and she thought I was very brave.'

'And…?'

'Dad says if someone lobs bricks through the synagogue window you report it to the police. You don't deal with it yourself unless you want to get done for assault.'

'That's not fair. The rabbi didn't try and stop you, did he? I bet he never even reported it. You acted on the spur of the moment, Jack, and I still think it was a brave thing to do.' Fay stood and smoothed the bedclothes. 'Don't worry about Dad. He'll have forgotten all about it in the morning.'

'No he won't,' said Jack. 'He thinks it's my fault that Mr Feldman got beaten up. They threw stones at him. They called him a filthy Jew and Mr Feldman said that the boy who punched him was a big lump with greasy hair. I'm certain it's the same boy. You know, the one I thought I'd killed.'

'I know who you mean, but how could it possibly be your fault?'

'Well, if we'd gone to the police in the first place, Dad says the boys might have thought twice about getting into trouble again and then they might not have had a go at Mr Feldman.'

Fay shrugged. 'He might be right, but then again it might not have made the least bit of difference. They might have done it anyway, and I still agree with Mrs Feldman. I'm proud of you, and I bet Dad is proud, too.'

'He's got a funny way of showing it,' said Jack.

Two hours later they were huddled together in the Anderson, Fay, Jack and their father, while her mother settled down in the cupboard under the stairs. For a while nothing happened. Then it began. There had been other nights but none like this. The drone of aircraft grew louder and louder until it was right above her head. Explosion followed explosion with hardly a gap between. The ground shook. The sky flashed and crackled and sparked with light as the anti-aircraft guns began firing. No one spoke and Fay wondered if her father and brother were thinking what she was thinking: that sheltering under a corrugated iron roof was like being trapped in the middle of a battlefield. Her father sat between them, his arms wrapped around them. A bomb landed so close that she was sure their house had been hit. She covered her ears with her hands. It was Jack who was the first to say what had been on her mind and, she suspected, on her father's mind, too.

'Mum will be terrified. Can we go inside, Dad, please? We should be together, all of us. I mean…if our number's up…'

They waited until there was a brief lull and raced across the garden. The house was still standing but her mother was not in the cupboard under the stairs. She was in the kitchen. The kettle was on the stove and the teapot and four cups were on the table. She made toast and with the questionable safety of the Anderson abandoned and the raid still going strong, they all retired to their beds. Each time another bomb landed, Fay opened her eyes and watched her wardrobe wobble and shake; heard the hangers rattling inside. Eventually, too exhausted to care, she fell asleep.

It was only when she was on her way to work the next morning that she realised how lucky they'd actually been. Only a couple of streets from her house a group of people were staring at the huge mound of rubble where the chemist had once stood, and on the opposite side of the road three houses had been completely destroyed. A woman was sifting through the ruins while her children squatted in the wreckage watching her. The front wall of their home – Fay assumed it was theirs – had collapsed into the street. She could see inside. The wallpaper, a fireplace, the stairs, a bath hanging precariously through the ceiling of the room below, everything exposed like the inside of a dolls' house.

That could have been us, she thought. Luck. That's all it was. The luck of the draw. Another night, another bomb and it would be someone else's turn. Maybe next time it would be them sifting through the ruins of their home.

Rita was waiting at the bus stop. Fay gave her a hug.

'I thought we'd had it. Are you all okay? Any damage?'

'Broken windows. A hole in the roof,' said Rita. 'Could be worse.'

Near Maida Vale a gas mains was on fire. The road was blocked and the bus was forced to make a diversion, which took them around the back doubles. It was late when they finally reached the top end of Edgware Road. They held hands and raced down Oxford Street.

'Danny starts his training soon,' said Rita as they reached Selfridges. 'He's going to be stationed somewhere near Sidcup. I'm so proud of him but I'm going to miss him like mad, and I don't even know when I'm going to see him again.'

Fay muttered something about the war being over soon…with a bit of luck. She didn't think it was true and she was sure Rita didn't believe it either.

'See you on Thursday,' she said. Rita looked at her blankly. 'In shul. It's Rosh Hashanah.'

'Oh dear,' said Rita, 'I haven't asked for time off yet. I hope they don't make a fuss.'

'Tell them you'll work on Christmas Day. That should do it,' said Fay.

She was lucky and she knew it. Miss Greenwood never made a fuss about the Jewish holidays. She even had the dates ringed on her calendar and ever since Fay had worked at the shop it had been Miss Greenwood's custom to search through the stock and provide her with a new hat for synagogue.

'You must look smart, dear,' she would say. 'You are representing Paulette's of Mayfair.'

That day, though, it was difficult to drum up much enthusiasm for Paulette's or for the idea of selling hats for a living. Surely, she thought, there was something more useful she should be doing.

'It was seeing that woman this morning, Miss Greenwood. Sifting through the ruins of her home. She'd lost everything and here was I off to work in a hat shop. I love my job, I really do, and I understand how important it is that everyone does their best to carry on as normal. But I can't help feeling…well, a bit useless, I suppose.'

Miss Greenwood nodded. 'Of course you must do what you think's best, dear, but unless you intend signing up for the armed forces, I would think twice before throwing the baby out with the bathwater. There's a new scheme coming into effect soon. It's for part-time war work. You only have to do a few hours each week and you don't have to give up your main employment. There's a leaflet somewhere, if you're interested.'

Fay was pleasantly surprised by the list of part-time work she might apply for without giving up her job at the shop. Was this what she was looking for? Would this satisfy her need to do something really useful? Assembling parts in a munitions factory? Operating a switchboard? Did it actually matter what she did as long as she was contributing something to the war effort?

She was still thinking about it when Sam put his head round the shop door. He was clutching a bunch of marigolds.

'Fay,' he said. 'I've been worried about you. I heard it was really bad round your way last night.'

'It was quite scary. Are the flowers for me?'

'Indeed they are. Picked them myself from my mother's garden.'

'And what would you have done with them if I hadn't been here?' she said.

'That's obvious, isn't it? I'd have given them to Miss Greenwood, instead.'

Miss Greenwood smiled and offered to make him a cup of tea.

'Sorry. No time. I just wanted to make sure Fay was okay and to find out if she got my letter. Shall we go to the pictures, Fay? Tonight?'

'Yes,' said Fay. 'I'd like that very much.'

He told her he'd pick her up from the shop at half five and was halfway out the door when he turned and before she could protest, in front of Miss Greenwood, he kissed Fay on the lips. As he marched out of the door Fay frowned.

'Sorry about that, Miss Greenwood.'

Miss Greenwood sighed. 'Perhaps it was a tiny bit forward, but my goodness me, he certainly is a handsome young man.'

At quarter past five she suggested Fay might like to freshen up. Fay retouched her make-up, fiddled with her hair and straightened the seams of her stockings while Miss Greenwood chose a hat for her. It was a particularly nice hat. Plain and simple, but very elegant. Miss Greenwood tugged the brim to a slight angle over Fay's left eye and nodded approvingly.

'Perfect,' she said. 'Do wear it this evening.'

Right on time, Sam's car pulled up outside the shop. He asked her if she was hungry.

'Not terribly,' she said.

They ended up sitting on a bench on the Embankment, looking at the river and sharing a bag of chips.

'My fingers smell of vinegar,' she said. He took out his handkerchief and wiped her hands. He asked how her brother was getting on with his boxing lessons. She told him about Mr Feldman and the incident at the synagogue, and how angry her father was with Jack for tackling the boys himself instead of reporting them to the police.

'Sounds like a little hero to me,' he said.

'That's exactly what I think,' said Fay.

He was, as Miss Greenwood had pointed out, extremely handsome, but handsome is as handsome does and Fay had yet to make up her mind about Sam Cassell. She was inclined to think that kissing her in front of Miss Greenwood suggested that he was taking rather a lot for granted and she wasn't entirely sure how she felt about it. She certainly wasn't ready to tell him about her visions, but she did mention the conversation she'd had with Miss Greenwood.

'I don't mind what I do, even if it's just for a few hours a week. It's wrong to do nothing. Not when other people are out there doing their bit.'

'So you think working in a shop is doing nothing?' he said.

Fay turned and looked at him. 'Don't you?'

He shrugged. 'And I suppose you think I should be doing more than making military caps?'

'It's not my place to tell you what to do but, since you ask, yes, I do.'

'You'd like me to join up?'

'Why not?' she said, and the second the words were out of her mouth, she couldn't believe she'd said it.

She of all people should have known better. When Bernard wanted to join up she'd begged him not to go. Yet here she was telling a man she hardly knew that he should do a lot more for his country. She might as well have handed him a white feather. It was wrong. It was none of her business and apologising would only have made it worse. Attempting to make up for her thoughtless comment, Fay rambled on about the Jewish holidays. Which synagogue did he belong to? Were they closing the factory until after Yom Kippur? Did he fast for the full twenty-four hours? After a few minutes the conversation fizzled out.

'Well,' he said, 'we better make a move. The film starts soon.'

They sat in the back row. She wouldn't have minded in the least if Sam had put his arm around her, but he didn't. The film was about the early life of Abraham Lincoln. It had just got to the part where Mr Lincoln was about to take his first case as a lawyer, when the sound began to slow down like a record that needed winding. The screen flickered, then went blank. The audience began booing and stamping their feet. Fay and Sam joined in until the lights came on and a man stepped in front of the screen.

'Ladies and gentlemen, I apologise for interrupting the film but an air raid is in progress. You may, if you wish, make your way down to the basement. For those of you who prefer to watch the film, our projectionist will continue showing it in a few minutes.'

She noticed that hardly anyone moved. A few people made for the exit. The rest stayed in their seats. The screen filled. The film sprang into life again. The audience cheered and the projectionist increased the volume to drown out the sound of the sirens. No one paid any attention to the muffled rumbling outside or to the vibrations and the flakes of plaster that fell from the ceiling.

When the film ended Sam drove her home in the pouring rain, all the way to her front door. The slight awkwardness between them had gone. She was secretly hoping that he would kiss her but he just took her hand and brought it to his lips. The flowers were on the back seat. He handed them to her as she got out of the car. She thanked him for a nice evening and waved as he drove away.

The raid ignored, everyone was in bed and Fay wondered if they'd ever use the Anderson again. It hadn't stopped raining for hours and she guessed their shelter was awash with rainwater. She found a vase for Sam's flowers and sat there staring at them. Marigolds, bright and brash, just like Sam. Bernard gave her violets. Tiny, dainty posies of violets, and she wondered what he'd think of her now. They'd known each other since childhood but in the year since he'd died, she had changed. Not as shy as she'd once been. More open. More prepared to take chances. She even looked different. She'd grown up and she wondered if she and Bernard would find much in common now. And Sam? Apart from taking the liberty of kissing her in full view of her boss, he hadn't really put a foot wrong. She liked him and she wished she'd kept her mouth shut. It was not her place to tell him what to do.

Chapter 36

Rosa was wearing her new frock. Her shoes weren't new but apart from that everything else had been bought especially for Rosh Hashanah, and hanging in her wardrobe was an equally smart outfit for Yom Kippur. It was a source of irritation that the dentist had been unable to supply Lionel with a false tooth in time. He had a large gap, right in the front where it showed. His mouth had never been his best feature. The teeth were uneven and discoloured but at least he'd had a full set.

'Try not to smile too much, dear,' she said as they stood outside the synagogue.

'I'm not likely to am I, Rosa? Not with a sore eye and my ribs hurting as much as they do.'

'Poor darling,' she said. 'I am sorry and you do look very smart, all things considered.'

Morris Feldman went inside with one of their neighbours, but as always Rosa waited until the last moment. She liked to greet people as they arrived. She liked to get a proper look at what they were wearing. She took a lot of trouble over her own outfit and it was important that people noticed.

But today it was Lionel who was the centre of attention and Rosa didn't mind in the least. Everyone knew what had happened. The telephone hadn't stopped ringing. The rabbi had visited them every day and Rosa had been delighted by the way everyone had rallied round. Lionel was well liked. He was respected and she was proud of him, but no one understood him like she did. He didn't need to say anything. She knew that the attack had left him feeling nervous and vulnerable and had been trying to find a way of gently building up his confidence again. She was certain she would think of something eventually.

'Look, Lionel,' she whispered. 'Here come Mr and Mrs Ebstein. Who's that fellow with their daughter?' Without giving him a chance to reply, Rosa waved. '*Shanah Tovah*, Mrs Ebstein, Mr Ebstein. Happy New Year, Rita. How lovely you look.'

It was Sam Ebstein who made the introductions. 'Mrs Feldman,' he announced proudly, 'this is Danny Da Costa. Rita's young man. He's just signed up.'

The young man smiled and raised his hat.

While Rosa asked the young man which synagogue his family belonged to, Mrs Ebstein was talking to Lionel. Rosa heard her say how shocked she'd been when she'd heard what happened to him.

'What kind of people would do something like that, Mr Feldman?'

'The kind that hate Jews,' said Lionel.

Rosa wished he hadn't said that. There was something about the way he said it that upset her. A kind of sad acceptance. As if he was just shrugging his shoulders. She wouldn't have minded so much if there'd been a trace of anger in his voice. But there was none. When she saw the Abrams family walking through the gates, Rosa smiled and beckoned them over.

'Ah!' she said, 'Here he is. Jack, my little hero. *Shanah Tovah* to you all. Hetty, how smart you look.' And it was true. Hetty was looking very nice indeed. Rosa noticed that her shoes and bag matched perfectly and her dress was rather flattering. 'Fay, my dear, what a wonderful hat. How well it suits you.'

Lou Abrams peered at the bruise under Lionel's eye. 'Does it still hurt?'

'Not much,' said Lionel. 'Here, Jack. Take a look at this. How's this for a smile?'

Rosa turned in time to see Lionel grinning at the boy. Jack was laughing.

'Lionel,' she said. 'You'll give the child nightmares.'

Linking arms with Hetty, Rosa walked into the synagogue and

took her seat. The days between Rosh Hashanah and Yom Kippur were meant to be a time for reflection; a time during which forgiveness was sought for the wrongdoings committed in the past year. Rosa always found this particularly difficult. She wasn't perfect. She didn't need anyone to tell her that, but how could she demonstrate that she had learned from her mistakes and would not be repeating them, when she couldn't actually remember doing anything wrong? Every year it was the same. She would look about her at the faces of the members of the congregation, wondering which of them had a nice, long list of terrible things that needed God's forgiveness.

Hetty, she noticed, was having no trouble following the service in Hebrew. Rosa was never sure if she was on the right page and now, instead of paying attention to the service, she found herself thinking about Hetty's mysterious mother, until a sideways glance at Hetty's prayer book told her that she was on the wrong page again. She tried to concentrate. Rabbi Shultz was warbling away like a nightingale. He really had the most beautiful voice. She looked across to where the men were sitting. She could see Lionel. He was sitting between Rosa's father-in-law and the Abrams boy. Such a lovely boy. He reminded Rosa of her nephews. Thank God they'd finally written to their mother. Perhaps Rosa's sister would stop worrying now. She'd begun to lose patience with her. Maybe that was something she should ask forgiveness for. Yes, she thought. She would do that. She would promise herself and God that in future she would be kinder and more tolerant.

Fay was watching her mother's finger move from right to left across the page. She glanced at her face. Her mother's lips were moving. Fay knew enough Hebrew to recognise certain words. It was a bit like being able to read music. If you knew the basics you could at least figure out where you were but her mother, who only attended shul on high days and holidays, read Hebrew perfectly.

She wished she knew about her mother's childhood. She'd always envied the closeness Rita enjoyed with Mrs Ebstein but it hadn't seemed to matter much before. Without thinking, she reached for her mother's hand. Her mother looked at her. Fay smiled. Her mother nodded as if she understood what Fay wanted. With her prayer book resting on her lap, she took hold of Fay's finger and began guiding it across the page and together they followed the service until the rabbi paused to lift the shofar to his lips. As he was blowing the long note, her mother let go of her hand. Fay glanced across the hall. She could see Jack watching the rabbi, paying attention to everything that was happening. A slight movement beside her made Fay turn in time to see her mother's prayer book slide from her lap. There was a thud as it dropped. Heads turned towards them.

She heard Mrs Feldman whisper, 'It's gone under the chair, Hetty. I don't think I can reach it.'

Her mother didn't respond. She sat perfectly still, her eyes open, staring off into the distance. Fay might have been alarmed had she not seen it happen before.

'It's all right, Mrs Feldman, I'll get it,' she said. As she bent forward and stretched her arm under the chair, her elbow brushed against her mother's knee. Her mother turned her head slowly towards her.

'Mum, are you all right?' she whispered. 'Do you need some air?'

Her mother nodded.

It was common practice for people, especially the women, to take a breather during a service, to change seats, to visit the toilet or to go outside for a quick natter, so no one took much notice as Fay gently led her out of the synagogue and round the side of the building where they couldn't be seen. There was nowhere to sit. Her mother leant her head against the wall. Fay waited for her to recover. It took a few minutes before she was able to speak.

'It was another one of those feelings.'

'What sort of feeling?'

'A bad one, Fay. A really bad one.'

'You saw something?'

Her mother frowned. 'No, I told you already. I don't see things. My mother saw things. You see things. I just have feelings.'

'Premonitions?'

'Call it what you like. Does it have to have a name? It's a feeling.'

'Tell me about it.'

Her mother sighed. 'What's there to tell? Something bad is going to happen.'

'Mum, bad things are happening all the time. You don't get feelings about all of them, do you? So what's special this time?' Her mother, who'd looked so well before, was looking quite pale and washed out. 'I think I should take you home,' said Fay.

'And miss the end of the service? I can't do that. What will everyone think?'

'Mum, they won't even notice.'

'Your father will, and Mrs Feldman certainly will.'

Fay took hold of her arm. Her mother brushed her hand away and with her shoulders thrown back, marched into the synagogue with Fay following behind her.

'Ah, Hetty, there you are,' whispered Mrs Feldman. 'Can you show me which bit we're up to? I've lost my place again.'

Her mother opened her prayer book, studied it for a moment, listened to the rabbi and turned to the right page.

'You're supposed to be on this page, Rosa,' she murmured.

Fay was beginning to see another side of her mother. There was a streak of courage that she'd never noticed before, and now she was wondering if perhaps they were more alike than she'd realised.

Chapter 37

Jack was in his room reading his new comic, her father at the depot training a bunch of new recruits for the Air Raid Protection unit. Fay was alone with her mother and she wondered if it was worth raising the matter of her odd behaviour at the synagogue. She could so easily slip back inside her shell if she didn't like the way the conversation was going, so for the moment Fay said nothing.

With the sewing box on her lap, her mother was turning the collar on her father's old work shirt. 'Tell me about this young man of yours,' she said. 'What's he like?'

Fay thought for a moment. 'He's different to Bernard. More sophisticated. Not so serious.'

Her mother frowned. 'Bernard was a good man, Fay.'

'I know he was. Sam's a good man, too, but I don't know him very well yet.'

'And is he going to sign up?'

Fay sighed. 'He doesn't have to. He's in a reserved occupation, but I suppose he's thinking about it.'

'Is that what you want?'

'It's not up to me, is it? He has to make that choice for himself.'

'Yes, but you could let him know how you'd feel about it.'

'I don't know how I feel, Mum. How would you feel if Jack was old enough to fight? Would you be proud or would you want to keep him safe?'

Her mother smiled. 'If it was Jack, nothing I said would stop him.'

'You're right, and if it was him and not Sam, I'd definitely want to keep him at home.'

'But it wouldn't be your decision, would it? So, let's be thankful that he's not old enough.'

Remembering that it was Jack's idea that they leave the shelter so they'd all be together if the worst happened, Fay couldn't resist saying something about her mother's remarkably calm behaviour that night.

'You know the other night, Mum, when me and Dad and Jack came into the house in the middle of that raid and you were making toast? How come you knew we weren't going to stay in the shelter?'

Her mother shrugged. 'I didn't know. Not for certain, but I had a feeling.'

'Like the one you had in the synagogue?'

'No, not at all like that. That was a bad feeling. This one was good.'

'And have you still got that bad feeling? I mean, do you still think something awful is going to happen?'

Her mother peered at Fay over the top of her glasses. 'It doesn't go away, you know. It's not like a bad dream. You don't wake up in the morning and it's gone.'

'So basically you feel anxious but you don't know why?'

Her mother nodded. 'That's it in a nutshell.'

At nine, the wireless was usually on. Henry Hall and the BBC Dance Orchestra, coming direct from Broadcasting House in the centre of London. Fay was about to switch it on when her mother shook her head.

'No, Fay. Not tonight. I'd rather talk.'

'Really? That's not like you, Mum.'

Her mother shut the sewing box and stared at her. 'You think you know me, but you don't really.'

Fay thought nothing of the kind. She didn't know her mother at all. It was only in the past few days that she'd even begun to understand her a little better.

'Okay, so what do you want to talk about?'

Her mother sighed and closed her eyes. Such a long sigh. What she said next took Fay completely by surprise.

'Your grandparents,' she whispered. 'Now it's all out in the open, I mean, now you know that your grandmother was like you, it's time you knew the rest.'

Fay sat up and waited. Her mother sighed again.

'You have no idea how blessed you are, Fay. Your father's a good man. He's kind and patient and gentle. Your grandfather wasn't like that. He was...' Her voice faltered. 'I don't want to speak ill of the dead, but...'

Her eyes opened and by the time she'd finished talking, her mother was sobbing and Fay was close to tears, too.

Her grandfather was a bully. A deeply religious bully whose response to his wife's visions was to terrify her with quotes from the Bible. "Suffer not the witch to live. The Lord thy God turns his face from you." He called her a Jezebel and told her that the dogs would gnaw at her bones. Life for his daughter was not much better. Under his strict supervision she'd learned to read Hebrew. He thought nothing of striking her if she made a mistake. She'd grown up watching her mother's spirit slowly crushed.

'God forgive me for saying it but the day the telegram came... the day I found out he'd been killed in action...I felt nothing except relief.'

'And my grandmother,' said Fay, 'how did she take it?'

Her mother sniffed and wiped her eyes with the corner of her apron. 'Your grandmother started talking as if she'd never stop, telling anyone who'd listen about her visions, and she kept on talking until they came and locked her up. And you know what, Fay? She was always right. Everything she said was going to happen happened just the way she said it would. But she never knew they were coming for her. She didn't know that was going to happen.'

'And did you know something bad was going to happen, Mum?'

Her mother nodded. 'A couple of weeks before they took her away I started having these feelings. Horrible feelings. I didn't want to let her out of my sight. I was frightened and I didn't know why and I felt sad, terribly sad all the time.'

'I wish I'd known all this before, Mum. I always thought you were a bit...'

'I know what you thought, and I'm sorry. I wish I'd been kinder. I kept hoping that your visions would stop. I didn't want you to be like her. Those visions ruined her life, Fay, completely ruined it.'

Fay reached for her hand. 'But they won't ruin mine, Mum. I won't let them.'

'I hope you're right, Fay. You're certainly much stronger she was and she was never a particularly clever woman. Not smart like you. Anyway, that's enough. All this talking, it's made me thirsty.'

Fay followed her into the kitchen. They drank Horlicks. Fay picked at the crumbs in the bottom of the biscuit tin and for a few minutes neither of them spoke. She thought about her grandmother. She wished she'd known her. She wished they could have talked about what it meant to have visions. To her grandmother they'd been a terrible curse. How different it might have been for both of them if they'd been able to share their fears. An image flashed in front of her. Her grandmother, peering lovingly into Jack's cradle, and instantly Fay knew what had to be done.

'I'd like to visit her grave. I'll go on my own if you don't want to come but I think it would be a good idea if we went together.'

Her mother was staring at her. 'When do you want to go?' she said.

'Soon. Before Yom Kippur. Sunday, if you're not doing anything.'

'I don't know what good it will do but if that's what you want, we'll go. Right then. You can wash the cups. I'm off to bed. Goodnight.'

Fay watched her as she shuffled towards the door. 'Goodnight, dear' would have been nice. 'Goodnight, sweetheart' like her father always said would have been even nicer.

'Goodnight, Mum,' she murmured.

Chapter 38

At the top of Beaconsfield Road, with Willesden Jewish Cemetery just ahead of them, her mother took hold of her arm and led the way through the cemetery gates towards the main central path.

'Look over there,' she said. 'That's the Rothschilds' family plot.'

Fay glanced across to where a group of tall, white monuments glistened in the sun. 'My grandmother's in good company, then,' she said.

'There's all sorts buried here,' said her mother. 'Your grandmother's grave is further down at the end of the path.'

'And when was the last time you were here, Mum?' she said, fully expecting to be told that it had been quite a while.

'July.'

Fay stopped walking and looked at her.

'What? You're surprised? You think because I don't talk about her that means I've forgotten her? She was my mother.'

'I had no idea you were coming here. How often do you come?'

'Not often. Two or three times a year. It depends how I feel.'

'Dad's parents aren't buried here, are they?'

'No, they're in Westcliffe.'

'And your father?' said Fay, suddenly aware that these were things she ought to have known.

'A war grave in France.'

'Like Bernard,' Fay murmured.

Her mother patted her hand. 'Perhaps the Ebsteins will bring him home, Fay.'

'But your mother never wanted to bring my grandfather home, did she?'

'I don't think for one moment that the thought even crossed her mind. She had more than enough problems without worrying about someone like him.'

There was no pretence, no attempt to hide the disdain in her voice. He was mourned by neither his wife nor his daughter, and loving her own father as she did, Fay couldn't help feeling just a little sorry for her grandfather. Halfway down the path she noticed that her mother had begun to walk faster.

'Look straight ahead, Fay,' she said. 'Don't turn your head. Just keep walking.'

She did as she was told. A few yards further on, her mother slowed down.

'What was that all about, Mum?'

'The last time you were here,' said her mother, 'the place we just passed, you made quite a scene.'

'But I've never been here before,' said Fay.

Her mother nodded. 'Yes, you have. You came here with me. Just once. I thought it would be all right. And you were fine. You behaved beautifully until you saw some of the graves, the really old ones back there. The headstones are broken and the ground's sunk and you got it into your head that the dead had escaped. You yelled blue murder.'

'Did I? I honestly don't remember a thing about it.'

'Just as well,' said her mother. 'You were scared stiff.'

'Well, I'm a big girl now, Mum, and I'm glad we're here.'

Her mother smiled. 'Me, too.'

At the end of the central path, she led Fay along a row of graves and stopped in front of a headstone that bore the inscription, "Zofia Anja Kroll. Born January 14th 1881. Died October 7th 1923". The grave was clean and cared for. On top of the headstone was a small, flat pebble.

'You leave a little stone to show you've been here,' said her mother. Fay watched her remove the stone – her little calling card. 'We'll leave two more before we go.'

Fay glanced at the graves on either side of her grandmother's. They too had small stones balanced on their headstones. Little calling cards that showed they weren't forgotten. She looked at her grandmother's headstone and read the inscription again.

'It says nothing about her being a mother and grandmother. Is that deliberate?'

Her mother nodded. 'It seemed the right thing to do at the time.'

'And now?'

'I don't know. You think it was wrong?'

Having noticed the sentiments carved on other headstones – "loving wife, devoted mother, much-loved grandmother" – she was quite certain it was wrong but she considered her reply carefully.

'I suppose I can understand why you did it, but even so I...' She hesitated, but before she could stop herself she touched the headstone and said, 'I can't understand why you were so ashamed of her. She didn't do anything wrong. What happened to her was terrible but it wasn't her fault, was it?'

Her mother stared at her, then turned away so that Fay couldn't see her face. Before she realised what was happening, her mother let out a wail and dropped to her knees on the ground beside the grave. To Fay's horror, she began to cry, sobbing loudly like a child. Fay bent beside her and wrapped her arms around her. She stayed like that, holding her until she was quiet. Then gently she lifted her mother to her feet and brushed away the leaves that clung to her skirt.

'I'm sorry, Mum. I'm sure you did what you thought was right.'

'But it wasn't right. I should have stood up for her. They all thought she wasn't right in the head and I was ashamed of her.'

'She had visions, Mum. Like me. She couldn't help it.'

'I know that now but it's too late, isn't it?' Her mother sniffed and Fay found a handkerchief and told her to wipe her eyes. 'I let her down, Fay. My father was so unkind to her and then I let her down, too.'

'But you can put it right. It's not too late. Change the wording, Mum. "Zofia Kroll, mother to Esther, grandmother to Frances and Jack Abrams".'

'But Jack was born after she died.'

'So what? She's still his grandmother, isn't she? We could have a little ceremony. A belated stone setting. The four of us.'

Fay watched as her mother's expression changed. She was smiling now, her eyes still wet with tears.

'We could, couldn't we? We'll do it. We'll change the inscription.' Her mother traced Zofia's name with her finger. 'There's enough room for a few more words,' she said, and before they left, they found two smooth little stones and balanced them on top of the headstone.

Walking back, arm in arm, along the central path, her mother, quite unprompted, began talking about the weeks leading up to Zofia's death.

'I was only a few years older than you are now. Married with a small child. My mother loved you. You gave her such pleasure but she was terribly ill by then. Such awful pains in her head. They got worse and worse. She was in Whitechapel Hospital. She wanted to see you so I took you there and she stroked your cheek…then she smiled and closed her eyes and she was gone.'

'I wish I'd known her,' murmured Fay.

Passing the Rothschilds' monuments she became aware of a sense of detachment. Her neck and the back of her head tingled with the all-too-familiar sensation which always accompanied the beginning of a vision. Somehow she managed to ignore it until they came to the buildings near the cemetery gates. There was the basin provided for visitors to rinse their hands before they left. A symbolic ritual; the removal of the air of death from the living. Unable to stop herself, Fay turned on the tap and, in a desperate attempt to halt the vision, began frantically splashing her face and neck with cold water.

Later, she remembered her mother's shocked expression; remembered that she'd looked round to make sure no one had seen what Fay was doing. She remembered stumbling through the gates, leaning with her back against them, eyes closed. How long it lasted she couldn't say, but when it was over, her mother was standing in front of her, her hands on Fay's shoulders, steadying her, keeping her upright, whispering to her, soothing her as if she was a child.

'There, there. It's all right.'

'I have to find a telephone box,' Fay murmured.

'Not now, you don't. I'm taking you home.'

'But it's important, Mum. What I saw...I have to tell Sir Thomas. I promised.'

'Don't argue, Fay. I'm sure it can wait until we get home.'

Her legs still unsteady, her mother's arm around her waist, Fay allowed herself to be led away from the cemetery, down Beaconsfield Road to the bus stop. Neither of them spoke again until they reached the house. Not once did her mother ask what she'd seen. She seemed to understand Fay's need for silence.

Chapter 39

Mary Langbourne was upstairs in her dressing room. Downstairs, Gerald was growing impatient. Twice he'd asked how much longer she'd be and twice she'd promised she'd be down in a minute. The outfit she'd finally chosen was perhaps slightly too dressy for lunch at Edwina's, but it suited her so well and she was determined to look her absolute best, especially once she'd discovered that Sir Thomas had also been invited. A touch more colour to her cheeks, a final glance at her reflection and, having swept downstairs expecting to find Gerald waiting for her in the hall, she found him instead in his study. He'd removed his jacket and was sitting at his desk reading the Sunday papers.

'I thought you were in a hurry, darling,' she said.

'And so I was, but you were taking so long to get ready I almost gave up.'

'Well, I'm ready now. Shall we go?'

He sighed, folded his paper and slipped his jacket on. They were in the hall when the telephone rang.

'Leave it,' she said. 'Elsie will answer it. She can take a message.'

But Gerald ignored her. He picked up the phone, listened for a second and Mary was appalled to hear him snarl, 'What do you want, Miss Abrams?'

'Must you be so rude?' Mary whispered.

Gerald gave a loud snort of annoyance and handed her the receiver. She waited until he'd crossed the hall and disappeared back into his study.

'Hello, Miss Abrams,' she said, 'how are you?'

The girl was agitated. She'd had another vision and telephoned Sir Thomas as requested, only to be told that he was not expected back for several hours.

'I promised I'd let him know immediately anything happened,' she said. 'I don't know what to do.'

'Well, it's lucky you caught us. We were just on our way out and I shall be seeing Sir Thomas myself in a few minutes. Why don't you tell me what you saw and I'll make sure he gets your message?'

She listened as the girl described her vision. What she heard caused Mary serious concern. Sir Thomas needed to know straight away.

'You did the right thing, Miss Abrams,' she said. 'Be assured I shall deliver your message personally.'

A few moments later, ignoring his ill-tempered scowl, Mary took hold of Gerald's arm and walked towards their waiting car. Gerald sat silently beside her but less than five minutes later, just as she'd expected, his curiosity got the better of him.

'Well,' he growled. 'What was that all about? More nonsense from your little friend?'

'Yes, darling, just as you say. More nonsense.'

She was tempted to say that it was quite possibly the same kind of nonsense that had already saved their lives once. Instead, she gazed out of the window and imagined how Sir Thomas would receive her news.

Arriving at Edwina's house, Mary glanced round and, satisfied that her choice of dress was entirely appropriate, she wandered outside to the terrace, where Edwina was talking to Sir Thomas.

'What kept you?' said Edwina. 'You look marvellous, by the way. I'll see you both later. There's someone over there I simply must talk to.'

As Edwina glided across the terrace towards the drawing room, Sir Thomas took Mary's hand and raised it to his lips.

'Shall we sit over there?' she said, pointing to a table at the far end of the terrace. 'I have some news for you.'

They sat together, away from the other guests.

'From the expression on your face I assume it's something serious.'

Mary nodded. 'Miss Abrams. She's had another vision. She telephoned about fifteen minutes ago.'

His knees brushed against hers as he moved his chair a little closer. 'She told you what she saw?'

'She did, and it's lucky she caught me. We were just about to leave.'

Glancing over his shoulder, Sir Thomas lowered his voice. 'All right, Mary. Tell me exactly what she said.'

Their heads close together, she whispered, 'Pall Mall. And more particularly the Carlton Club. Buildings demolished. Choking clouds of dust and ash. A brass sign lying among the rubble. The address, 100 Pall Mall. That is the Carlton, isn't it?'

Sir Thomas, his face suddenly pale, stared at her. 'Indeed it is. Good lord, Mary, the entire War Cabinet dine at the Carlton.'

'So does my husband,' she murmured.

'Do we know when it's going to happen?'

Mary shook her head. 'I asked her the very same question. She didn't know, but even so she seemed to think it was imminent. What can we do? Could the club be closed for the time being?'

'No, I don't think that's the answer. The problem is finding the right balance. Adequate precautions for everyone's safety without arousing suspicion or panic. I'm quite certain it can be done, but it has to be done quickly and with the minimum of fuss. I don't need to remind you to say nothing of this to anyone. Not even your husband.'

Mary smiled. 'You needn't concern yourself about my discretion, Sir Thomas, and if you knew Gerald as well as I, you would understand why he would be the last person on earth with whom one would discuss Miss Abrams' visions.'

'Then you'll forgive me if I take my leave as soon as I decently can. I shall stay for lunch but then I'll go straight from here to the Carlton. I want to take a closer look at the layout of the building.'

There was something so reassuring about the way he spoke that Mary was utterly convinced that left in his capable hands, a potential disaster would be averted. Such confidence. Such power. A heady combination in any man, but in one prepared to accept the unexplainable without dismissing it as nonsense...if only Gerald was a little more open-minded, she thought. Sir Thomas was looking at her. Did he know what she was thinking? Forcing herself to look away, she curled her fingers round the stem of the glass but before she could raise the glass to her lips, he reached across the table, touched her wrist and stroking it with his thumb, asked if she remembered what else Miss Abrams said. My goodness, she thought, the man's an outrageous flirt, and she suddenly began to feel a little annoyed with herself for responding so easily to his charm.

'Of course I do. I made a point of remembering. But apart from what I've already told you, everything else Miss Abrams saw was so vague as to be quite unhelpful.'

'But Mary, I want you to tell me everything, my dear,' he murmured.

Brushing his hand away, she leant back in her chair, so his face was no longer close to hers, raised her glass and took a sip of champagne.

'All right, but I've already told you none of it's terribly helpful. A blue light swinging backwards and forwards. Muffled voices. She couldn't say what it meant and to tell you the truth, Miss Abrams sounded quite weary of the whole thing. I asked her if she was all right and she said she didn't think she'd ever be all right as long as she had visions. It was rather sad, really.'

'Nevertheless, we are indebted to her. When you see her again perhaps you'll tell her how much I value her help. Will you do that for me?'

'I'm unlikely to see her soon, Sir Thomas. I think you should tell her yourself. A little thank-you note perhaps? You have her address?'

Hearing footsteps behind her, Mary turned and saw Gerald walking towards her. She smiled up at him.

'A private tête-à-tête or can anyone join?' he said.

Sir Thomas rose to his feet. 'Lord Langbourne, I was just saying it's about time we all got together.'

'Indeed,' said Gerald. Mary felt his hand on her shoulder. 'Darling, you do look lovely but you must be feeling dreadfully chilly in that dress. Won't you come inside? I believe lunch is about to be served.'

As he led her across the terrace, Mary was aware of the warm pressure of his hand on the small of her back. Gentle but deliberately possessive. During lunch he was attentive and amusing. Conversation flowed. Mary was at her best; witty and charming. The meal had barely finished when Sir Thomas, who was seated at the far end of the table, made his excuses and left. Only Mary knew where he was going, but by then – assuming Miss Abrams was not mistaken, and why should she be, since up to now she'd always been right – Mary was satisfied that the time had come when Gerald would have to accept that her faith in her little friend's visions was entirely justified.

Chapter 40

The next morning, the queue at the bus stop stretched right back to the newsagents. Rita was there. Fay squeezed in next to her. No one complained. There was no point being annoyed. Nowadays no one got into trouble for being late for work as long as they made the effort to turn up.

'Look at this bloomin' queue,' said Rita. 'I could have had an extra twenty minutes in bed.'

As she spoke the queue shuffled forward. Two buses pulled up at the stop. With all the seats quickly filled it was standing room only, all the way to Maida Vale. When they eventually found two seats together, Fay asked if her manageress had kicked up a fuss about time off for Yom Kippur.

'No, I was expecting an argument but she was fine about it. Look, they stuck this in my wage packet.' Rita unfolded a Ministry of Information leaflet and handed it to Fay. 'All the girls got one. All the single ones. It's about part-time war work.'

'Yes, I know,' said Fay. 'I got one too.'

Rita had already decided what she was going to do. Smith's, the factory in Cricklewood, manufactured clocks but according to Rita they were taking girls on to assemble instruments for aircraft. Surprised that she'd acted so quickly, Fay asked if she'd tried anywhere else.

'No, I haven't bothered. Smith's is as good as anywhere else. Why don't you apply, too? It would be fun if we were both working there.'

The idea of working side by side with Rita on an assembly line, even for just a few hours a week, wasn't quite what Fay had in mind. She didn't say so but she was hoping to find something just a bit more interesting. Something in Whitehall perhaps, with a view across St. James' Park.

As she walked towards the shop she thought about her telephone conversation with Lady Langbourne. She had tried. She'd done her best to describe what she'd seen. The vision of the bombed buildings in Pall Mall was vivid and, from Lady Langbourne's reaction, a valuable piece of information. But those other things – the half-seen, flickering images, the muffled sounds – Lady Langbourne had dismissed them as being too vague to be helpful and Fay had to agree. She'd even begun to hope that it signalled the end of her visions. Perhaps they'd get fainter and fainter until they just faded away to nothing and stopped forever. But then perhaps that was just wishful thinking.

The visit to her grandmother's grave had given Fay a connection to the past. The feeling was new and she wondered if her mother understood how much it meant to her. It had already altered her perception of who she was and she was determined that the inscription would be changed. There would be a proper ceremony. They'd all be there. They'd say a few prayers and Rabbi Shultz would give a blessing. When Miss Greenwood asked if she'd done anything special at the weekend, Fay smiled.

'Yes, Miss Greenwood. I did something very special. I visited my grandmother's grave.'

Miss Greenwood stared at her. 'Your grandmother, dear? I don't think you've ever mentioned her before. When did she pass?'

'Years ago. I don't remember her at all but I'm ever so glad I went.'

Miss Greenwood nodded. 'Sometimes we need to be reminded of where we came from. There are always lessons to be learned, don't you agree?'

Yes, she agreed. There were lessons to be learned and wrongs to be righted.

*

Not on the front page. No big headlines. But it was there in her father's newspaper. He had spotted it and folded the paper so the article was immediately visible. He was watching her as she read it.

> The Carlton, Pall Mall, London's oldest established Conservative Club, was one of several buildings destroyed in last night's raid. More than thirty members were dining at the club when the building was struck by high explosive bombs. However, a spokesman reported that due to the last-minute decision to move the dining hall to the basement there were no fatalities.

'Well, darling,' he said, 'you were right, weren't you?'

Her mother spread her hands and gave a little shrug. 'What did I tell you? Of course she's right.'

She should have felt gratified. Whatever Lady Langbourne had said to Sir Thomas, he had taken the information seriously. His response must have been almost immediate but Fay was filled with a peculiar sense of dread, as if she'd started something she might come to regret. Nor did her father's excitement do much to dispel the feeling.

'Maybe they'll give you a medal, *buballah*,' he said.

'A medal?' said her mother. 'She doesn't need a medal. She did the right thing. I'm proud of her. We're all proud of her. I just…'

Fay smiled. 'I know, Mum. You just wish I was normal, like you.'

Later, when the telephone rang, Jack rushed into the hall and answered it. He came back, looking wide-eyed with excitement.

'It's him. Sir Thomas Poulton. He wants to speak to Miss Abrams.'

Out in the hall, Fay picked up the receiver. Her parents and Jack perched on the stairs, listening.

'Good evening, Sir Thomas.'

Jack was grinning from ear to ear. It put her off. She turned and faced the wall so she didn't have to look at him.

'Miss Abrams speaking,' she said.

Sir Thomas thanked her. He told her he was more grateful than he could say. He thanked her again. He wanted to show his gratitude. How would she like to work in Westminster, in the Ministry of Information? He could offer her a permanent position. Decent salary. Generous pension. Mostly administrative work.

'I've never worked in an office before, Sir Thomas. I can't type and I'm no good at maths.'

Apparently that didn't matter in the least. There were other people to do those jobs. She didn't need to give him an answer straight away. His secretary would send details, duties, salary, etcetera, and two copies of the contract of employment if she decided to accept the position.

'I don't know what to say, sir. Thank you. Thank you very much. It's very generous. I'll need a few days to think about it.'

'Of course you will, but can I ask you, in the meantime, to keep me informed if there are any more visions?'

'Of course. That goes without saying, Sir Thomas.'

He thanked her again and wished her a good evening. Fay replaced the receiver and faced her audience.

'He offered you a job?' said her father.

'In Westminster,' said Fay. 'Two hundred and twenty pounds a year.'

Her mother frowned. 'So why did you tell him you can't type and you're no good at maths?'

Fay shrugged. 'Because it's true. I'm a shop assistant. I sell hats. So why offer someone like me an administrative job?'

'I'd rather have a medal,' said Jack.

'Look,' said Fay, 'must we have this conversation in the hall?'

They followed her into the kitchen. Fay's mind was racing. A full-time job for life and a pension. It was worth a small fortune. Wouldn't anyone give their eye teeth for a job like that? So why hadn't she jumped at the offer?

'I'm not taking it,' she said. 'The job. I'm turning it down.'

Her father was the only one who looked surprised.

Her brother shrugged. 'I don't think you'd like being a civil servant, Fay.'

Fay glanced at her mother. She couldn't tell what she was thinking. She thought she was trying not to smile.

'Mum, what would you do if you were me?'

'What would I do? I'd think about it, then I'd turn it down.'

'Why?'

'Because it doesn't feel right.'

'You think it's some kind of trick?'

Her mother stared at her. 'Did I say that? No, of course I didn't. You asked me what I'd do and I've told you. It's not for you. A job like that? You're better off where you are.'

'If you ask me, I agree with Mum,' said Jack.

Her father had been quiet up to then. Fay looked at him. He was frowning.

'Am I the only one who thinks this might be a golden opportunity for Fay? Tell me. How often does a chance like this come along?'

Of course he was right. A shop girl with no experience in ministerial matters. It sounded like a once-in-a-lifetime opportunity but Fay knew there was no job. No real job. No real duties. They'd move a desk, stick a telephone on it, a notepad and pencil and call it Miss Abrams' office and they might find a few things for her to do while they waited for the next vision. Jack was right. A medal would have been nicer.

Chapter 41

Alone in the meeting room at the back of the synagogue, Rosa Feldman silently bemoaned the lack of support from the Ladies' Guild. They'd cooked and baked, they'd lent the crockery and cutlery she needed but, as always, everything else had been left to her. There were tables and chairs to be set out, food to be laid out, flowers to be arranged and where were they? Most likely still at home deciding what to wear. Surely, it wasn't too much to expect a bit of help. Did they think the work would somehow get done without them having to lift a finger? She was thinking about what she would say to them at the next Ladies' Guild meeting when Hetty Abrams put her head round the door.

Rosa sighed. What did she want, she thought, but before she could ask, Hetty wished her *Tzom Kal*, removed her hat, took an apron from a large shopping bag, tied it round her waist and rolled up her sleeves.

'What would you like me to do, Rosa?' she said. 'I've brought the chopped liver and I made three loaves as well. Shall I start with the tablecloths?'

Tzom Kal. An easy fast? Rosa's cheeks grew hot. It was not midday yet and her fast had already been broken. Not deliberately. She'd had every intention of lasting out until Yom Kippur was over. Every intention. But that morning, in a hurry to get to the synagogue, she'd been packing leftovers from last night's feast and quite absentmindedly, without thinking, she'd bitten into a slice of apple strudel. Such a nice, moist slice. It seemed a pity to waste it.

'And *Tzom Kal* to you too, Hetty,' she murmured, quickly turning her attention to a sad-looking bunch of chrysanthemums. 'And bless you for offering to help.'

Her ladies, she vowed, were certainly going to get a piece of her mind. Hetty Abrams wasn't even a member and yet here she was ready and willing to give Rosa a hand, without even being asked. They made a good team, too. Hetty was stronger than she looked and Rosa was impressed at how quickly she arranged the tables and chairs. She had even thought to bring clean tea towels. But Rosa simply had to put her foot down when she saw Hetty's tablecloth. A snowy white cloth with deep lace borders.

'No, Hetty,' she said. 'I can't possibly let you use it.'

'Why ever not?'

'It's far too nice. That's why.' Rosa was not prepared to take responsibility for what might happen once the service finished and the mad stampede for food began. From the cabinet she pulled a bundle of oilcloth table covers. 'Trust me, Hetty. They might not look anywhere near as nice as yours but we've used them for years. A quick wipe with a damp cloth and they're as good as new.'

Hetty shrugged. 'Well, if you're quite sure. You know best and I really wouldn't like anything to happen to it. It belonged to my mother.'

Before she could stop herself the words were out of her mouth. 'Your mother? Would that be Zofia Kroll?'

Hetty stopped what she was doing and stared at her. Rosa primed herself for an angry outburst, but none came.

'Sorry. It's none of my business, is it?'

Hetty didn't reply.

'Sorry,' she said, again.

When Hetty spoke her voice was quiet but calm. 'You're quite right, Rosa,' she said. 'It is none of your business, but since you ask, yes, my mother was Zofia Kroll. And, as I'm quite certain you already know, she was in prison for almost a year. Would you like to know why?'

Did she want to know? Of course she did. She tipped her head to the side. 'Oh dear,' she said, 'how awful. Surely it was all a frightful mistake?'

'No mistake, Rosa. My mother was just like Fay. She saw things before they happened and they locked her up in case she said something they didn't want anyone to know.'

'They can't do something like that, can they? It's inhuman. Unlawful.'

Hetty smiled. 'Oh, you'd be surprised what they can do. Especially when the country is at war. Any law can be twisted to suit their purpose and they don't need an excuse. Sometimes it's enough just to have a foreign-sounding name.'

Rosa pulled out a chair and urged Hetty to sit down. If she wanted to talk, Rosa was more than ready to listen. Slowly at first, Hetty began to tell her story. She talked about Zofia, about Fay, about the fears she'd been nursing since the moment she realised that her daughter had visions too. By the time she finished, Rosa had nothing but admiration for this woman she'd once thought so mousy and unfriendly. She reached for her hand.

'Honestly, I don't know what to say. How on earth have you managed to cope so well?'

'I haven't. I haven't coped well at all. I've been a nervous wreck for most of my life. A bundle of nerves.'

'You needn't worry, Hetty. You can trust me. I promise you this won't go any further. It's just between us two,' said Rosa, and she meant it. Every word. This was Hetty's secret and the fact that she'd chosen to share it with her felt to Rosa like something of an honour.

But Hetty just laughed. 'You don't understand. I don't care who knows. I used to care, but not anymore. Everything's changed. It's all out in the open now and I'm glad.'

'Nevertheless,' said Rosa. 'They won't hear about it from me.'

A slight frown appeared on Hetty's face. Her eyes narrowed. 'Do you know something, Rosa?' she said. 'I was always terribly worried about you finding out. You more than anyone. Ridiculous, isn't it?'

Uncertain what to make of that, Rosa chose not to ask. Instead she patted Rosa's hand and suggested that they'd better get a move on and finish getting the room ready. A little later when everything was more or less done, Hetty mentioned Jack's bar mitzvah.

'Such a lovely boy,' said Rosa. 'Not long now, is it?'

'January. I thought we'd do afternoon tea at home. Bridge rolls and cake,' said Hetty.

'Don't have it at home, Hetty. You must have it here. Lionel will take care of the music, and the top table, well, that can go over there just under the window. You could use that lovely tablecloth of yours. I'm sure Mrs Shultz would help decorate the room. She's ever so good at that sort of thing and…' Noticing Hetty's amused expression, Rosa paused. 'I'm interfering, aren't I?'

Hetty nodded. 'You certainly are.'

'I don't mean to,' said Rosa, apologetically.

'I know you don't. You just can't help it, can you? Okay, Rosa. Let's do it. Let's hold it here.'

Rosa grinned. She liked this woman. She really did. With the sound of Rabbi Shultz's voice floating towards them, she and Hetty looked around the room and satisfied with what they saw, removed their aprons, put on their hats, crossed the hall and took their places in the synagogue.

With just over an hour to go, Fay had developed the kind of headache that could only be cured by having something to eat. Unless you counted the glass of water and two surreptitious bites of a cream cracker, nothing had passed her lips since the previous night. She felt a bit faint, and when the image of a single blue light swung backwards and forwards in front of her eyes, had she not seen it before she might have thought her hunger was causing her to hallucinate. Just for a second she closed her eyes but her mother, sitting beside her, reached across, turned the pages of Fay's prayer book and tapped the page with her finger.

'Concentrate,' she whispered.

Perhaps that was the answer. Focus on the service. Fay watched her father step forward. He helped lift the Torah scroll and Mr Feldman carried it over and placed it carefully inside the ark. Everyone was standing now, facing the ark, and Rabbi Shultz, his voice still remarkably strong, considering how long the service had been going on, was singing with all his heart when the wail of sirens sounded. Fay searched his face for any small sign of alarm. There were none. He simply carried on, his voice soaring, perhaps a little louder now than it had been before. But nothing could drown out the sound of that siren.

She saw the look that passed between her father and Jack; the worried glance that Mr Feldman threw in his wife's direction; she could feel the pressure of her mother's arm against hers. All of Fay's attention was on the sound of the siren. And then it stopped and she was listening to another sound. The drone of approaching aircraft. But the rabbi sang still louder. Explosions, one quickly following another, shook the building to its foundations. The light above the ark, the eternal light that was supposed to symbolise God's presence, flickered and spluttered but it remained lit. Above the heads of the congregation, the ornate chandeliers bounced and shook violently. And still the rabbi sang. Unhurried, each word clear and filled with emotion. Fay gripped her mother's arm tightly. Her mother's eyes were closed. Her lips were moving.

It was not until they heard the voices outside in the street, screaming and shouting, that the rabbi showed signs of speeding up, skipping over entire sections. When he put the shofar to his lips, the note that marked the end of the service was thin and weak. He tried again. It was better but nowhere near as long or as loud as his congregation had come to expect. Moments later, the doors were opened and Fay joined the immaculately dressed army of helpers as they streamed out of the synagogue and into the darkened street.

Chapter 42

On either side of the road, most of the houses had suffered some damage but all were still standing. In one house a small fire was threatening to take hold. As Fay ran past it, a group of neighbours were forming a chain and trying to put out the fire with saucepans and buckets full of water. At the far end of the street, in the spot where the communal shelter had stood, a group of people had gathered together. They didn't appear to be doing anything. They just stood there. One man moved aside to let her pass and, as her eyes became accustomed to the dark, Fay saw the figure of a woman lying face down on top of the rubble. Her father had already removed his jacket. He'd just begun barking out orders when the woman lifted her head and screamed.

'They're still alive,' she howled. 'My boy. Get him out. Get him out.'

It was Rosa Feldman who helped her to her feet. Rabbi Shultz removed his prayer shawl and Mrs Feldman wrapped it around the poor woman and gently led her off to the side of the road. Kneeling on the spot where the woman had been lying, Fay held up her hand and signalled for silence. Coming from deep below the rubble, she heard the muffled sound of groans and cries. In seconds, everyone, young and old, was frantically moving bricks, still hot from the explosion. She was aware of Jack, his sleeves pulled down over his hands to protect them from the heat, kneeling next to her. She saw her mother and Mr Feldman working side by side with Mr Ebstein and Rita. Her father encouraged them to keep going.

'The rescue team should be here any minute,' he said, and a little later Fay heard the sharp sound of a whistle. She looked up and saw a boy in a tin hat racing towards them.

'Ah! The cavalry,' said her father. 'Where's the rest of the crew?'

The boy pushed his hat back. His face was filthy. He was not much older than Jack. Fourteen at the most. His clothes were wet and he was shivering violently.

'Sorry, sir. There's only me.'

'Where the hell's the rest of them?'

'Kilburn, sir. Kilburn Police Station. Direct hit, sir.' The boy's voice cracked. Fay saw her father put his hand on the boy's shoulder.

'It's all right, lad. I'm glad you're here.'

'I ran all the way, sir. They could only spare me. I've brought a couple of torches.'

'Good lad. We could do with some light.'

'The officers took cover in the basement, sir, but the bomb fractured the mains water supply. They're trapped down there.' The boy's voice cracked. 'I think they drowned, sir.'

Fay glanced at the boy's face. 'Can someone please get this lad a hot drink? Quick, before he passes out.'

How long they'd been digging she couldn't tell. It seemed like forever, but then someone shouted.

'Light. Over here. Quickly!' And moments later, two, then three, then four bodies, cut and bruised but still alive, were pulled clear of the rubble and carefully laid on the pavement. As more of the bricks and mortar were removed, Fay lost count of how many had been rescued, how many were already dead. Her hands were raw. Her knees and back were aching. Her father selected the half-dozen helpers who still had the strength to carry on and ordered the rest to deal with the injured.

Fay stood and stretched and turning, saw the woman, the rabbi's shawl still round her shoulders, kneeling on the ground beside an injured boy. The woman looked up.

'Thank you,' she said. 'God bless you for saving my son.'

Fay managed a weak smile.

'Don't try and move anyone whose injuries might be serious,' said her father. 'Leave that to the ambulance crew, but if they can stand and walk, get them inside the synagogue as quickly as you can. Fay, I'm putting you in charge.'

The procession back to the synagogue was slow. The rescuers were exhausted, the injured shocked and in pain. Mrs Feldman and Fay's mother went on ahead and by the time Fay led the procession into the hall her mother was cutting tea towels into strips and Mrs Feldman had three catering-sized kettles on the boil. The tables had been pushed against the wall and the chairs had been set out in rows. The room smelt of Dettol. On the floor in front of the chairs, bowls of hot water sat waiting to clean wounds. They'd thought of everything. Fay looked across at her mother and nodded.

'Well done,' she murmured.

'Where's Jack?'

'He wouldn't come. He wanted to stay with Dad.'

There was no time to say anything else. Those who needed to lie down were either supported on three chairs or they lay on the floor. The rest sat quietly as their injuries were assessed and decisions taken about how to give temporary relief. Rabbi Shultz was all for treating burns with margarine but it was Rita's mother who stopped him.

'Cold water, rabbi. Just plain cold water.'

He didn't argue. Neither did Mrs Feldman's team of ladies when they were tasked with providing endless cups of hot, sweet tea for everyone. The boy's mother, the woman who'd been wrapped in the rabbi's shawl, took on the job of filling the kettles as fast as they were emptied.

Rita had earned herself a badge in first aid when they'd been in the Girl Guides. She took over the worst injuries. Fay and Mr Feldman and Mrs Ebstein took care of cleaning wounds but there was so much dirt to be cleaned off before they could even see what they were dealing with. The girl Fay had just been attending to had a deep gash above her eye. Her face was covered in blood. Underneath all that blood the girl's face was a most peculiar colour, and Fay noticed that her eyes did not seem to be focusing properly. It was

Rita who, after a cursory examination, told her that the girl had probably fractured her skull and moments later when the girl threw up and passed out, it was Rita who put her in the recovery position.

What skills had she got? None that she could think of, but she could find out who needed hospital treatment. She could compile a list of names and addresses and next of kin. It would save the ambulance crew time when they arrived. Rabbi Shultz found a notebook and pencil for her and she was making good progress with her list when Mrs Ebstein called her over.

'Another one for your list, Fay,' she said, pointing to the boy's arm. A white, splintered bone was poking through his shirt. 'He says his mother's here somewhere.'

Fay was about to go and find her when Jack and her father staggered into the room. Covered in dirt and brick dust and looking utterly exhausted, they sank down on to the nearest chairs.

Mrs Feldman pointed at one of her ladies. 'Two teas over here. Quickly now.'

'Rescue team's finally turned up. They've taken over. Ambulance will be here soon,' said her father.

Someone asked if there were any more bodies still down there. Fay turned and saw her father nodding. It was then that she noticed the way Jack was staring at the boy. She tried to stand between them, blocking the sight of that splintered bone from his view, but before she could move he was out of his seat and standing next to her.

'It's all right, Jack. It's probably not as bad as it looks. Go back and sit with Dad,' she said. He ignored her. He was looking at the boy. Not at his broken arm, but staring straight into his eyes. And then he smiled and put his mouth close to the boy's ear.

'Remember me?' he whispered.

Fay watched as a look of slow recognition crossed the boy's face. His eyes widened. His mouth opened, but Jack turned away without saying another word and, taking a seat next to his father, sat quietly talking to him.

'You know my brother?' said Fay.

The boy didn't reply. His lips trembled. His eyes were tightly closed.

Fay patted his hand. 'Don't worry. The ambulance will be here soon. Shall I go and find your mother?'

He nodded.

Fay found her in the kitchen. She was refilling a kettle.

'Do you know, I've never set foot in a synagogue before? Honestly, I can't believe how kind you all are,' she said.

What did she expect, thought Fay? She nearly asked. Instead she shrugged and said, 'Your son – I think you should keep him company while he waits for the ambulance.'

But the boy already had company. Her father and brother and Mr Feldman were all standing in front of the boy, looking down at him.

'What's going on?' she asked.

'Ah! Fay. Meet the sorry specimen who attacked Mr Feldman. He broke the synagogue window, too. Didn't you? Answer me or I might be tempted to break your other arm.'

'Dad, stop it. That's enough now,' said Fay. 'Leave him alone. You can sort this out later.'

'I just want to hear it from him, Fay. That's all. Why did he do it? He doesn't have to like us, but this…this thug…attacked an innocent man and left him alone and unconscious in the middle of an air raid.'

Forgetting that his mother was standing there listening, Fay was taken by surprise when the woman pushed her aside and raised her hand as if she was about to slap the boy. Fay grabbed her arm and pulled her away.

By the time the ambulance arrived, with his mother glaring at him as if she was just waiting for an opportunity to give him a good hiding, the boy was forced to apologise for his disgraceful behaviour. First to the rabbi for breaking the window. Then to Mrs Feldman for throwing the rock that only narrowly missed her head, and lastly to Mr Feldman.

'Show him, Lionel,' said Mrs Feldman. 'Show him what he did to your poor teeth.'

Lionel obliged.

When the last of the injured had been dealt with, Fay's mother and some of Mrs Feldman's ladies made up parcels of food for the rescuers to take home with them. The room stank of Dettol. No one wanted to stay to break the fast. Everyone was exhausted.

Fay's hands were in an awful state. One of her fingernails had been ripped off and the skin on her knuckles had been scraped away to the bone. But as she staggered home, knees burnt raw from the heat of the bricks, the sights and sounds of that day etched themselves into her mind.

The following morning, hand bandaged and knees stained purple with iodine, she called Sir Thomas Poulton's number and told him she was grateful for the offer but she'd decided not to take the job at the Ministry of Information.

'I wonder, Sir Thomas, could you tell me what's being done about providing better shelters?'

'Shelters?' he said. 'I suggest you leave that to the politicians, Miss Abrams. The situation is a potentially volatile one.'

'I'm sure you're right, sir,' she murmured. 'Leave it to the politicians.'

She smiled as she replaced the receiver. Something momentous had happened to her, and what he didn't realise was that being the girl in the hat shop who had visions was no longer enough for Fay Abrams.

Historical Note

Inspiration for this book came first from my aunt's wartime diaries. I owe much to her for those precious snippets which so vividly describe the manners, language and social history of the times. During the war, my aunt worked in a hat shop in Mayfair and from her diaries, written in cheap exercise books from Woolworths, I learned about attitudes to class and discovered how people carried on with their lives in the face of danger.

It was when I began researching this period that I came across the extraordinary story of Helen Duncan. In 1944, tried by jury at The Old Bailey, the unfortunate woman was found guilty of contravening the 1735 Witchcraft Act. The discovery that such an archaic Act was even still on the statutes and not actually repealed until 1951 caught my imagination. I read everything I could find about the case, learned that Winston Churchill, in a memo to the Home Secretary, Herbert Morrison, described it as "obsolete tomfoolery" and it was then that the story of *Girl in the Hat Shop* began to take shape.

www.leilacassell.com